Truth, Lies, and Second Dates

Truth, Lies, and Second Dates

MaryJanice Davidson

ST. MARTIN'S
GRIFFIN

First published in the United States by St. Martin's Griffin, an imprint of St. Martin's Publishing Group

TRUTH, LIES, AND SECOND DATES. Copyright © 2020 by MaryJanice Alongi. All rights reserved. Printed in the United States of America. For information, address St. Martin's Publishing Group, 120 Broadway, New York, NY 10271.

www.stmartins.com

Library of Congress Cataloging-in-Publication Data

Names: Davidson, MaryJanice, author.
Title: Truth, lies, and second dates / MaryJanice Davidson.
Description: First edition. | New York : St. Martin's Griffin, 2020.
Identifiers: LCCN 2020028416 | ISBN 9781250053176 (trade paperback) | ISBN 9781466855458 (ebook)
Subjects: GSAFD: Love stories.
Classification: LCC PS3604.A949 T78 2020 | DDC 813/.6—dc23
LC record available at https://lccn.loc.gov/2020028416

33614082139659

Our books may be purchased in bulk for promotional, educational, or business use. Please contact your local bookseller or the Macmillan Corporate and Premium Sales Department at 1-800-221-7945, extension 5442, or by email at MacmillanSpecialMarkets@macmillan.com.

First Edition: 2020

10 9 8 7 6 5 4 3 2 1

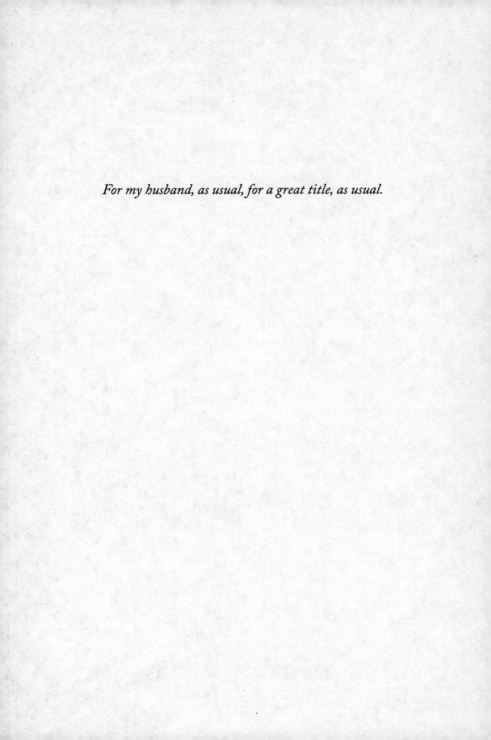

For my husband, as usual, for a great title, as usual.

You know what a great pilot would have done? Not hit the birds. That's what I do every day: not hit birds. Where's *my* ticket to the Grammys?

—Captain Carol Burnett, *30 Rock*

Fate was cruel to play this trick on her, although if she were honest she knew she only had herself to blame. She had taken the chance and now she had to pay the price.

—Emily Arden

When pilots have a bad day at work, it's not a small thing. The margins for error are microchip thin and the smallest of vagaries can result in a catastrophe.

—Jane Macdougall,
"'I Got Everyone Home Today': How Real-Life
Pilots Feel with Our Lives in Their Hands,"
National Post, September 2016

Half a pound of tuppenny rice
Half a pound of treacle
That's the way the money goes
Pop goes the weasel.

Every night when I go out
The weasel's on the table
Now I take a stick
And I knock it off
Pop goes the weasel.

—"Pop Goes the Weasel"

Forensic pathology is the branch of medical practice that produces evidence useful in the criminal justice administration, public health and public safety. Under this definition are three key elements: Cause of Death, Manner of Death and Mechanism of Death.

—"AUTOPSY PROTOCOL,"
INDIANA STATE CORONERS TRAINING BOARD

Slough (plural *sloughs*): A type of swamp or shallow lake system, typically formed as or by the backwater of a larger waterway, similar to a bayou with trees.

—WIKTIONARY

Author's Note

This is the third book in the Danger series, which came about because my editor and I love romance tropes and wanted to write a love letter about . . . well . . . love. And tropes! (But also love.)

Tropes are walking, talking figures of speech. A trope is when you're watching a new show about a cop who's set to retire next week/month/year, and you immediately understand the cop will never retire. It's when the pretty teenager in a horror movie says, "I'll be right back!" and you know you've seen the last of her. It's a way for the writer to let the audience know what to expect without having to, you know, write.

A trope is the thing that brings you back to the same genre again and again, because the stuff you loved in the first book will pop up in other books and you're always chasing that feeling, the giddy excitement of reading about a hero and heroine, or hero and hero, or heroine and—you get the picture, whoever they are—and you know they are destined for love, and you want to watch. (Not in a creepy way.) Even more: you want to fall in love, too.

And that's how the first two books in this series came about. Romance novels that pay respect to romance novels, where the readers are in on the joke. Unless you skipped my Author's Note, in which case you're not in on the joke and you think I hate romance novels and I cannot help you.

This time I switched it up a bit and made it about horror/serial killer tropes, too, because I'm a weirdo and romance and horror are my first loves.

For those of you in a hurry, there's a trope list at the end. This is partly to make it easier for my readers, but also because I like making lists. (The strangest things give me a thrill, for which I make no apologies.)

While researching this book, I discovered that the minimum age for a commercial pilot is eighteen. Now think about a teenager piloting a five-hundred-foot-long wide-body carrying seven hundred passengers and try not to lose your shit. (It's impossible, right? Just *typing* that gave me the chills. My beloved and intelligent son is nineteen, but the thought of him piloting a wide-body . . . and now I've got the chills again.)

New Jersey gets a bad rap but is in reality a beautiful state.

MAGE, the Massachusetts Association for Gifted Education, exists and they do great work. You can check 'em out here: www.massgifted.org/events.

Circus Day at Hazelden is, unfortunately, a real thing.

Hazelden is also a real thing and, Circus Day aside, is a wonderful nonprofit dedicated to helping addicts reclaim their lives. You can check them out here: www.hazelden.org.

Not to sound like a commercial, but J.Jill clothing really is comfortable, you really can crumple it into a ball and it'll still look great, and they ship anywhere overnight.

Again, not to sound like I'm hawking clothing, but the designer my fictional airline hired is a real person: Lisa

Hackwith of Hackwith Design House. Simple, stylish, comfortable, a little pricey but nothing you need a second mortgage to finance. Check her out here: hackwithdesignhouse .com/product-category/sustain-shop/.

Some of Ava's pilot announcements are based on this article from Snopes.com: www.snopes.com/fact-check/pilot -light/. I don't know about you guys, but I love a pilot with a sense of humor.

Unfortunately, in our post-9/11 world, most airlines don't let civilians into the cockpit when the plane's in the air. For the purpose of this story, I ignored that regulation. You don't own me, FAA! But thanks for helping keep the skies safe.

Nepal's Lukla Airport is apparently one of the worst airports to fly into. It's elevated, it's in the middle of the mountains, the runway is unbelievably short, there aren't any lights, there's very little electricity (!!!), and there are no air traffic controllers. It's basically nightmare fuel for pilots.

There isn't a comedy club in Boston called Konichi-ha, but there should be.

I love Minnesota, even if Ava does not. Just wanted to get that on the record. Don't @ me.

Truth, Lies, and Second Dates

Prologue

Ava Capp came awake in another anonymous hotel room and thought, *If this was a book, I'd be thinking about how empty and aimless my life as a single woman is and how I need to make a change.* If *this was a book.*

She shivered; Blake was awake and was doing that thing where he ran a finger up and down her spine like an erotic chiropractor. "God. You know that gives me the shivers."

A deep chuckle from behind her. "More effective, perhaps, than an alarm."

The voice. Ummmm.

Blake Tarbell, careless heartbreaker, had many fine qualities, beginning with the Voice and ending somewhere lower. He was a guaranteed good time when she was in port, which made him valuable, but not indispensable.

Meanwhile, his spine skimming was turning into buttock grabbing, which she would normally welcome. However.

"Forget it." Ava flopped over and sat up, moving so quickly Blake put out a hand. *Whoa. Easy. No need to sprint just because you don't want to have That Particular Conversation.* "I've gotta get back, so just holster the morning wood already."

He smiled and let his hand drop. "Holster it where?"

"Dunno. It's a guy thing; you figure it out." She bounded from the bed, already running through checklists (and creating new ones) in her mind, and grinned to see Blake shiver. He'd once accused her of being a morning person in the same tone people accuse politicians of grifting, like it was *that* bad.

She ducked into the hilariously opulent bathroom (loads of free toiletries plus a bidet plus a towel warmer, which was wasted on her because she used room temperature towels like a savage) and figured today would likely be the last time she saw Blake. She felt bad that she didn't feel bad.

As was their habit, they'd met in the lobby for drinks (never dinner). As she had explained the first time she let him pick her up, "Don't ask me out. Don't buy flowers. That's not what this is."

"What is it, then?" he'd asked, amused. They'd met at McCarran four months ago: she was a pilot for Northeastern Southwest ("We fly everywhere!"); his flight had been delayed. He was gorgeous and smart and a practiced flirt (being one herself, she could spot the breed). They'd had drinks and then they'd had each other.

"What is it?" she parroted. "This is me enjoying myself. This is you being the sexual equivalent of a Fun Run. Less talking, Blake, and a lot more stripping."

Finished with her minimal makeup and reminiscing, she stepped back into the bedroom. "I need to get moving if I'm going to make the run to Boston." She was slipping into the clean set of civvies she'd brought—she kept clean uniforms at LAX and MSP, among other things—while Blake watched her with a heavy-lidded gaze. "God, sometimes I think it'd be

easier to keep a spare set of clothes and some toiletries *here*."
She looked up at the exact moment, caught him. "Ah-ha!"

"What?"

She pointed at him with one hand while zipping her slacks
with the other. "You should see the look on your face. I've only
seen people go pale that fast when the oxygen masks drop."
She could see him preparing a denial and cut him off before
he embarrassed himself. "S'fine. Really. I was teasing. I know
you're cemented in your bachelor ways." *I am, too.*

He opened his mouth again.

She shook her head, which made her curls bounce, which
reinforced the love/hate relationship she had with her hair.
What sick twisted god had given her blond curls and sallow
skin? Long limbs but fragile ankles and wrists? She'd shatter
like a bathroom mirror if she tripped at the wrong moment
in the wrong place. A love for flying but a hatred for enclosed
spaces? "Nope. Don't even try that. And don't go on about
how you're just waiting for the right girl, and maybe that girl
could be me—"

"I wouldn't have used the word *girl*," he pointed out.

"It's *fine*. This"—she gestured, indicating him, the suite,
the empty champagne bottle, the remote control, yesterday's panties—"What we do? It's great, really. It's just . . . I
need something more. And . . . there's this woman—oh. You
didn't know?" He hadn't, she realized. And he was getting
That Look. The *wait, I could have been in a threesome with two
hot women* expression, like he was simultaneously thrilled and
crushed. And like she'd ever have sex with a girlfriend solely
for the amusement of a random man. "I'm pretty flexible between the sheets."

"Figuratively and literally. Why would you wait until now
to bring that up?"

She laughed, bent, kissed a stubbled cheek. "For a chance to see that look on your face. Hey. You're great, Blake. This was, too, y'know? But I never go back for seconds."

"Fourteenths."

She rolled her eyes. "Right. But I want to keep liking you, if not fucking you. So: you don't pretend you're going to miss me, and I won't pretend you can't fill my spot in your sex suite with one text."

He grinned, and she almost wavered. Of the many things she liked about Blake, his smile was in the top five. "Fair enough."

She had everything together—overnight bag, purse, the Godiva sack (they'd devoured the chocolate-dipped fruit, but there were some truffles left)—and slipped into her shoes. "Might not see you again. But if we do, it'd be great to keep it friendly, okay?"

"You're wrong," Blake replied.

Wait. What? She was halfway to the door, then stopped and turned. "Wait. What?"

"I *will* miss you when you're gone," he said solemnly, still sitting in a puddle of sheets.

"Awww." She came back, kissed him again, the last kiss. "But not for long, I bet."

She left. A remarkably painless breakup. If that's what it even was. Though she'd fudged a little. The woman she'd told him about wasn't a girlfriend. For one thing, they'd never dated. For another, she was long dead.

One

"Hey, Ghost Baby."

"Dammit, Cap Capp!"

Nuts. Need a new list already. Ava tried to pretend the thought of coming up with a new list so early in the day made her sad. "C'mon, Graham," she said as he fell into step beside her. "It all worked out fine. Nobody died. Nobody was even inconvenienced."

"Oh, like it was *my* fault that idiot thought babies needed to be stowed with laptops," G.B. (known by Graham Benjin until last August, now forever known as Ghost Baby) retorted.

"You're doing that thing where you respond to a point I didn't make. And maybe don't refer to our customers as idiots? Also, lighten up. It was her first flight." Ava chuckled into her hot chocolate. "Why wouldn't she think a small snug dark cave above her seat was the perfect place to stow her dozing infant?"

G.B. muttered something under his breath, hands stuffed in his pockets to the wrist. He was a tall, dark-skinned man in wonderful shape who bore more than a passing resemblance to the actor Terry Crews (except with hair). He got jittery and snappish before every flight, which was tolerated as he magically transformed into an efficient and unflappable crew chief once he boarded. (Except when he thought the flight was haunted by a baby ghost. But even then, it had to be said, he kept his cool.)

"You're just upset because it took you so long to find the poor thing." This was tactful in the extreme, because when G.B. couldn't immediately find the baby, he had wondered aloud if he was hearing a ghost and pondered the pros and cons of an in-flight de-haunting.

("Not an exorcism?" Ava had asked, amused.

"In flight? Ridiculous. Too many variables and we're fresh out of Bibles.")

"There are so many things that upset me about that flight. I don't have the time and you don't have the patience for me to go into any of it."

"Sounds about right," she agreed. "I assume we're doing a Sorkin walk-and-talk to pre-flight because you're running my flight crew?"

"Yeah. A bunch of us lost the coin toss."

"You're full of shit. I'm a great captain and you love flying with me."

"First, low bar. Second, love is an exaggeration. Third . . ." G.B. had slowed, then opened the door to the crew room for her. "Why are you in such a good mood? Is this my cue to make inappropriate guesses about your sex life?"

"Better not."

"Aw, c'mon, roomie. Spill."

"I let you camp on my couch for two weeks and that was months ago!" she protested. "That doesn't mean we're roommates."

"And after the Easter thing last year."

"Well."

"And we've shared hotel rooms too many times to count."

"Three, G.B. We've shared rooms three times, and the fact that you can't count that high is deeply troubling to me as your captain and your . . ."

He raised his eyebrows expectantly.

". . . occasional roommate." She sighed, giving in.

"Ha! Also, after you."

She swept inside and tossed her now-empty cup of hot chocolate into the garbage. "Morning."

A chorus of "Good morning!" and "Hi, Captain Capp!" greeted her. Her senior first officer, India James, was printing off the flight plan and waved. "Weather looks good, Cap."

"I love when the weather looks good." She parked her carry-on to the left of the table and dropped her purse on the chair. "How's your newest?"

"Fat," India replied with satisfaction. He was a brown-eyed blond who hailed from Chicago, almost exactly her height at five feet, ten inches and—pardon the cliché—skinny as a rail. In fact, by comparison rails looked a little thick. "Ninety-fifth percentile."

"Excellent." India's new daughter had been born five weeks premature. He and his wife were taking great pride in the infant's journey from scrawny wrinkled preemie to cheerful blond butterball.

"Do you tell her she should enjoy the fact that it's only acceptable to be fat until you hit first grade?"

"No, G.B.," India replied patiently. "I talk to her about the stock market and how I think the economy is going to rebound."

"Weird." Then, to Ava: "Cap, this is Becka Miller, who lost a bet with God and must now fly with Northeastern Southwest—"

"We fly *every*where!" everyone else sang, which was terrific.

"It wasn't a bet with God," said the team's newest flight attendant, a redhead whose hair was so vibrant, it was hard to look her in the eyes. "I've wanted to do this since I was a teenager. It's very nice to meet you, Captain Capp." Becka said this with more intensity than Ava was used to, but she shrugged it off—some people were nervous around captains.

"Back atcha. Don't mind G.B. He's exhausting but skilled, so it all works out. Eventually. Probably. Look, nobody wants to do all the paperwork necessary to fire him, so we're all just dealing."

"Had to ruin it. Had to tack something on at the end. Just couldn't help yourself."

"Nope. Couldn't." As she turned away to consult with India, she heard Becka hiss to G.B. "She's the one who did the belly landing!"

"Hey, I was there, too. I was integral—I had the booze cart."

"Um, I also heard . . . I mean, is she the one whose friend got m—"

"Yeah," he muttered in reply. "But time and place, okay?"

Yes, I'm the one whose friend got m—, Ava thought. *Also, why do people think whispering works when I'm only three feet away?*

"How about we get started?" One of the nicer things about

making captain is that it may have sounded like a request, but everyone in the room understood it wasn't. "India, you want to take us through the briefing? G.B.?"

"Got it," G.B. replied, then shooed Becka toward the cabin crew as they filed into their own briefing room. "See you on deck."

"Will do. So then." She settled in with a fresh cup of tea. "Where are we going today?"

"If *you* don't know, we're all fucked."

"Oh, shut up."

Flight Deck
McCarron International Airport

"Another day in the relatively friendly skies. Not to jinx us."

"No, don't do that," Ava replied, mildly alarmed. "Though it might be too late. Thinking the *j* word almost always brings on the *j* word."

India was finishing entering the specs needed to calculate takeoff speed—weather, runway conditions, weight of bags, fuel, angst, existential crises, etcetera—when Ava heard a bubbling laugh and made the mistake of looking for the source. For the thousandth time, she saw someone who could have been Danielle if she'd survived. Same glossy black hair. Same freckles, dark eyes, infectious giggle. She was one of the last ones on, holding up the boarding to flirt with G.B., who was loving it while politely urging her toward her seat.

She'd be twenty-eight this year.

Irrelevant.

And Dennis would be, too.

Also irrelevant. And speaking of irrelevancies, was that Dennis behind the doppelganger of his dead twin?

Why, yes. Yes it was.

"Excuse me," she said, rising, and then stepped out of the cockpit. "Dennis?"

He turned at once and his eyes widened. "Ava! Wow! You—" He cut himself off and looked her up and down. "You look great! Captain. You look great, Captain . . . uh . . . Capp. Huh."

"Believe me, colleagues have pointed out the alliteration," she said dryly. *Shake his hand? Hug? What's the etiquette for running into your secret crush ten years after his sister's murder?*

Ah, she thought as he bent toward her. *The A hug. Arms around shoulders, pelvises at least a foot apart, butts sticking out just a bit. Completely awkward and joyless. So, perfect.*

"It's great to see you," she said, pulling back from their sterile hug. "But time's not on your side, cutie."

"Rude." Oof, that grin. It made Tom Cruise's look like Donald Trump's. "Pretty sure it's not on anyone's side."

"So follow your friend's example"—she nodded at the woman who had preceded him on the plane—"and plant your butt in your seat."

"That's my cousin, Xenia. But aye-aye, Cap Capp. Consider my butt planted," he replied, and then—

Oh, shit. Here it comes.

—let out his patented giggle. Which never failed to make her snicker. Dennis Monahan was as close to a cliché as a man could be and not work in movies or ads as central casting's rugged-yet-sensitive guy: tall, with sleek runner's muscles, thick dark tousled hair, just the right amount of stubble, bright blue eyes, light tan—Dennis Monahan was an absurdly good-looking man.

So the giggle, which sounded like a noise an effeminate cartoon character might make if someone poked them in the belly, was always incongruous. And she had never been able to resist it.

"Jesus Christ," she muttered before she could stop herself, which made him giggle harder. And like that, it was ten years ago, her best friend was alive, and she had a crush on the cutest guy in town. "Go sit down already. I can't be having that weird tittering in my head for the next three hours. My God. The idea."

With a smile and a wave, he obeyed.

"Weird tittering?" India commented, staring straight ahead as Ava took her seat. "Good call. He sounds like a cartoon villain on helium."

"Yep." Fortunately, there was no need for further small talk, because she got the high sign from G.B. just as they got their authorization and picked up the mic.

"Northeastern Southwest 402, cleared for takeoff. Contact Departure on frequency."

She clicked in. "Roger, Tower, Northeastern Southwest 402 switching to Departure."

So began another day in the sky, and she wasn't hiding.

She wasn't. She didn't love flying out of some silly half-formed notion that no one could corner and kill her in the air. She loved it for other reasons. *Lots* of other reasons. The, um, uniforms, for one. And the food. And the long hours. And the drunken unruly passengers who thought she was an overpaid cab driver.

No question.

At all.

$\mathcal{T}wo$

Minneapolis–Saint Paul International Airport
Terminal 1, Lindbergh

". . . and we've just landed in the Twin Cities, where the temperature is sixty-four degrees despite being high summer because Minnesota. Which is just . . . bleah. Anyway, we at Northeastern Southwest—we fly everywhere!—appreciate your business and wish you a pleasantly frigid day."

Ava could hear G.B. bitching from the jump seat ("Oh my God with the weather again. She will *not* let it go.") and the new crew member laughing softly.

"No comment from the copilot?" Ava asked sweetly.

India shook his head and quirked a smile at her.

"Oh boy, I know that look. Out with it."

"You know it's not in my nature to pry into my captain's personal life."

"Oh my God."

"Right. Now that *that's* out of the way . . ." He cleared his throat. "That guy. The last passenger to get on. He looks, um, familiar." When Ava said nothing, he added, "He looks like Danielle Monahan. In fact."

"Dennis is Danielle's twin," Ava replied. Or would it be *was* her twin? Were you still twins when one was in the grave? Not that Danielle was in a grave; there'd been precious little of her left to bury. And there was no point asking how India knew what Danielle looked like. Sooner or later, everyone in her flight crew eventually found out about Danielle and how her murder literally propelled Ava into the sky.

"Tenth anniversary of the, um."

"Yep."

"And you don't like the Twin Cities under the best of circumstances, never mind now. So," he finished, "no wonder you're grumpy about the weather."

"The weather sucks."

"It's actually kind of ni—"

"I don't like MSP because most of the time I have to crosswind taxi. And that's *after* we navigate the OPDs."*

"Uh-huh."

"And there's no need to look at me like I'm about to set you on fire. We've been flying together how long? You know I'm not gonna bite your head off. Most likely."

"That's true. In fact, you seem kind of, um, detached about the whole thing. The murder. And what happened after. Or at least like you don't mind."

She made an exasperated noise. "Or because I've had a decade to come to terms with it."

Alas, India wasn't having it. "New employees are skittish about it because they assume it's an unbroachable subject."

---

* optimized profile descents

India jerked his head to the side, indicating the jump seat. "Takes 'em a few flights to learn it doesn't seem to bother you at all."

"Aaaaand again: it's been a decade, India."

"A long time to be alone."

"Ah-ha!" Then she realized what he was getting at. "Oh, *no*." Abort, abort! This was worse than an unwanted-yet-casual chitchat about *feelings* with a colleague. Much, much worse. "No. No, no, no."

"It's just that I really think you'd love my wife's cousin. He's a great—"

"No. No. No. No. No. No. No." Then, wary of alarming passengers even with the cockpit door shut, she whispered, "No. No. No. No. No. No."

"Just one double date."

"No. No. No. No. No. Stop or I'll hurl you out of this plane."

"We've docked, so I'm pretty sure that wouldn't kill me."

"Who's talking about killing you? I just want out of this conversation." And this plane. And this city. State. The Midwest in general. And the unreasonable gym contract she'd signed on January 2. "Enough. Pretend you care about flying—"

"I *do* care about flying."

"—and let's finish up here."

"Finish up," he said, and snickered. She bit back a groan; though she hadn't lived here for years, her dialect was peppered with various Midwesternisms. Same reason she couldn't stand to watch even one season of *Fargo*. Screw their quirky characters and exquisitely timed dark humor. "Then have a hotdish."

"It's just hotdish. It's not *a* hotdish. You're not going to *a* school, you're just going to school. Same thing."

"Oh, you betcha."

"Stop that. Do I mock your Chicago patois?"

"Not that I can recall. You save most of your mockery for my fix-ups."

"As I should. Now don't take this the wrong way, India, but I'd like to race through our exit protocol and cabin checks so I can get the hell away from you."

"Can't set foot on Minnesota terra firma fast enough, huh?"

"Oh my God." *Should have known when I gave Blake the boot—that was going to be the best part of my day.* "I'm going to sabotage your next simulator eval."

"Bring it. I love a challenge."

Three

THE LIST
Avoid India for at least a week
Get out of memorial
Meeting?
Pick up moisturizer

As she had feared, Dennis and his cousin were waiting for
her at the gate. Trying to combine dithering
    ("Did you check the toilet for corpses?"
    "That happened *one* time!")
with racing through checklists
    ("Not much left now and then we can get out of here."
    "Seriously, though, if you gave my wife's cousin a chance . . .")
had not worked.
    Dennis greeted her with, "It's so great to see you! Again."
And another awkward A hug.
    "You too."
    "And I don't think you ever met my girlfriend, Xenia."
    Ava shook the woman's hand, marveling again at the

resemblance. "So nice to finally meet you," Xenia said, smiling. "You probably don't remember—we crossed paths at the funeral, but . . ."

But she'd been numb. She could have run into Angelina Jolie and not remembered later. Then his words hit her. "I thought you said you were cousins."

"Well, I figured it'd be easier for you to place her."

"We're not *really* cousins," Xenia broke in. "Or at least, not close ones."

"Our great-grandparents were siblings," Dennis said.

"So that's . . . what? Second cousins? First cousins once removed? Or twice?" Ava started counting on her fingers, which was dumb—how would fingers help here?

"We can legally bang," Dennis said. "Which is what counts." And Xenia giggled, which was irritating.

"What a relief," Ava replied, deadpan. "For a second I was super worried about your sex life."

"It's fine," he replied.

No doubt.

"We can talk about the elephant in the room," he continued.

Kill me, please. "We can?" *Yes, but should we? No. We should not.*

"Absolutely."

Argh.

They both nodded at her, which was unsettling. "Go on. Ask us anything," Dennis prompted.

"I honestly don't have any questions. At all." They waited, clearly not believing her, so she sighed and added, "Fine— Dennis, you're banging someone who looks like your dead twin sister. You don't think that's a little weird? You don't think *other* people will find that a little weird? Like your mom? Which, I imagine, is why you're feeling me out on the subject, no pun intended?"

"*What?*" From Xenia.

"Oh my God!" From Dennis, eyes bulging in distress. "We were talking about the memorial! We know you don't want to come!"

"*That's* the elephant in the room?"

"Of course it is!"

"If you know I don't want to come, then why even bring it up?"

"We're hoping to persuade you! Which is why it's an elephant!"

Annnnnnd it gets worse. "That's not the actual elephant."

"Well, I know that now, obviously!"

"We should stop yelling! Especially in an airport!"

"Good point," Xenia put in, doing a credible job of sounding less horrified than she'd looked a minute ago.

"Okay, so. The memorial." Ava coughed. "Danielle's memorial. Ten years. Right. I don't think I was invited."

"Of course you were invited," he snapped. "After family, you were the first one on the list." Which would have been flattering, except there were a thousand Monahans. Being guest number 1,001 was not flattering in the least. Not that it was about being flattered. Right?

"Well, I'm on the road a lot," she said, gesturing to the bustling to-and-fro of the Minneapolis–Saint Paul International Airport. "You know, with . . . the flying."

"Which is why we sent multiple invites."

"But, again: on the road."

"The last two were sent certified. We know you got them."

"Oh. Well. That settles it, I guess." There was a long, difficult pause. "So, you guys can legally bang, huh?"

Four

THE LIST

Feign appendicitis to get out of memorial

Never ever ever stay in Minnesota longer than ninety minutes ever ever again

Seriously, skin is flaking like a snake—moisturizer!

After googling appendicitis symptoms, Ava decided to bite the bullet (which, if done literally and then swallowed, might have mimicked appendicitis symptoms) and just *go* already. She had nowhere to be until 0700 tomorrow—another pilot had asked for her Boston and D.C. hops.

Which is why she was pulling into the Crisp and Gross Funeral Home (after a quick stop at CVS to pick up some lotion—all that time in the air wreaked havoc on her skin) at 6:30 P.M. on a Saturday night.

Who are you kidding? It wasn't like you had a hot date lined up.

No, it wasn't like that. Though she'd never had any trouble finding someone to fill a spot in her (hotel) bed, seeing Dennis had thrown her off her game. And speaking of . . .

"Thanks for coming." He was standing on the sidewalk in front of the two-story building that looked like one of those older Tudor-style buildings: dark roof, stone instead of bricks, weathered. Dennis had changed and looked smart in dark slacks, a pale blue shirt, navy blazer, matching tie, all of which artfully set off his stubble. Dennis was a master of "scruffy on purpose while pretending it's not on purpose."

"Gotta admit, I had my doubts."

"How else would we have continued our incredibly awkward conversation about whether or not you're committing incest if I didn't come?"

"Yeah, God forbid we put *that* to bed. So to speak."

She groaned. He smiled back, stepped aside and gestured, then courteously followed her in.

The first thing she saw was a huge blowup of Danielle's senior picture, the one where her brunette hair looked like a cloud instead of pulled back in her habitual ponytail, her eyes were artfully smoky with a professional makeup application, and her long fingers (tipped with artificial pastel-pink nails) were cupping her chin, emphasizing the point. The photo she fucking *hated.* "It's what they want me to look like," she'd explained. "Not what I actually look like."

And there it is in a nutshell, she thought, staring at the poster. *Her folks didn't get it then, and they don't get it now.*

The second thing she noticed was the banner hanging over the door into the chapel: WE CELEBRATE LIFE!, which was a cold lie.

Still not too late to feign appendicitis.

No, no. Better to suck it up and endure. And it wasn't like there would be much interaction—to her surprise, there were only about a dozen people milling around, speaking quietly.

"Isn't that a *wonderful* picture of dear Danielle?"

and saying absolutely nothing.

"Hello, Ava."

She turned and saw a short, slender man about her own age, dressed in a beautifully cut black suit, blinking at her through Versace eyeglass frames and holding out a small, slim hand.

"Oh. Hello." She shook his hand and wondered if it would be better to pretend to know him or admit straight-out that she had no idea—

"It's Pete. Crisp?"

Dilemma overcome. "Of course, sure. Pete Crisp." Of the Crisp and Gross Funeral Home, no less. His generation was the second or third to run the place. "How are you?"

"Bewildered." He glanced around the funeral home. "I haven't been back here for years. Not since my cousin took over."

"Oh, God, tell me about it. Why do people think nostalgia is so great? Everything about this place is . . ."

"Yes."

"And it's all so . . ."

"Yes."

"So what have you been up to? Are you a pharmacist now? Or a drug rep?" She had a vague memory of him wanting to invent the cure for cancer or, if not, to market the cure for cancer.

"No, I moved to Scotland after I got my computer science degree. Liked it so much I never came back. These days I move around depending on the job." He shrugged. "I'm never in the same place for long. So we have something in common, Captain Bellyflopper."

"Nope. Not discussing that right now. Today is about Danielle."

"You don't have to discuss it. I read all about it online," he teased. "Did you know Buzzfeed made a quiz about you?"

"Buzzfeed has made quizzes out of literally everything on the planet, including onions and soup. I'm one of a crowd."

"No, not you. You've always been singular."

True enough, in the literal sense. It was why she loved hanging out at Casa Monahan. And she was beginning to place Pete, who had been a year or two ahead of her in school. He'd volunteered at the same nursing home. Speaking of . . .

"Did you hear Shady Oaks finally had to shut down?"

He nodded. "I was astonished it took as long as it did."

"Right? I mean, those guys were shady when *we* were there. I guess the drug thing—the latest drug thing—was a bridge too far."

"Hey, Pete. Here, Ava."

"Thanks. Nice talking to you, Pete." She accepted a cup of water from Dennis, profoundly wished it was vodka

(No one understood the Atomic Blonde's love of vodka like I understood the Atomic Blonde's love of vodka.)

and sucked it down. She had just decided that getting sloppily drunk at that point in time would be an error of judgment when she heard, "Look what the cat brought . . . haw!" and turned.

There was Xenia, blinking her big doe fuck-me eyes

(low-cut sparkly black cocktail dress? really?)

while pushing a wheelchair that held, at first glance, Methuselah. Or one of his close relatives.

"My God," Ava said, staring. "You're still alive? How is that possible?"

For that she got another "Haw!" from the man in the chair and an expressive eye roll from Xenia. "Welcome home, you sassy brat."

"It's not home and it's nice to see you again, Pat."

"You too, girlie girl—and I hear it's 'Captain' Capp these days."

"Wow," Ava marveled. "You didn't even use them and I could *still* see the air quotes."

Darren Monahan, the patriarch (only Ava got away with calling him Pat for short), though wheelchair bound for years, had the broad, deep chest of a man who used his upper body far more than his legs, as well as the Monahan dark hair and eyes. He was a retired salesman—cars, used cars, farm equipment, furniture, copy machines, insecticide—and in his prime could sell anything to anyone. And had, as half the state could attest.

"Yes, it's Captain Capp now. Also, keeping tabs on me? Not too creepy, Pat. I'm young enough to be your great-great-great-great-great-granddaughter."

"Oh, *hell* no. Think I got nothing better t'do than look you up? That boy Dennis was blathering about you when we got here. And while it's nice to see your beautiful blank face again—"

"For God's sake. Three lies in one sentence fragment."

"—this is one of them times I'm glad my sister isn't here to see this." He looked around at the mourners, the poster of Danielle, the flowers. "This woulda killed her. As opposed to the cancer that killed her."

Ava decided the focus should stay on Danielle and let that pass. "Xenia, did you lose a bet? Is that why you're on chair detail?"

Xenia laughed. "Yes. And yes!"

"No one needs to be on chair detail," Pat fussed. He was wearing a black suit, clearly new, with scuffed black dress shoes, clearly old, and couldn't stop fiddling with his shirt cuffs. "*I'm* on chair detail."

"You know those two things can't be true at the same time, right, Pat?" She made an effort not to stare at his shoes. They made her sad—scuffed, clearly ill cared for—in a way the wheelchair didn't. Who needed to take care of shoes when you never really used them anymore? They were just . . . foot decorations.

"That's enough out of you," he commanded. "Make yourself useful. Here comes That Boy Dennis. Go see what he wants."

"Hey, Grandpa." He turned to Ava. "You know, I was nine before I found out That Boy wasn't actually part of my name? *Nine*."

Ava tried to convey sympathy, exasperation, and gentle sorrow at the same time without saying anything and doubted she was pulling it off. But, just then, most of the group started moving toward the chapel doors.

She let Dennis, Pat, and Xenia pass, then filed in behind them and took a seat toward the back of the chapel. The stone windowless room with the dark wood altar at the front matched her mood. She wasn't sure she was up to sunlight splashed through stained glass windows and the accompanying clichés about God's plan and how Danielle was in a better place.

Someone who had never met Danielle talked. And talked. And Ava was meanly glad to note that sitting in the back was making it harder for the gawkers to gawk. You couldn't subtly stare at someone when you had to twist halfway round to see them. She met every guarded look and side-eye with a wide, toothy smile and raised eyebrows. She decided giving them a double thumbs-up would be overkill.

After a while, the stranger stopped talking and Danielle's mother talked. Then Xenia, who liked the "out of death comes my boyfriend who is also a distant cousin so it's not all bad" theory and expounded on it for five minutes.

And then it was over. Ava tried (and failed) not to leap to her feet and bolt for the foyer. She'd have to do some glad-handing, perhaps accept a few more awkward hugs, maybe extra banter with the grumpy patriarch, and then she'd be free. Then it was back to the Hyatt to pay eighteen bucks to watch a *Fast and Furious* movie and suck down at least two room service sundaes.

"We couldn't believe it when we saw you come in." This from Dennis and Danielle's mother, Mrs. Monahan, a bird-like woman whose hands were so small they were like flesh-colored bundles of twigs. "After all this time."

"Yes, I flew with Dennis here."

"Oh, that's right. You're a flight attendant."

"Pilot."

"Oh, a copilot? Already?"

"Pilot pilot. Yeah."

"And how are your folks?"

"Dead."

"Oh."

"Yeah."

"Ma, did you forget how bad Ava is at small talk?" This from Dennis, who had come up behind her. To Ava: "Seriously, you are the worst. I'm sorry about your mom and dad, though. You got my card?"

Ava nodded. Car accident on the way to her college grad-uation. Toyota Camry vs. snow plow = send flowers. They'd outlived Danielle by two years almost to the day. Her folks had been only children, and children of only children. Ava was an only child; the Capp family had always been small. It was part of the reason she'd been drawn to the Monahans;

there were, at rough count, a zillion of them. Which made the memorial's turnout (only about a dozen people) puzzling.

Well. Ten years. The best and worst thing about life is that it goes on. Any number of Monahans have been born since Danielle died. She might as well be a page in a history book to them. "Here's a chapter on women getting the vote in 1920. And here's a picture of your long-dead cousin. These will seem equally ancient to you."

"I'm surprised there aren't more people here."

"That's why we're doing it all over again tomorrow," Mrs. Monahan replied. "The family's scattered. This way, more of us can say our goodbyes."

If they haven't managed to say goodbye in ten years, why do you think a memorial marathon would help? Ava realized she'd been looking at this all wrong. It could have been worse. She could have had to go both nights.

"Terrible business," Mrs. Monahan was saying, small hands fluttering like she didn't know where to put them. "All of it. And then you went away."

Flew away. Immediately. At the speed of sound, never to return except for the occasional layover and/or memorial service. And to stock up on moisturizer.

Dennis gently caught and held his mother's hands; she looked distinctly relieved. She was a smaller, shrunken, older version of her children, the trademark dark Monahan hair streaked with gray. "Ava, what are you doing after?"

"After? You mean right now?"

"Cripes, you're the worst. Stop being so literal. Listen, Xenia's already left to get Grandpa settled at the hotel, and my ma's gotta get back, too, but I was hoping you and I could grab a drink or something."

"Oh." Wait, without Xenia? And why was her heart suddenly pounding harder? "You—really?"

That glorious, idiotic giggle. "Yeah, *really*. Don't look so shocked. C'mon, I haven't seen you in years. I'd love to catch up with you. Xenia won't mind."

"Xenia doesn't mind a lot of things." This muttered by Dennis's mother, because, like many natives to this land, she was an Olympic-level passive aggressor. "But she's *such* a lovely girl."

"Ma, don't start. She's great. We're doing great."

Huh. Emphasized great and used it twice.

"Really great," he finished.

They are not doing great.

Well, who knew? Perhaps this was meant to be (a phrase she loathed until this moment). Perhaps she and Dennis would rekindle something. Out of mourning comes love. Out of death comes life. Out of Xenia comes Ava.

Wait, that's not right . . .

(Perhaps this was her very own romance novel.)

"Sure I will," she said. "I mean, I'm free. That sounds—that'll be great. Really great. *Fine.* I meant fine. It'll be great to catch up."

"Great!" *It's official: we all need to find a synonym for great.* But Dennis was oblivious to her need for a thesaurus. He let go of his mom's hands, held up one finger. "One sec. I've gotta grab something and then we can go. Ma, you're good? Car's outside?"

"I'm fine, Dennis. I should be getting back, too."

"I'll see you tomorrow before church, okay?" To Ava: "Don't fly away this time, okay?"

"Great! I mean, I won't. Fly. I'm—my feet are here. On the ground. Definitely not flying, heh." *Oh my God. Staaaaawwwpp.*

Dennis darted off and Mrs. Monahan bid a listless farewell

to the stragglers. Far too soon it was down to her and the missus.

"I was surprised to see Pat made it. In a good way," Ava added, since, with Pat, the grouchy buzzard, it could have gone either way. She'd always gotten along with him, though not being related helped. The other Monahans had always walked wide around him.

Mrs. Monahan shrugged. "He'd never miss a family gathering."

"Yep, only death could have thwarted him, and maybe not even that." In fact, Ava wouldn't have wanted to bet on the outcome of a mano a mano with the Grim Reaper and Pat Monahan. Death would be down for the count by the fourth round. "But why's Xenia taking him to a hotel?"

"He sold the farm some time ago."

"You're kidding." The Monahan farm was family legend. Started by Pat's father—or was it grandfather?—it had seen countless births, deaths, and baby showers. Danielle had hated the place, so Ava had only been there a couple of times. "It's hard to imagine him letting it go."

"He *is* nearly ninety, Ava. And no one in my generation wanted to take it over. We don't even like corn."

Wait, you had to like the crop you were growing? Is that a secret farmer rule? The things you learned on the rare trip home you had desperately wanted to avoid!

"And Danielle and Dennis never liked it."

"No, they were always trying to get out of visiting when they were teenagers," Ava recalled.

"Yes. Exactly. Even if she was—was still alive, she would have had no interest."

"Yeah, I can't really picture her *or* Dennis in overalls."

Mrs. Monahan ignored her silly-ass attempt at humor

(understandable) and continued. "Grandpa M. rents the house and sold the rest of the land a couple of years ago. I think it was a relief. He lives up in Saint Cloud now. It's just easier to spend the night, then start home fresh in the morning."

"Yes, that's a good system." *Ugh. This conversation. I definitely should have downed some vodka.*

"So do you get very homesick, all your time on the road?" Mrs. Monahan made a vague gesture that encompassed the funeral home. "Do you miss Minnesota?"

"Of course I don't miss fucking Minnesota. Are you out of your goddamned mind? The weather sucks and for every pleasant experience I had here, I had nine more that ensured PTSD, substance abuse, lefse, or a stomach virus. The only reason, the *only* reason I'm in town is because I gave another pilot my hours, and the only reason I'm in this room with you is because I wasn't fast enough and then slow enough to give Dennis the slip, and then wasn't smart enough to come up with a credible excuse for missing this horror show. Do I miss Minnesota? Are you clinically insane? *Jesus.*"

She stopped herself, appalled, but when Mrs. M. just kept blinking at her and waiting, she realized none of that had been out loud. Thank *God*.

"Oh, sometimes," she lied. "The, um, fall. Is nice."

"All the colors," was the vague reply.

"The lakes are nice."

"All the lakes."

"Yes, and—shit."

"Beg pardon?"

She was looking around. "I've misplaced my purse. I just had it—I *think* I just had it—" She tried to remember when it was in her hands last. Just after the memorial was finished, she'd set it aside to gulp down more water. "Shit!"

"I'm sure it's around here somewhere," Mama Monahan said, giving off clear "not that I care in the slightest" vibes. Not that Ava could blame her. If the shoe/purse were on the other foot, Ava wouldn't care, either. But then—

"Hey. Ava." Dennis emerged from wherever he'd been, waving a black clutch at her. "This what you're looking for?"

"Yeah, thank goodness." After a quick scan, she was reassured nothing was missing. "You ready?"

"Yep."

And just like that, they fled the Crisp and Gross Funeral Home for the dark sanctuary of the bar. A bar. Any bar.

Five

". . . and then Grandpa Pat literally threw the guy off the porch. Grabbed him and hoisted him and *heaved* and the guy went flying and kicked up a bunch of dust when he landed."

"Probably should have taken Pat seriously when he said 'no comment.'"

"Right? Like trying to set the guy's rental car on fire wasn't enough of a hint? Anyway, that was the height of the media mess."

"Nightmare."

"Yeah. But it didn't get any worse, and after that there were fewer reporters, and then one day, we got up and saw they'd all left."

"Like the swallows on their way to Capistrano."

Dennis snorted. "Sure. Exactly like that."

They were imbibing in the Tamarack Tap Room, because Ava could get behind a place with the motto "Beer, Burgers, Bourbon." Dennis was sucking down a liquid that was so dense and black, it looked like something he had to drink because he lost a bet; Ava was content with rye and ginger.

"Hard to believe it's been ten years."

"Agreed," Ava replied. "Depending on the day I'm having, it either seems like too long a time or not enough time. And I can't imagine—I mean, this had to have been hard for you."

"It wasn't a boatload of chuckles for you, either."

"Yeah, but you lost a twin." She shook her head. "Can't imagine. You know I'm an only."

"I know that's why you hung out at our place all the time," he teased. "You were literally the only person in town who envied Ava for having too many weirdo relatives."

"I think 'weirdo' was unnecessary."

"Hell, for a time people thought you and Danielle were twins. Remember when you both got the same haircut and matching dark dye jobs?"

"Argh, don't remind me. It took so long to grow out." As soon as the words were out, she could have bitten her tongue. Because Danielle's never had a chance to grow out. And the reminder of how desperately Ava was looking for an identity back then made her cringe. Hell, they'd even dressed alike more than once.

"Aw, c'mon." Dennis nudged her, doubtless picking up on her mood. "It was cute. We all thought so. Even the nursing home you guys volunteered at—remember?"

"Vaguely," she lied. She remembered everything: Ava volunteering at Shady Oaks—which provided neither shade nor oaks—and quickly realizing it wasn't going to be what she thought. She'd been picturing grandparental figures, loving proxies. Instead, the residents were real people, and weren't there to fulfill Ava's fantasies of living in a big extended family. The third time she'd had to wipe shit off Mr. Wilkin's ass, she'd decided enough was enough and told her folks she was quitting.

Which led to the "you took on this responsibility and will see it through" lecture, hilarious given how often her parents shirked their own responsibilities. Oblivious to the irony, her mom and dad had then left for their semiannual trip to Vegas.

After crying (and ranting) on Danielle's shoulder, her friend suggested they take turns being Volunteer Aide Ava. It was such a silly, sitcomesque idea, so of course Ava was all over it. So while Volunteer Aide Ava was on the schedule three afternoons a week, the *actual* Ava only went once or twice, while Danielle picked up her other shift. The work was still gross and grueling, but knowing they were "gaming the system" made it interesting.

Ava shrugged off the memories, started to ask something, then cut herself off.

"What?"

"No, it's—okay, well, I'm sure you got asked this all the time, but—was there anything that last day? Anything at all?"

"No, Ava. Trust me. I've been asking myself that for a decade. If anything, you spent more time with her that day than I did."

It was true—she and Danielle had spent most of the day together, divvying up the Volunteer Ava shifts for the next two weeks and gorging on pizza. Ava had finally left to pick up her parents at the airport. And sometime in the four hours that followed, Danielle was butchered like a veal calf in her own bedroom.

Dennis had been out of town for twenty-four hours—an overnight kegger followed by a day trip to the U of M. By the time he got back, it was all over, and not just for Danielle.

"Senseless crime, *fuck*," Dennis said, startling her with the abrupt comment. "Hate that phrase the most, I think."

He was staring into the dregs of his black drink. "The reporters loved that one and it's so stupid. Who'd stand over a stranger's mutilated corpse and say, 'This crime makes perfect sense.' Obviously it's senseless. Christ." Dennis, finished with his third black drink, looked around for their waitress.

"Maybe you want to take a break from the tar?" she asked, smiling so he wouldn't think she was taking his inventory.

"You mean switch to bourbon?"

"Uh . . ."

Half an hour later, Ava was helping Dennis out to the parking lot, if "helping" meant "staggering under his weight."

"Gggggnnnn work with me, Dennis! We might be the same height, but I'm pretty sure you've got at least twenty pounds on me."

"Haven't lost my winter weight," he slurred, which made her laugh, which made her lose her grip, which meant Dennis's ass was about to meet pavement.

"Captain Capp?" Suddenly most of Dennis's weight was gone. "May I be of some assistance?"

"*Some,*" Dennis mumbled to . . . someone. "But don' go overboard. With the . . . uh . . . the assist-tancing. Assisting. We could use a little. Of the assistancing. But not too much."

The man who had come to her assistancing—wait, now *she* was doing it, and she wasn't even drunk—was over six feet tall, with the broad shoulders and overall musculature of a regular lifter. His eyes were deep brown (probably—it wasn't a well-lit parking lot) and his nose was a blade; he was clean-shaven and unabashedly bald, with broad wrists

(Why am I noticing his wrists?)

and casually dressed in tan slacks and a navy-blue dress shirt. His voice was a deep rumble, almost a baritone, as he quietly answered Dennis's questions.

"You're super tall. And *big*. Are you a skyscraper sometimes?"

"I am not."

"Well, you should drink about it. Think about it. Is what I
meant. Not drink. D'you want to get a drink and tell me how
you became a skyscraper?"

"No, thank you."

"Thanks a lot," she told the mystery hunk after he'd man-
handled Dennis into the car with about as much trouble as
she'd have with a sack of groceries. "We've had a long day."

"Not as long as Danielle's!" Dennis shouted from the back
seat. "That day, I mean. Her last day. Not today. Ava, is this
a rental car? Cuz I might have to throw up in it. So much.
Not right this second. Prob'ly later. Just so you're apprised of,
y'know. The situation."

"Thanks," Ava said to the mystery man, and she could feel
her face getting warm. Drunken ex-boyfriend shouting inappropriate observations? Check. Long-ass day including her
best friend's memorial? Check. Mysterious hunk seeing her and
Dennis at their worst? Mark that one off, too. Vomiting im-
minent? Of course! "I'm not sure I could have gotten him in."

"Where do you have to go?"

"The Hyatt next to the mall. But we'll be fine. I'm sure
I can manage." Her confident tone was immediately contra-
dicted by the sound of retching from the back seat. "Anyway.
Thanks again."

He chuckled, a wonderful rumble that she practically felt,
then held up a finger in the universal gesture for "give me a
minute," and sprinted away. Yeah. *Sprinted*. If she wasn't seeing it, she wouldn't have believed a large man could move so
quickly. And he was back in seconds, reaching through the
open back seat door and handing Dennis a . . .

"What is that?"

"Emesis basin."

"Thanks, man! If my dead sister wasn't dead, she'd really like you! She's dead, though. So. There's that."

Ava tried to shut out the drunken babble and focus. "Emesis? Those things you find in hospital rooms?"

"Yes."

"Why are you traveling with an emesis basin?"

"Don't worry. I've got plenty. I don't need that one back."

Plenty? "Thank God," she replied with no small amount of relief, because from the sounds, Dennis was using the hell out of the thing. Or he was being devoured by dinosaurs.

The weight-lifting track star smiled and said, "Why don't I follow you? The Hyatt is less than ten minutes from here. I'll help you so you can get him up to your room."

"We're not sharing a room," she said quickly, because she'd decided it was important to establish that for some reason. "I mean, it's not necessary. Don't put yourself out."

"I wouldn't be, Captain Capp. I didn't imply I would aid you without payment."

Hey! "Hey, that's right! How'd you know who I was? Wait, don't tell me . . ."

"Belly landing," they finished in unison. "Argh, they're gonna chisel that into my tombstone."

"As well they should, if the stories are accurate. In return for my assistance with your friend this evening, I ask that you allow me to buy you a drink in the hotel bar and tell me the tale of the belly landing."

She stared at him. "I don't even know you."

"Yes, that's correct."

She thought about trying to wrestle a vomit-spattered

Dennis out of her car, through the parking lot, into the lobby, up the elevator—

You know what? Fuck it.

"Deal," she said.

From the back seat: "I'm done throwing up if you two wanna bone in the back seat."

"Jesus Christ," she muttered, but the mystery hunk just laughed.

Six

"Of course I recognized the infamous Captain Bellyflop—"

"Oh, for—I do *one* interview with Buzzfeed . . ."

"—and had to introduce myself."

"There's really not that much to it."

"I have found that when someone says that, ninety-five percent of the time it's demonstrably untrue."

"What, you've done a scientific study? Besides, it was. And it was ages ago. I can't believe people still remember."

"It was two and a half weeks ago. Which in news-cycle time is about forty years, I grant you."

"Ages ago," she insisted.

"Next you'll tell me you were simply doing your job—"

"Well, I was."

"—and your training kicked in—"

"It did."

"—and it was a group effort, and thus your crew is equally entitled to the public kudos."

"It's true! My friend G.B. didn't hesitate to take over the booze cart."

They were in the Bar Urbana, but the drinks made up for the terrible name and uncomfortable chairs. The courteous/yummy stranger had been true to his word, helped her get Dennis up to his room (miraculously, Dennis hadn't missed the emesis basin), got him to drink a big glass of water, left another for him on the nightstand, put his phone in reach, and left him dozing off to the Weather Channel.

Now they were back in the lobby, and Ava was appreciating that the dim lighting of the parking lot had not done the man justice. *Two words: oofta. No, wait . . .*

"So, then," he prompted. "What happened?"

"Well—" She stopped, embarrassed. "I just realized I don't—"

"It's Tom Baker." He stuck out his hand and, amused, she shook it.

"Good enough. Well, my friend G.B.—he's a flight attendant—we were deadheading to Vegas. That's when employees of an airline who aren't on duty take a flight for free. And everything was pretty quiet right up until the aneurysm . . ."

Seven

Ages ago

"It sounds so . . . unceremonious. I can't believe she just up and dumped you like that."

"I can," G.B. replied gloomily. "I knew she was an up-and-dumper *and* a superficial wench when we got together, but even so, I didn't anticipate—"

"Falling in love?"

"No, you idiot. Have we met? I got used to the perks that come with the 'Influencer' lifestyle."

"Wow. I actually heard the capital *I*. And you see the irony in you calling *her* superficial, right?"

"So much free shit," G.B. moaned, ignoring Ava's 100 percent on-point observation. "Much of which was passed on to me. See?" He held out his wrist, displaying a Power Rangers wristwatch. "She didn't even *like* Power Rangers. That's when I knew we'd never be long-term."

"What a heartbreak," Ava observed. "Well, you're welcome

to stay at my place while you look for a new place. You've still got my key from last time."

"Thanks, and that's another thing. I have to go from a McMansion with high ceilings—the place was basically one gigantic loft—and a pool *and* a home gym back to that hovel my mom's letting me squat in."

"The hovel would be the mid-six-figure condo at the Platinum? One of the three she owns?"

"Only one bedroom." He sighed. "And no home gym."

Given the excellent shape the man was in, Ava could understand his woe. For all his frivolous bitchiness when he wasn't on duty, and all his calm, polite efficiency when he was, more than once a woman had moved her purse when she saw him approach. Or crossed the street. Or wouldn't get on an elevator with him. A clueless coworker had once suggested G.B. not work out so much, not look so imposing. G.B. had fixed him with a cold stare and said, "They're judging me on skin color, so *I'm* the one who has to change my life. Got it."

Long story short, a home gym and free watches would induce G.B. to tolerate an "Influencer" for months. Which he had. However, to everything there was a season. Or something. "I'm pretty sure you're gonna land on your feet."

His reply was a snort, but before she could form a devastating rebuttal, they both heard the odd noises from the cockpit. They were in seats 3A and 3B, and the cockpit was less than ten feet away. And it wasn't soundproofed, so it was easy to hear the thuds.

"Flight Attendant Evans to the cockpit, please."

Ava could not recall ever being in a cockpit and doing or seeing anything that would result in the noise they were hearing followed by the immediate summons of a senior flight attendant.

"Maybe he spilled hot coffee . . . ?"

"Maybe," she replied.

Flight Attendant Evans, a short brunette with a fixed smile, hurried past them and disappeared into the cockpit, reappearing almost immediately and going for their seats like she was laser guided. Ava reached for her seat belt just as she heard the click of G.B. unbuckling his. "We're up," he said under his breath.

"Pardon me, Captain Capp, the first officer would like to see you on the flight deck."

"Of course," she replied. To G.B.: "Stand by."

"I'll be here," he replied dryly.

When she stepped onto the flight deck she saw at once what had been making those odd thuds: the pilot appeared to have had a full-on stroke at the controls, and the copilot had tried to shift him. He was slumped, semiconscious, and his right arm and leg were limp. When he turned with great effort to look at her, she noted his right eye was drooping and the right side of his mouth was drawn down. She felt a fist clench just above her stomach and begin to squeeze.

"Captain Lewis, may I be of assistance?"

He tried to answer her, couldn't. The first officer glanced at her, then back at the controls. "Ma'am, I think he's had a stroke. But the thing is, this happened when we were trying to deal with a hydraulic leak."

The fist tightened. "I see. And when you say 'leak' . . ."

"Major fluid loss. And I—" The first officer looked at the pilot, down at his instruments, up at Ava. He cleared his throat. "I've only been doing this for four months."

The fist tightened . . . then relaxed. Not knowing had been the worst of it.

"I understand, First Officer Wilson. As the manifest advised,

I'm Captain Ava Capp, and I've been doing this for six years." Which in pilot time meant she was a bratty teenager as opposed to a teething toddler, but there was absolutely *no* point saying that out loud. To the flight attendant: "Please bring Flight Attendant Benjin to the flight deck." To the pilot: "Sir, I'm relieving you as of"—a glance at her phone, which she'd set to RECORD the moment she stepped on deck—"thirteen hundred hours." She was reasonably certain he knew exactly what she was doing, but there was no telling how severe the stroke had been, so it was worth elaborating. "We're going to make you comfortable and get you medical assistance ASAP, and since you decided to goof off, I'll be helping your first officer land the plane today. I won't tell you not to worry," she said, squeezing his shoulder. "But we've got this."

And here was G.B., who took in the situation at a glance. "How can I help?"

"The captain is in difficulty. Please assist Flight Attendant Evans in moving him to an empty row, then assist the crew as needed and stand by for further instructions."

"Right away."

"I'll be making an announcement to the passengers shortly; I'll want you back on deck when you hear it. You know what to do until then. And after then, actually."

He smiled. "Yes, ma'am." Then: "Ooch over, Evans. I'll shift him out of there for you."

Ava was at the controls seconds later, and after a thorough check, turned to her pale but calm first officer. "Everything else looks good, aside from that pesky matter of no hydraulics."

He blinked and almost smiled. "Yes, ma'am. Aside from that."

"All right. I'm showing we're forty-four minutes out from Vegas, but Salt Lake City is closer. Your captain needs an ambulance, so I'm going to advise SLC of our situation and we'll go from there."

"Yes, Captain." He nodded stiffly and she realized just how frightened he was. It would have been horrifying to see his captain go down for the count, even without the hydraulics issue. His eyes were so wide they showed the whites all around, like a crisply uniformed horse about to bolt, and he was sweating. But his ass was in the seat, he was paying attention and following his checklist, and he'd called her within seconds of his captain's stroke.

She tapped his wrist. "It will be fine," she said. "I'll bet you dinner on it."

He tentatively smiled back. "You're on."

She clicked in. "SLC, this is Northeastern Southwest flight 729 bound for Las Vegas, Captain Ava Capp, Northeastern Southwest employee number 293, at the controls. Captain Lewis appears to have had a stroke and First Officer Wilson has requested my assistance. I have had Captain Lewis moved to the First Class section and will initiate an emergency landing."

There was a short, startled silence, followed by, "Copy that, Captain Capp, NS 729."

"We also have a hydraulics issue. EICAS* indicated a drop in pressure; extent of damage unknown."

"Copy that, NS 729. Where would you like to go?"

"Salt Lake City."

"NS 729, we understand. Please advise when you want to come in."

"Copy, Tower."

---

* Engine-indicating and crew-alerting system.

Wilson let out a breath. "Okay. So. There's a plan."

"There's always a plan, First Officer Wilson."

"How about the passengers?"

Passenger announcements were at the captain's discretion. This wasn't her first emergency landing, and experience had taught Ava not to say a word until she'd taken care of the essentials and had a plan for landing. Which she now had, so she clicked into the PA system.

"Ladies and gentlemen, my name is Captain Ava Capp. Captain Lewis has had a medical emergency, so we are keeping him comfortable and diverting to Salt Lake City. We'll be landing in a few minutes, and, needless to say, I've turned on the fasten-seatbelts sign. The flight attendants are standing by to assist you, and I will update you as often as I can. And remember, once we're safely on the ground, you'll have a good story for your friends and family."

There was a quick rap at the cabin door, and then G.B. was poking his head in.

"How's Captain Lewis?" she asked.

"There are no medical personnel among the passengers, so we're giving him oxygen and monitoring his vitals." Which was about all they *could* do, but it was better than nothing.

"Very well. I need a head count, passengers and crew," she replied without looking up.

"Got it right here," G.B. said at once, because he was terrific. "Two hundred twenty-two passengers, crew of seven, including us."

"Copy, leave the manifest where I can grab it in a hurry."

"Copy. I also have a number of passengers requesting drinks service. Specifically booze."

"Oh, I'm sure. But that's a negative."

"I figured." Then, lower, "I wanted to request booze, too, but you're heartless so I have to do this sober."

Startled, Wilson let out a bark of laughter as G.B. exited.

"NS 729, this is the SLC tower."

"SLC, this is NS 729. Go."

"Report SLC when in sight, please."

"In sight," Ava replied, because yay! It was. Never had the clay valley of Salt Lake City looked so inviting. "Tower, SLC airport is in sight."

"Very good, NS 729. Runway four is available."

"Copy that, descending to runway four. Please roll an ambulance."

"Got it, NS 729. Rolling ambulance."

"Okay, Wilson, let's see what's going on with the hydraulics. Starting descent." But because it was that kind of day . . . "Landing gear is not deploying." She tried again. Nothing. So the hydraulic system was fucked. "Accessing electrical system to deploy landing gear." Gotta love all the redundancies the engineers thought up . . . except that wasn't working, either. No hydraulics + no way to bypass and use the electrical system = no landing gear. No landing gear = belly landing. What fun. "Tower, our landing gear will not deploy. Repeat, attempts to lower landing gear have been unsuccessful. Can you verify with a visual?"

"Negative, NS 729; all incoming flights were diverted."

"Copy. We'll be making a gear-up landing. Are we still go for runway four?"

"Affirmative, NS 729. Runway four is ready for you. Rolling more ground emergency crews."

"Copy, Tower. I'm going to circle up here for a while, use up some of our fuel."

"Copy, NS 729."

Wilson cleared his throat. "We're still on for dinner, though, right? Because everything's going to be fine?"

"Of course." She clicked into the PA system. "Ladies and gentlemen, we are unable to lower our landing gear, which means we'll be making what's called a belly landing. I know that sounds scary, but I can tell you that in twenty years, there have been only three belly landings and all resulted in zero injuries. I'm going to circle for a bit while they get ready for us. Follow the crew's instructions *to the letter* or you're in for a *major* scolding. I'm not kidding. I'll use foul language and everything."

She clicked off and looked at Wilson. "Ready?"

"Of course."

"Atta boy. Y'know, the chances of a pilot emergency *and* a hydraulics issue have to be millions to one. When we get on the ground, I'm buying a lottery ticket."

"When we get on the ground, I'll buy you all the tickets you want." While they were talking, Wilson had been going over the emergency landing checklist—airlines have lists for everything—and Ava set a course to keep to her pattern and burn fuel. Might as well minimize the chance of them all going up in a blazing fireball, which would be unpleasant and inconvenient.

A familiar rap, and G.B. was there. "We're getting set up back there, Captain. Anything I can do for you?"

"How's our other captain doing?"

"Laughed his ass off when he heard your announcement. Which got the passengers in First laughing, so it wasn't all bad. He says the odds of a pilot medical emergency and a belly landing are millions to one."

"See?" she said to Wilson. "Today's the day to buy a Powerball ticket. G.B., get back there and you and everyone else assume the position."

"Way ahead of you. Good luck, my friend."

"He's only saying that because he's terrified and homeless," she confided to Wilson.

"Well, he's got company. On the first one, anyway. How much more fuel you want to burn?"

Twenty-five minutes' worth, as it turned out. By then, the Tower had summoned what looked like every fire truck and ambulance in the state, and she didn't dare linger—there was also Captain Lewis to think about.

"NS 729, we can see you. Your landing gear is *not* down. Do you need a repeat?"

"Negative, Tower, thank you for the visual verification," she replied, unsurprised. Faint hope, and all that.

"You are cleared for low approach."

Well, I certainly hope so, since I'm in one. "Thank you, Tower. On approach."

"NS 729, when able, please report SOB and remaining fuel."

"Tower, we have two hundred twenty-nine souls on board including a crew of seven, and forty minutes."

"Copy. Wind calm and we have emergency trucks standing by."

"Very good, Tower."

As they descended, Ava realized she was white-knuckling and loosened her grip. Belly landings tended to do major damage to the aircraft, but almost never the passengers—that was the good news. The bad was that there was a risk the plane would flip, break up, cartwheel, catch fire, or any hellish combo of the four. Hell, keeping the aircraft straight and level was a must even *with* landing gear.

As they descended, she breathed silent thanks for good visibility and low crosswinds. Runway four seemed to be racing up to meet them, and when they hit, there was a terrific bounce and a horrifying noise, like the plane was screaming as its belly was scraped to shit while Ava and Wilson fought to keep seven hundred thousand pounds under control. The plane slid for another two hundred meters, then came to a shuddering, grinding stop.

Ava turned to her first officer. "I probably should have anticipated the smell."

"Jesus Christ, we're not dead!"

"That's the spirit. Tower, we've landed and the crew is evacuating the passengers."

"Copy, NS 729. Welcome to Salt Lake City."

They could already hear the flight attendants deploying slides and barking instructions, and Ava opened the cockpit door in time to see Captain Lewis actually kick G.B. back with his one working leg as he pointed furiously to the passengers and shook his head. Clearly the idea of deplaning before his passengers was beyond unthinkable.

"G.B., see to the passengers." She could see the plane was rapidly emptying and decided it would be safer to unload Captain Lewis in forty seconds as opposed to upsetting him (and the passengers) by carrying him off now. "Wilson and I will see to the captain."

"Yes, ma'am." Later, at the bar, G.B. would drink to Lewis and say, "For a guy who was barely conscious and could only use half his body, he put up a hell of a fight."

Afterward, Ava found out they had everyone off the plane in 102 seconds, with zero injuries aside from Lewis. She was amazed when she realized the time lapse from Evans asking her into the cockpit to deplaning was fifty-eight minutes.

A final head count had shown everyone was out, and then she was sliding out of the plane *(wheeeeeee!)* where G.B. was waiting for her. "Idiot," she told him. "You're not supposed to wait."

"You're not supposed to land without wheels." With that, he grabbed her and swung her around in an exuberant hug— he was one of the few men who made her feel doll-sized— and when she threw her head back to laugh, Buzzfeed had its photo of the week.

But like an idiot, or someone born before social media, she'd thought that would be the end of it. Not on the airline's part, of course—there would be months of investigation, meetings, PR damage control, more meetings, interviews, debriefings, meetings about debriefings, etcetera. But she assumed the public wouldn't be terribly interested past the first day or so.

When she and G.B. finally left the debriefing room, they were astonished to find hundreds of people waiting to see her, most of them refusing to be budged by airport employees. And many of them *were* airport employees. Suddenly everyone wanted to shake her hand.

"You seem surprised," G.B. said as they tried to make their way through the crowd, shaking random hands thrust at them and smiling rather fixedly. "What, did you forget that literally everyone is walking around with a portable television studio these days?"

"Kind of," she replied, blinking at all the cell phone lights. "Probably a bad day to wear shorts and my PILOTS: LOOKING DOWN AT PEOPLE SINCE 1903 T-shirt."*

"Naw. Shirt's the best part of this story. You wait and see."

---

* This is a real shirt!

Eight

"It *was* the best part of the story," Tom agreed.

"You've heard of the miracle on the Hudson? G.B. called it the unlikelihood in Salt Lake City."

"Did you ever find out why you couldn't deploy the landing gear?"

"The FAA guys found out that a circuit breaker popped. Nobody knows how, just that it would have happened after takeoff. Since they could use hydraulics to retract the gear, we didn't know the breaker popped until we tried to direct to that system. They closed the breaker and poof! Landing gear worked. Well. As well as it could since the belly of the plane was scraped to shit."

"I knew you weren't telling me the truth."

She nearly fell out of her chair. They'd moved from the bar to the back corner and the place was getting empty. "Excuse me?"

"You said 'there's really not that much to it,' when there was a great deal to it."

She shrugged. "Well. It was literally my job, so I can't get too smug about it."

"What happened to Captain Lewis?"

"Aneurysm. He's on medical leave and getting a ton of physical therapy. They're optimistic. I got a really nice card from his whole family."

"And did you go out to dinner with First Officer Wilson?"

"Him *and* his husband. And his husband works for the local paper, so he was the first guy I gave an interview to." It hadn't been her favorite way to pass the time, but she did each and every one, knowing it was helping the company's bottom line. "You can probably guess that after anything like this, the company's bookings drop like a rock."

"Unless there's a personable, charismatic spokeswoman for them to flock around."

"Yeah, or me. Heh. Get it? Too obvious?"

"Very much so."

She smiled and looked down at the dregs of her Irish Shirley Temple, then back up. "Well."

"It's late."

"Yeah."

"And you have an early start tomorrow."

"As a matter of fact, I do. But first this." And then she leaned in and kissed him.

Nine

The impromptu kiss had promptly morphed into a good old-fashioned make-out session, complete with hickeys. They'd made it out of the bar and to his truck, because she'd decided walking/kissing/groping him to his truck would be the polite thing to do, and when she finally came up for air they were both breathing hard.

"Wow."

"Agreed," he said, smiling.

"I *never* do that."

"That's demonstrably untrue."

She gave him a playful whap on the shoulder and her fingers promptly went numb. It had been like trying to smack a tree trunk. "No, really. But it's been an odd day and a long one and you're gorgeous and smart and a good listener, but now it's time to go back to our lives and I'm really glad I met you but goodbye."

His eyebrows arched. "You're remarkably blunt, but charming enough to pull it off."

"Thanks?"

"I assume you don't live in Minnesota."

Perish the goddamned thought. "Vegas."

"Well. You have my card. If you'd like to get together the next time you're passing through, please consider reaching out."

Puzzled, she shook her head. "I don't have your . . . wait." She pulled a white business card out of her back pocket, then tucked it back—too dim in the parking lot to read, anyway, and it wasn't like she planned on seeing him again. "Damn, that's slick. I thought you were just grabbing my ass."

"Multitasking," he replied with a straight face, and she had to laugh. She heard a familiar buzz-whir and he produced his phone, unlocked it, looked at the screen. "Ah. My niece is wondering when I'll be back. It's ridiculous that she's up this late." At her expression, he asked, "Problem?"

"Nope. I didn't know you had a niece, but why would I? We only met two—holy shit, we've been talking for three hours."

"Time flies."

"And so do I. But remember, I was already slipping out of your life before she texted you, so it's nothing to do with her and everything to do with my emotional immaturity."

"Blunt," he said, leaning in for a chaste kiss on her cheek. "But charming."

"Finally a title for my jazz ensemble," she said, and that was the last she saw of him. Or so she truly thought at the time.

Ten

"Get up! I'm dying."

Ava spat toothpaste into the sink, wiped her mouth, opened the door, recoiled. "Jesus."

"Back atcha." Dennis pushed past her and sat on the bed before his knees buckled. "I'm not gonna make it to lunch. Just so you know. I've updated my will and I'm leaving you nothing."

Despite the chaos of his appearance, Ava was relieved to see him. She'd been staring at her reflection in the bathroom mirror, eyeing the hickeys Tom had planted on her throat and shaking her head. She looked like she'd been attacked by a friendly, toothless Burmese python. And remembering his pliant mouth and skilled hands (slipping that card into her pocket had been a neat trick—guy probably paid for college by picking pockets), how the two of them had taken turns playing the aggressor, how her heart was pounding so hard she was sure everyone within a mile of the parking lot could hear it, how she came *this close* to hauling his ass up the stairs and finding out if he tasted as good as he looked . . . ummmm. Nice guy, great bod, smart, wonderful kisser, demonstrably responsible if the niece was any indicator. So naturally she kicked him from her life as soon as she could. Why did she pull this shit? Was it simply a matter of—

"Get up! I'm dying."

So, yeah, she'd been glad for the interruption. She'd pulled a high-necked sweater on to hide the worst of the hickeys and went to Dennis. However . . .

"You," she said, staring at this pale, red-eyed, odiferous version of Dennis, "are barely cute right now."

"I'm barely alive right now."

"You've never looked worse. Well, maybe the morning after junior prom." Memorable if for no other reason than it was the first and last time Dennis had spent the night drinking chocolate milk with tequila chasers.

He flopped back onto the bed. "What happened last night?"

"You drank about a gallon of dark black something or other, then had a couple of shots."

"That's it? Because I either had some pretty fucked-up dreams last night or I was abroad actually doing the fucked-up things."

"Uh-huh. Don't read into this, but have you thought that you might have a problem with alcohol?"

"You're only saying that because I'm drunk just about every time you see me."

"I know some people you could talk to." Carefully, carefully. She was on tricky ground, and given her own problems with substance abuse, it was possible Dennis would assume she was projecting. "I could put you in touch with some people. If you wanted."

"I know some people I could talk to, too. Don't sweat on my behalf. I'm not a full-fledged alkie. I'm a binge drinker."

"You know it's possible to be both, right?"

"Change of subject, please."

Got it. Case closed . . . for now. "Fine. After the tar and the shots, I brought you back here."

"And then?"

"And then nothing. You conked out after I left."

"Abandoned me, you mean." He let out a piteous moan, then peeked to see if she was moved. "Anything else?"

"You had the common courtesy to *not* barf in my rental car, for which I thank you. Well, you did, but it all hit the basin."

"I could have died! What basin?"

She restrained herself from rolling her eyes. "Don't worry. A total stranger helped me get you to drink a glass of water—"

"I hate water."

"How can you hate water? It doesn't taste like anything— never mind, I'm not having the H_2O argument with you again. Then we turned you on your side so you wouldn't choke and die and left you snoozing." She'd forgotten that Dennis was a creature of drama even before his twin sister had been murdered. "Now what were you babbling about on the phone?"

"Something happened at the funeral home. My ma's freaking out and wants both of us over there ASAP."

"What? Both? She's not the boss of me." Right? Right. "And what's 'something'?"

"I. Don't. Know. I basically said yes so she'd stop screeching. We've gotta go; my life's now measured in minutes."

Ava drove and fumed while Dennis hung his head out the window and gulped fresh air, periodically ducking back inside to drink from one of two bottles of water she'd brought for him. A return to the funeral home was not on the agenda. Nor was dealing with more Monahans. Not to mention she was due in preflight in a couple of hours. Well, nine. But still. What *had* been on the agenda was to wake up, hate herself for kicking Tom to the curb, eat oatmeal, use all the hotel moisturizer she could get her hands on, then hang out at the airport until preflight. It was an odd life, but it was hers.

Her (mostly) inaudible grumbling turned to real anxiety when she swung into the parking lot and saw the cop cars and ambulance.

"Oh, fuck," Dennis said, which just about summed it up. They parked, got out, and at least one of the cops seemed to know who they were, because yellow caution tape was pulled aside for them and they were waved right in.

And stopped short once the doors closed behind them. In the twelve hours since she'd last been there, someone had radically redecorated the Crisp and Gross Funeral Home in graffiti, broken glassware, upended chairs, and overturned tables, and there was some kind of dark dust all over the—the—

"Is that . . ." Ava started to reach out just as Dennis seized her wrist and yanked.

"Don't," he said hoarsely, which was good advice. She should have caught on quicker, or at least recognized the upended urn. Someone had come in and made a grand fucking mess, and finished by flinging Danielle's ashes all over the room.

On the wall, written in her ashes: WRONG.

Eleven

"You!" The word wasn't shouted so much as shrilled, and Ava jumped like she'd been poked. She realized she'd been so transfixed by the bizarre scene she hadn't realized the room was full of cops (yikes) and Mrs. Monahan (quadruple yikes). It was amazing how she saw everything when she was in the cockpit, and nothing out of it. "This! Explain yourself!"

"I—what?" Was she looking for a critique? *Well, the up-ended tables clearly represent chaos, but I feel the artist went too far with the ashes.* "I can't explain this. How could I explain this?"

"Exactly." Mrs. Monahan was still in yesterday's dress, which was surprising—had the woman been up all night? "How could you?"

"You think I had something to do with this?"

Something happened at the funeral home, Dennis had said, and yeah, something had. *My ma's freaking out and wants both of us over there ASAP,* he'd said, and yeah, she was. Ava should have realized they'd be looking for a scapegoat, because it's what they'd done ten years ago.

"Miss Capp?"

"Yes," she said, too distracted to correct him. "And this is Dennis Monahan, Danielle's brother."

The tall blond with a sunburned forehead—not often something you saw in early Minnesota spring—and tan suit showed them a badge. "I'm Detective Springer. Can you help us figure out what happened here?"

"I have no idea what's happened here," Ava replied, and she was pretty sure it was the truest thing she'd ever said.

"Goes double for me." Dennis looked even worse than when she'd first seen him that morning, which she'd honestly thought was impossible. And he smelled worse, too. Could he still be drunk? Stranger things etcetera. "When did this—I mean, who even called you guys? And Ma? What *is* this?"

"I told you not to invite her." This from the always-helpful Monahan matriarch, who when she wasn't wringing her bird-like hands, was cracking her bird-like knuckles. Wait. Did birds have knuckles? "I said, didn't I?"

"It's not like he was doing me any favors," Ava mumbled, wishing she'd faked appendicitis or amnesia or blindness or a coma or scurvy—anything that would have gotten her out of the Monahan madness. Because here they all were, again. Upset and finger-pointing like they'd been paid. Again.

"Ma!" From Dennis, who was clearly Fed Up. "Not now with that, okay?" Wait, *with that*? Mama Monahan had said something like this before? Then: "Detective, I don't get any of this." Dennis was raking his fingers through his hair and looking not a little deranged. "Can someone please run down the sequence of events for me? Quietly? And super, super gently?"

"Sure. An employee of the funeral home got here at seven thirty A.M., saw the mess, called 911 to report a break-in and vandalism. When we got here we realized it was a little more than random vandalism. We contacted your mother, and she suggested you and Miss Capp might have some insight."

"No, my ma suggested that *Captain* Capp might have done it. Or been in on it." He turned to the older woman, who was lingering just on the outside of their small circle, now clutching her purse so hard the knuckles were dead white. "Ma, Ava and I were together last night. *All* night. There's no way she did this."

"Not 'together' together," Ava put in hastily, and Mrs. Monahan looked slightly less appalled. "We just hung out. For hours. But we didn't do anything else. Besides drinking. If you were . . . y'know. Worried."

"Or you got him drunk so you could dump him and come back and do . . ." Her lip curled as she eyed the devastation. "This."

"No one," Ava replied dryly, "has to 'get' Dennis drunk." She wasn't sure if he was an alcoholic, but the boy liked his booze and no mistake. "Besides—" *The total stranger I was throwing myself at can verify I'm telling the truth. Argh. There's just no way to make that sound unslutty. Not that I owe this harpy an explanation. The cops, though . . .*

"Ma! Is this why you told me to bring Ava?" Then he slapped his forehead. "Dumb question, *of course* that's why." He gave Ava an apologetic shrug.

"You were keeping things back ten years ago, and you're withholding information right now, young lady!"

"I am not! And I'm pushing thirty, for God's sake, so feel free to drop the always-condescending 'young lady' nonsense."

Detective Springer had been watching the squabble with the air of a man watching a tennis match where the players hit each other instead of the ball. "Is there anything you can tell us, Captain Capp?"

"I didn't even know about this until I drove Dennis here. Last night we hung out, then went to bed late." If push came to shove, she'd bring Tom into it. Better that Mrs. Monahan think she was a hussy than a . . . what? Vandal? Upender of tables and spreader of ash? "That's it."

"Captain Capp has an alibi until 1:50 A.M."

"Yeah, what he s—Tom?" She gaped—she'd almost used up her gape allowance for the month, but it was definitely warranted. There was her make-out buddy *du nuit*, freshly showered and shaved and wearing a crisp, white button-down with black slacks. "What the hell are you doing here?"

"And what were you doing to Ava until 1:50 A.M.?" From Dennis, who had a knack for making things worse.

"This is Dr. Tom Baker from the Ramsey County Medical Examiner's Office," the detective explained.

"But . . . there's no body."

Springer coughed. "Technically there is."

"It's nice to see you again, Ava," Tom said with textbook-perfect politeness.

"Uh," she replied, because what the hell?

Definitely should have read that card last night, she realized, *bad lighting be damned.*

Twelve

"Son of a buggering switch!"

Oh, good, Ava thought. *My surreal weekend isn't over yet.*

She was in the small waiting area of the Ramsey County Medical Examiner's Office, and wasn't *that* macabre? She had no idea they had waiting rooms. For dentists, sure. For auto repair, of course. For morgues . . . huh. One of those things you never think of until you're in it.

After giving her statement to Detective Springer, and further squabbling with Mrs. Monahan, she had seen the morgue truck pulling out and, before she consciously realized what she was doing, had hopped in her rental car and followed it to Saint Paul. Dennis could get a ride with his mom. Or a cop. Or thumb it. Or Uber it. Or live in the funeral home.

"Fuck!" she said aloud, because her thoughts hadn't been enough; she needed sound and volume. She'd rarely felt more vulgar in her life. Everything was filthy and ruined. Again.

So she'd carpe'd the diem and followed the rolling morgue. It reminded her of when she was younger and the neighborhood kids would run into their houses for money

("Wait for meeeeeee!")

and then trot behind the ice cream truck while it blared "Pop Goes the Weasel," occasionally stopping to hand out that holiest of holies, the ice cream sandwich.* The parallel was so ludicrous she started laughing, and somewhere between the exit for 494 and University Avenue, the giggles had turned to tears. And not the delicately beautiful ones, like Demi Moore's perfect teardrops rolling down her perfect cheeks in *Ghost*. No, ugly, noisy sobs, the kind that required multiple Kleenexes and lots of nose blowing.

Now here she was, after walking through hallways and trying to wrap her brain around the fact that Danielle, who had been laid to rest, was never laid to rest. It all got churned up again, and what the hell did WRONG mean? Wrong girl? Wrong funeral home? Wrong Monahan?

A month after Danielle's murder, she had told herself it was over. She did it again at the one year mark, the two year mark, five, eight, ten: years spent satisfactorily observing that everything was under control and it was definitely over.

Hokey as it was, she understood and was facing it now: it would never be over, no matter how far she flew.

WRONG.

She closed her eyes, but could still see the staggered, dirty-gray lettering on the wall, the accusation in Danielle's ashes for everyone to see.

"Captain Capp?"

---

* The only acceptable treat distributed by ice cream trucks. This is not opinion but established fact.

And there was Tom again, looking as delicious as he had last night, though he was absently rubbing his knee. She assumed that was why he'd yelled.

Now, as she had last night, she found him quite striking. Ever since she saw a buff Patrick Stewart in a tank top (*Star Trek: First Contact*—both her parents had been exuberant Trekkies), she'd equated bald with brainy/sexy. In particular, bald on purpose.

She realized she'd been staring at him without saying anything. "Oh, it's Captain now?"

"It's whatever you'd like," he replied coolly.

"Why'd they call you?"

He smiled a little. "They know I like the odd ones."

"Oh."

"You followed me here."

"Yes." He didn't seem alarmed or angry. He just looked at her and waited. And when she didn't elaborate, he added, "You have some questions for me."

"Actually, I think you probably have some questions for *me*."

"Come with me," he said, which should have been annoying—so perfunctory!—but really, it was comforting to have something to do. There were hierarchies everywhere, in particular her job (and perhaps his?) and sometimes knowing where everyone was supposed to be was . . . was nice. She didn't know why.

She followed him out of the waiting room, down a hall bare of everything but nameplates and an exit sign, and into a surgically neat office, presumably Dr. Thomas Baker's office, according to the sign.

"So."

"Yeah."

"You were a witness. Ten years ago, not last night."

"A piss-poor one," she admitted. "I never saw a thing. By the time I got back, she was—it was over."

"It must have been difficult."

Worst. Small talk. Ever. "I—yeah. Just a smidge. And then ten years roll by and suddenly it's like it happened yesterday. Like it's still fresh."

"For someone, it *is* fresh."

"Yeah." Because he was right. Someone had been pissed about the murder. Or the memorial. Or both. Then, "Son of a buggering switch?"

Tom flushed red. Which shouldn't have been adorable, but was. "Ah. I hit my knee when I heard you come in. I apologize. I'm trying not to use profanity around my niece."

"I think buggering is profanity."

"No. No?"

"Have you been to the United Kingdom? Pretty sure it is."

"Then it goes on the list at once," he replied, and to her surprise he extracted a small notebook from his shirt pocket, produced a pencil from somewhere, scribbled a note, put the pad away.

"Huh."

"Yes."

"You take that pretty seriously."

"She is insanely precocious and no one wants another Cokesucker incident."

"Yes, that makes sense." Then they just eyeballed each other as the silence stretched.

What are you doing?

Stalling so we can keep talking? If I stand here like a dummy long enough, maybe he'll tell me about the Cokesucker incident.

"Would you like to meet for breakfast later today?"

"Wh-what?"

"In a professional capacity," he said quickly, because of course he meant a professional capacity and was she trolling for *dates* now? Clearly their relationship was going to be purely business going forward, which was a good thing, a *very* good thing, a thing she richly desired, so it was fine. Everything was fine. "I'd like to do some more research and ask you some follow-up questions."

"Okay . . ." Something was off. They'd only been speaking for a few minutes, but he was bouncing from kind to businesslike and back again, like he couldn't make up his mind how best to deal with her.

Who cares? Talk to him. Spill your guts! He might help you think of something, he might find something that jogs your memory or—or—look, it's preferable to moping in your hotel room, isn't it?

It was.

"Ten thirty?" she asked.

He nodded. "The Black Dog? Down the street?"

Yes, because nothing said "time to mourn and then get back to getting on with the rest of your life yet again" like a specialty espresso sipped in a hip coffeehouse across from a medical examiner who was trying to cut back on the profanity.

"Absolutely," she said. "Yes."

So it was done, and she left Dr. Tom Baker to it (he'd gotten up to walk her out, banged his knee on the corner of the desk again, and yelped "crap on a cracker!" in his deep voice, and she had to bite her lip, hard, so as not to laugh), and within half an hour she was reacquainting herself with the hotel room bed. She was short on sleep and wanted to be fresh for breakfast, plus leave time for a trip to the drugstore, because though she'd had it less than a day, she'd already lost her moisturizer somewhere.

And she needed it, because even though she hadn't touched Danielle's ashes, she couldn't seem to stop washing her hands.

Thirteen

Tom Baker realized he was nearing a full-on sprint and forced himself to slow down. It wouldn't do to burst through the door of the Black Dog Café rushed and wheezing, then try to radiate calm disinterest while he had coffee with a possible murderess whose mouth and lush curves were sin personified.

It is deeply frigged that I am excited about this. And dammit, I am allowed to swear in the privacy of my own thoughts!

And there she was, Ava Capp, staring pensively out the window onto the street, either because she was pensive or because she was a sociopath who could mimic pensive, and he had no idea which it was.

He walked past the long counter and sun-splashed tables to where she was sitting in the back, though he could have picked her out from farther away. The mass of shaggy dark blond waves, the olive complexion, the eyes, and the elegant lines of her body were unmistakable. Not that he could see her eyes from this distance, but he remembered them: gray and remarkable. He was so intent on reaching her he hardly felt it when his hip slammed into the corner of the counter.

But she'd looked around at the sound and his muffled curse ("Heckfire!") and winced in what appeared to be perfect sympathy. She greeted him with, "How do you *not* have a limp? I've seen you do that three times in twenty hours."

"Irrelevant," he said, sliding into the seat across from her.

"Listen, I didn't say so earlier, but I wanted to thank you for giving my alibi to the cops."

"I didn't."

"You didn't?"

"I could only alibi you until 1:50 A.M. I didn't see you return to your room, though I assumed you had. And you weren't inebriated."

"No, Dennis drank enough for both of us," she said dryly. "Well, thanks for speaking up anyway. Besides, surely the funeral home has security videos."

"Not for the parking lot or the public area. Just the prep room."

"Prep—"

"Embalming area."

"They have cameras *there*? But hardly anywhere else? Do I want to know why? I don't want to know why." She sighed. "Too bad about the videos, though. Too easy, right?"

"So it would seem." Tom had no idea if Ava had caused the considerable damage to the funeral home, but he wouldn't rule her out as a suspect. Not last night, and not ten years ago. Though it would not do to let her know that just yet. "I would prefer to discuss your deceased friend now."

"Uh. Okay."

Darn it all to heck and back. A new record. "I apologize and will try to be less blunt."

"Please don't. It's refreshing. People have been tip-toeing around this for a decade. Understandably, but it gets old." She pushed her curls back with a sigh. "Also, now that I hear my-self, there's just no way to say that without sounding like a heinous wretch. So I'm just gonna own it."

He waited long enough to confirm it was his turn to speak, then said, "Danielle was stabbed repeatedly and died of exsanguination. She would have been in extreme distress before she bled out."

"Distress. Yeah. One way to put it."

"And ten years later, someone attacked her memorial and flung her ashes everywhere."

"Here's your salmon scramble!" As the waitress set the plate before Ava, she glanced at it, seemed to think about it for a few seconds, then picked up her fork. This made much sense to him; regardless of the topic of conversation, fuel was necessary. "And for you, sir?"

Breakfast? Or briefing? Breakfast briefing? Yes. More efficient. "Lox and bagel, please. And coffee. Lots."

As the waitress headed off, Ava said, "You must be ex-hausted. Up half the night, um, with me, and now here with me again."

"No."

"No, what?"

"I don't require much sleep."

"Okay."

"Tell me about the memorial."

"Besides the fact that it was a mistake?"

"Yes, besides that."

"I ran into Dennis on my flight. He knew I'd be at MSP and invited me. I was on the spot and didn't think about fak-ing scurvy until it was too late."

He blinked. "All right. But you hadn't planned to attend before that day, correct?"

"Yes."

"So the family and friends in attendance were surprised to see you."

"Yeah, I guess." She shifted uncomfortably. "I don't—I mean, the memorial wasn't about me. I imagine everyone's mind was primarily on Danielle, not my late gate crashing."

"And nothing unusual happened during the memorial itself."

"Well, I couldn't find any booze on the premises, but that might just be *my* definition of 'unusual.'"

He could feel himself blinking faster. Impossible to tell if she was teasing or being serious. "And afterward?"

"Awkward small talk."

He grimaced in sympathy; he'd sailed through medical school but could still get tripped up trying to discuss the weather with an acquaintance. What, precisely, was there to discuss? *It is sunny out. Perhaps there will be precipitation later. But perhaps not. So what brings you to the morgue?*

"So you didn't want to be there and didn't enjoy the socializing, but didn't leave right away."

"Dennis wanted to catch up. So I talked to his mom while I waited for him to finish up."

"And Mrs. Monahan never left your line of sight."

"Oh, if only," she groaned. "Ugh, that's awful. The poor thing's still mourning. I shouldn't still be annoyed by her passive-aggressive small talk. But I was. Am."

"Many mothers have lost daughters."

Ava, who had just taken another bite of her scramble, chewed, swallowed, and asked, "Are you saying that as a general observation—"

"People don't always like it when I make general observations."

"—or is it specific to this case?"

"The latter." She was remarkably unfazed; often at this point in the conversation, the other participant was, to use Tom's ex-girlfriend's words, "weirded out by all your weird weirdness." "I think the killer might have been at that memorial service."

Their waitress, a harried-yet-cheerful brunette in her forties, returned with his bagel and—excellent—his own pitcher of coffee, pouring him a cup before dashing off to deliver more food. He heavily sugared the brew. An all-nighter was nothing new for him, but his blood sugar was ridiculously low. It was the only explanation for how he couldn't take his eyes off her. The bounce of her curls was mesmerizing. Which was ridiculous. *It's hair, for God's sake.*

Meanwhile, Ava was staring at him with wide eyes. To his annoyance, this made her more attractive; her gaze was penetrating.

"You think the killer was there, and . . . what? Saw me and made a point of coming back after hours to throw an ashes tantrum?"

"If they even left the funeral home."

"Wait, so the killer spotted me, lurked like a creep, and when the place was empty he went on a table-tossing ash-spreading binge? That's what you think?" She'd paled, the fork dangling in her fingers ready to drop and make a clatter.

"I think the killer finally realized that he or she killed the wrong girl."

"Killed the wrong—" Now Ava *did* drop her fork, and it hit the plate. The café was noisy—cheerfully noisy, he supposed some would say, though the racket set his teeth on edge—so this brought no attention to them. Excellent. "Are you talking about me?"

That depends. Are you asking if I think you were the target, or if I think you were the killer? Because I myself don't yet know. "I think it's a strong possibility."

"A strong possibility," she reiterated, and for a second he wondered if she was hard of hearing. *No—it's shock. Or perfectly feigned shock.* "But why wait ten years? Why would someone have wanted to kill me all those years ago, somehow screw it up and kill Danielle by mistake, hibernate for a decade, then see me last night and get pissed off all over again? Because that would mean—poor Danielle—she went through that, and it was a *mistake*?"

He opened his mouth, but before he could answer, she gagged, dry-heaved over her salmon scramble, then lurched to her feet and rushed past him to the exit, leaving her purse, tea, and scramble in her dash for the door.

He'd been left behind, too, but that was nothing new. He had been on actual dates that hadn't gone so well. "Don't worry," he told the waitress, who had returned to tend to them and was staring after Ava. "It's probably the murder, not the salmon. May I have the check?"

Fourteen

THE LIST: THINGS I LOATHE ABOUT MN
The winters
The springs
The weather
The way I regress to a dim teenager whenever I'm here
The way someone I care about got murdered here
The lack of edible bibimbap
The fucking weather

"A mistake?" she cried as Dr. Tom Baker hurried into the alley behind the restaurant. For a moment, she was sure he was going to bang his hip on the dumpster—could almost hear the thud—but he avoided it at the last second. "This psycho fuckmuppet didn't just kill my friend, he missed? And then came back years later? And might want to fix his mistake? Because he didn't think he was enough of a gutless monster? His murder bingo card still has some slots left?"

"Yes," he said, handing her a doggy bag and her purse.

"Jesus!" She snatched her purse and started rooting through

it. She knew she had a small packet of Kleenex, but by the Law of Purses, she wouldn't be able to immediately find it. "And before you say anything, I didn't almost barf like some wimpy dolt."

"That's correct. It was a dry heave."

"It was the dill in my salmon scramble! It threw me off."

"Dill: the most diabolical herb."

She jerked her head up to stare at him and smiled in spite of herself. "No, that'd be cilantro. Who was the idiot who ate leaves that tasted like dish soap and declared, 'You know what we oughta do? Put this in a bunch of food!'? Ha! Got you, you little sucker." She grabbed a Kleenex and scrubbed her lips, then began what she suspected would be a vain search for Chapstick. "I hate this."

"A simple organizational system would make your handbag more manageable."

"No, I hate Minnesota."

"To be fair, killers operate everywhere."

"If you're trying to cheer me up, it isn't working."

"I am not trying to cheer you up."

"And if you're trying to talk up Minnesota it *also* isn't working." No Chapstick, but she did have a small dirty pot of Carmex, Satan's moisturizer, which she applied, then resisted the urge to scrub off. "Okay, you gotta tell me everything," she said, almost gagging at the taste of Carmex. "Beginning to end. Starting with how you knew about Danielle—I know I didn't talk about her last night."

"No, when I got home after our, ah, time together, I looked you up. I had recognized you from the Captain Bellyflopper stories—"

"Argh."

"—but didn't know you'd been involved in a murder when you were seventeen."

"*Involved* isn't the right word, I think, but whatever. Can we get out of here?"

"I believe we have," he said, gesturing to the alley.

"No, I mean leave the restaurant—"

"But we *have* left—"

"—and go somewhere else and you can give me the scoop?"

"It seems odd to linger," he admitted, adding, "especially as we've finished our meal."

"Yes. Right. Exactly. Inefficient to lurk and gag in alleys. C'mon. We're gonna go somewhere private and where my dry heaves will attract no undue attention and you're gonna tell me all the stuff I've studiedly ignored for the last decade and—and—"

"Yes?" His dark gaze never wavered; he just stood there holding her salmon scramble and waiting for her to finish, all tall and dark and broad-shouldered and intense and annoying.

"Well, I don't know. But we'll figure it out."

And she strode out of the alley like she had a clue where she was going. But hey—when you've committed to the dramatic entrance (and departure), you had to stay committed. It was the rule.

Fifteen

"This isn't what I had in mind."

"My understanding is that you had nothing in mind."

"Hey! Well, okay. Technically that's correct." Ava looked around the park and had to admit, it was a lovely day to talk about murder in a public place filled with frolicking children. But that was how Minnesota got you. It occasionally gave you a perfect summery day and tricked you into thinking it didn't suck the rest of the time.

The most duplicitous state in the union! Besides New Jersey, which has a bad rap but is actually pretty great.

They'd walked a half mile to the Lowertown Dog Park (so they were going to discuss murder near children *and* their beloved pets), and Tom had had very little to say, which should have been awkward but wasn't. When he did say something

("That's the building where the accountant was strangled with his ex-wife's bra.")

it was morbidly fascinating. Who knew the capital of Minnesota was such a hotbed of exotic/weird murders?

I should be alarmed. I should be very, very alarmed, or at least put off. But he's so earnest. He really wants me to understand the area's murder-ey history. He's like a ghoulish tour guide! A ripped, intense, ghoulish tour guide.

Before long they were sitting at a picnic table while Tom outlined what he'd learned from Danielle's case and last night's shenanigans.

"Wait, you just carry these around?" she asked, indicating the files.

"Yes."

Asked and answered. Dr. Baker is nothing if not straightforward.

"The police were unable to find a motive for Danielle's death. She wasn't pregnant, she wasn't seeing anyone, she was well liked and had a healthy family life. She was going to graduate soon—"

Ava nodded. "Yeah, our grad was coming up in another few weeks."

"—and was going to the U of M in the fall. No drama that anyone could find."

"Clearly you don't remember high school girls," Ava pointed out. "Let's amend that to 'no unusual drama.'"

"As you like. So I got to thinking . . . what if Danielle wasn't the target?"

"Well . . . maybe . . . but why assume I was? I wasn't pregnant or seeing anyone, and I might not have been homecoming queen, but I wasn't the school Igor, either."

"That's what I'd like to figure out. First we hypothesize—"

"Is that what we're doing?"

"—and then we prove or disprove."

"Well, what do the cops think?"

Tom sighed. "The police for the most part disagree with my theory. Which is understandable."

"Because . . . ?" Who could doubt this guy? This meticulous, efficient guy who pulled all-nighters and drove around with autopsy folders in his trunk and kissed like it was about to be outlawed? Someone like that wasn't prone to wild leaps of imagination.

"Because it's a cold case—though it's been dusted off due to last night's vandalism. I need more than a theory to rekindle their interest in solving Danielle's murder."

"Okay. But can I ask you something? Why this case? You knew all about Danielle before we met. You didn't just learn all this last night. Don't get me wrong. I'm glad you're going over and above, but you've gotta have bunches of unsolveds in your files."

He nodded. "Every medical examiner does. But I was only a teenager when Danielle was killed."

"Join the club. You're—what? Four years younger than me? Five?" So he would have been thirteen or so. Ouch.

He nodded. "Before Danielle was murdered, I thought I had understood the concept of death, if only from an intellectual standpoint. But that was the first time I truly understood that some people simply get away with murder, and often for no good reason at all. And"—he paused, then met her gaze and finished with—"it stayed with me. It always will, I think. Even if we solve it."

We?

She glanced down at his folder, saw an autopsy photo, looked away. But that wasn't enough, so she physically pushed the photos to the side and leaned forward. "Okay, so . . . what's the plan?"

Tom ran his hand over his bare scalp and frowned. She assumed he was either deep in thought or worried about sunburn. Or both. "In progress. There is little I can do on my own, and you'll be leaving the Cities by the end of the day. Would you consider making yourself available to me—"

Down, girl. Put your libido in park already.

"—via telephone and social media and the like?"

I can't remember the last time someone said "telephone" instead of "phone" or "cell." Adorable!

"Sure. I'd be glad to. But c'mon, Dr. Baker . . ."

"Tom, please. Unless you wish for me to use Captain."

She waved it away. "We're past that, Tom. I don't even know why I used your title." *Please tell me I don't have a latent* Little House on the Prairie *kink.*

"Not Tommy, though," he added with odd intensity. "Never Tommy."

"Got it. I am making a mental note to never call you Tommy. Okay? So don't worry. We're in a Tommy-free zone."

"Oh, Tommy?"

They both looked up at the same instant to see a smiling elderly man holding hands with a girl who looked about five. Tom's eyes widened and he was on his feet before she had time to blink.

"What—what are you doing here?"

Before Ava could ask if there was a problem, she was hit by something with enough force to knock her right off the picnic table bench. Because that's what kind of weekend this was. No matter where she was or what she was doing, something was always trashing her equilibrium.

Now what fresh hell is this?

Sixteen

"Ack! What the—agh, not there, that tickles!" Elbows flailing, Ava managed to heave the weight off her chest and struggle upright. She blinked up at the old man, the giggling girl, and an aggrieved Tom. She blinked down at the dog, who had rolled over for a belly scratch.

"I should have deduced you'd be here!"

"Why, Tom?" the elderly chap asked, extending a wiry arm. Ava was surprised at how easily he got her back on her feet. He looked like a stiff breeze would turn him into a human tumbleweed. "We haven't taken Turq here for a month."

"Five weeks, three days. Nevertheless."

Tom sank into thought (or was again worried about too much sun exposure), and the other man turned to her and said with a smile, "I'm Abe Simon. This is my granddaughter, Hannah. And that's our dog, Turquoise. *Out!*"

Ava, who had been brushing herself off, froze. "Out? Where—where do you want me to go? Oh. The dog. I've heard 'sit' and 'stay' and 'come,' but never 'out.'" Turquoise was a yellow lab the size of a canoe and, like all labs, her tail was equal parts wonderful and terrible. She frisked around them, tail lashing and, when it made contact,

"Ow!"

stinging. *It's got a five-inch circumference! That dog's butt should be registered as a deadly weapon.*

Tom had shaken himself out of whatever thought process he'd gotten lost in, because he broke in with, "Apologies. Captain Capp, this is my . . . friend, Abe, and my niece."

"Ma'am." Ava shook his hand, which was like shaking hands with flesh-covered cords of rope. *Was this guy a dockworker? Until yesterday?*

"Hello, Captain," the little girl piped up. "Is your rank a military designation or are you a civilian pilot?"

Ava tried not to gape at the child, whose eyes were the same deep brown as Tom's. "Uh. I'm a commercial pilot for Northeastern Southwest."

"You fly everywhere!" Abe said, delighted.

"Yeah, I sure do. The best money the airline ever spent was on those commercials. That jingle will haunt me to my grave." Then, to the child, "My copilot learned to fly in the navy, if that helps."

"Why would that help?"

"Uh. Good question."

"We have to go now," Tom said, abrupt even for him. "This is . . . we're working."

Abe, clearly familiar with Tom's habits, nodded at the file folders. While Ava made with the chitchat, Tom had tucked away the horrifying pictures (good call). "I'll bet. I was real sorry to hear about your friend getting killed. Tom's been following the case—"

"Abe."

"—and told me about it when he stopped in a few hours ago."

"Abe."

Ava ignored Tom's obvious unease. Which was fine; so was everyone else. Including the dog. "You all live together?"

"Yes, since my daughter-in-law passed away a couple years ago."

"That's nice. I mean about living together. It's a *Three Men and a Little Lady* thing. If the dog was a man. And if this was a movie." *And if I could shut the hell up for five seconds and STOP BABBLING.*

"If our lives were a movie, it would not be family friendly," Tom pointed out. "At all."

Ava almost laughed, because of course that was perfectly true. *Seven,* maybe. *Silence of the Lambs,* possibly. Nothing by Disney. Although Disney *did* like to kill the moms off pretty much immediately . . . and the kids were always cute and precocious . . .

"Uncle Tom is the best forensic pathologist in the Midwest," Hannah announced the way most children announced their love for ice cream: presenting it as immutable fact. "He'll catch the perpetrator. Well. He'll ascertain the perpetrator's identity and then the police will catch him. There's precedent to back that."

"Jesus, you're amazing!" She instantly remembered Tom's fake swearing and could feel herself getting red. "Sorry. I meant jeepers."

The little girl beamed, peeking up at Ava through dark blond bangs that were slightly too long. "You don't have to apologize for complimenting me. Or breaking the Third Commandment. Although if you're a Christian, you should probably apologize to God."

"Hannah."

"What? Those are the rules. If she identifies as Catholic, she would have to go to confession and tell everything to a male designated by the church hierarchy—"

"Hannah."

"I apologize for overstepping. I am not judging your spiritual belief system."

"Oh my God, you're awesome."

A triumphant beam revealed one missing front tooth. "See, Grandpa? Captain Capp doesn't mind."

"Captain Capp doesn't mind one bit and would love it if you called her Ava." She looked around at the wiry older man, the genius child, the frolicking dog, the weirdly compelling pathologist. "This is all really cool." *Except for the part about Danielle dying. But that probably goes unsaid. Right? Right. Jesus, I'm a monster. I mean jeepers.*

"We must leave," Tom said, though he'd calmed down a bit.

"Yeah, I get it, time and place and this is neither." Ava turned to say goodbye. "It was lovely meeting all of you. Even you," she added, scratching behind Turq's ears. "It'll be tough to explain why there's more dog hair than human hair on my clothes, that's for sure."

"Why? 'A strange dog jumped on me.' See? Easy."

"Thank you, Hannah. You're quite right."

"Oh, would your husband wonder about dog fur?" Abe asked with blatantly transparent intentions. She could smell a matchmaker a mile off, and Abe was only three feet off.

"I'm not married and I don't have a boyfriend." She spared a quick thought for Blake Tarbell, but they had never been boyfriend/girlfriend. Just bang buddies, a juvenile phrase she refused to drop because it horrified literally everyone who heard it.

"That's hard to believe, Captain Capp, a pretty girl like you."

Wow. Subtle this guy is not.

"I will see you at home. Abe, Hannah, good day," Tom said, and if he'd produced a hook to drag Ava offstage, his intent could not have been more clear. Lesson of the morning: Dr. Tom Baker did not like it when his personal and professional lives collided. Which, given his line of work, was understandable. "Please come with me, Captain."

"Ava."

"Yes." He bent, gave Hannah a hug, whispered something in her ear that made her grin, and then he was practically dragging her toward the park entrance. "I apologize."

"Why? Your family's great. How old is your niece?"

"Six years, four months, two weeks."

"I'm sorry about your sister." Ava wondered what could have happened, but held off asking. And she'd noticed the pause just before Tom introduced Abe as his friend. What *did* you call your late sister's father-in-law?

"Thank you. Now as I was saying . . ."

"You were begging me never to call you Tommy, and then your sister's father-in-law rolled up and called you Tommy. That's who Abe is, right?"

"Correct."

They were almost at the entrance and she was having to really move to keep up with Tom's long strides. "Actually, just before that—agh, slow down!—I was asking why you were telling me about your theories. I get the 'unique witness perspective' thing, but this isn't TV. Random pilots don't team up with random MEs to catch random killers. Although if that *was* a show, I'd definitely watch it. The pilot episode at least. Heh."

Tom smiled a little—and thank goodness, because he'd been clearly stressed by the park encounter. "As would I." Then the smile faded from his face and he stopped walking, doubtless to emphasize whatever he was about to say, so yikes.

"I'm telling you this because if I'm right, the killer is fixed on you and will try to rectify his or her mistake while you're still in town."

"He won't just let bygones be bygones, huh?" *Ugh. Not funny. You don't have to crack a joke* every *time like some deranged court jester.*

"Perhaps not. And if I'm right, the killer will now fixate on you. It's likely someone you know, even if only peripherally."

"Well, son of a buggering switch," she managed, because sometimes actual profanity was woefully inadequate.

Seventeen

THE LIST
Avoid killer
Return union rep's call
Sushi?

"You found *what* in my urine?"

"Marijuana, cocaine, meth, PCP, benzos, oxy, ecstasy, and PCP."

For a second, Ava thought she was going to topple off the hotel bed. The room actually tilted a bit as she took in the rep's words. "You . . . you said PCP twice."

"Yeah, well . . . there was a lot of it."

"Are you fucking kidding?"

"Oh, and you've also got a vitamin C deficiency."

Wait, so I might actually be getting scurvy? That's amazing!

This is not what you should be focusing on. "Jan, what the hell am I supposed to do?"

"Drink more orange juice?"

"I don't actually give a shit about the vitamin C thing, Jan!"

"Sorry." The union rep let out a polite cough. "Just trying to lighten the mood."

"The mood should not be lightened, Jan. At all. *What* is going on?"

"Well, you know how it goes. I got a call from the MRO* and your drop wasn't clean."

"That's putting it mildly," Ava muttered.

"I've never seen anything like it," Jan admitted. "I'm pretty sure there are full-on meth addicts who don't have as many drugs in their system as you do right now."

"Jesus Christ! Jan, I'm aware that most people who flunk a drug test instantly insist the lab must have made a mistake, but I'm telling you, the lab must have made a mistake!"

"Pretty big one."

"I know how it sounds. But I swear I'm telling the truth. If I was rocking on weed *and* coke *and* meth *and* PCP *and* ecstasy *and* PCP *and* . . . uh . . ."

"Benzos and oxy."

"Right! If I was high to my eyeballs on all that, don't you think someone would have noticed?"

"Yes."

"Look, I don't care what we have to—wait, you're agreeing?"

"Yes." Jan lowered her voice. "Ava, I'm willing to bet my reputation that it's a mistake. I mean . . . c'mon. That's just a ridiculous amount of drugs. I know you had a problem way *way* back in the day, but you've never flunked one of these

---

* Medical review officer.

in all the time you've been working here. Hell, I remember when you self-reported eating a non-pot brownie. You said it was so good it *might* be laced with something. That's how careful you are."

"That was a good brownie," Ava admitted. Moist, but with chewy outer edges and yummy and dense. *Two* kinds of chocolate . . . mmm. Which wasn't relevant. But Jan's tact *was*. Especially since "you had a problem back in the day" could also be described as "when you were barely old enough to vote, you were so hooked on Ambien you needed eight a night to sleep."

"Obviously, we're going to run another test ASAP. But . . . you know the rules."

"Yeah." Company policy—any dicey test results = grounded for seventy-two hours. Minimum.

"You're still at MSP, yes?"

"Don't remind me."

"Right. Well, stay put for a bit. There are two DOT-compliant NIDA labs in the area—Hastings and Cottage Grove. You know the area, right?"

"I grew up here." Hastings was a charming river town about twenty minutes away from Saint Paul. If she *had* to be in Minnesota, she could tolerate Hastings for the access to Emily's Bakery if nothing else.

Cottage Grove was where she and Danielle had lived. And where one of them had died. Cottage Grove.

"I'll get you an appointment wherever's quickest for another test," Jan was saying, "and we'll go from there."

"Okay, Jan. Thanks so much. Sorry for all the screaming. I know you didn't want to be the bearer of bad tidings."

"Actually, I get off on it. And it would have been weird if you hadn't screamed. That is a shit ton of drugs."

"Your delicate way with words is always an inspiration."

Ava hung up, still freaked but relieved Jan believed her and was being accommodating. Her cynical side pointed out that Northeastern Southwest had no interest in letting the world find out Captain Bellyflopper was possibly a raging meth/weed/coke/PCP/benzo/oxy/ecstasy/PCP addict. But whatever the reason, she was grateful.

And now that she was temporarily grounded, she could help Tom. Which should *not* have cranked her heart rate, but there you go. Or maybe it was the fake meth making her pulse spike. Either way, she had more calls to make.

"Good God, are you all right?"

A complex question that demanded an even more complex answer. But she doubted G.B. had that kind of time. "I'm fine if the bar is set at 'Were you murdered?' but much less fine if the bar is set at 'Did something weird and terrible happen last night?'"

"I saw it on the news." Doubtless while eating fistfuls of kettle corn, going by the chewing in Ava's ear. G.B. and kettle corn had a long and complex history. "Some loser actually vandalized the funeral home?"

"Yes. And the ME thinks it might have triggered Danielle's killer. Or been done by her—wait, it made the news in Vegas?"

"Yeah, tenth anniversary of Danielle's death and all that. I don't think it would have gone national if not for the whole trashing-the-place thing. And why are you talking to medical examiners?"

"It's a long story. Well, it isn't, but I don't want to go into it right now because I just got some bad news from Jan." She shared the gory details and heard G.B. nearly choke on his popcorn.

"Jesus Christ!"

"That's *exactly* what I said."

"That sucks! That is epically sucky to the nth degree!"

"Well put."

"So you're grounded. Right? Seventy-two hours?" Munch. "Which is a goddamned shame because you're one of our best—never mind." Crunch. "Look, deadhead home and we'll hang out." Munch-munch. "Don't be alone."

"Too late." She was touched by his offer, and she knew he'd overnight a canister of kettle corn to her if she asked, but he couldn't help her with anything nonpopcorn- or nonflying-related just now.

The person who *could*, though? Was right here in the Twin Cities. So for now she wasn't budging. Well, she was budging, but she wouldn't cross state lines. Yet. "But I appreciate it."

"Yeah, that's your code for 'I'm putting the emotional wall right back up and will retreat rather than engage.'"

"Huh. Pretty succinct of me."

"C'mon, you've gotta be *dying* to get out of there. Oh, shit, poor choice of words . . ." More stress munching. "Listen, it's not like you want to stay in the Twin Cities, right? You've probably spent the last couple days feeling like you had the DTs. So come here instead."

"I'm not sure Vegas is much better," she teased. "Besides, they didn't clip my wings for long; I could be back in the air by Tuesday."

"Jan setting up a new drop for you? Good."

"Yeah, and she doesn't believe the test, which was a huge relief."

"I fucking love our union, man."

They all did. (Well. Maybe not management.) As much as the Northeastern Southwest jingle grated on her, working for them was swell. Five weeks' vacation, unlimited brownies at HQ, dental (thank goodness—see: brownie policy), scads of family leave, and every lounge was stuffed with (more) brownies, milk, and cold cereal. (The negotiations over Raisin Bran, Frosted Flakes, granola, and Cocoa Puffs had taken weeks and had nearly resulted in a walkout.)

"Listen, Ava, you just say the word and I'll be there with my pee. I'm clean as a whistle! My only vice is hard cider."

"That's not your only vice. And you're sweet, G.B., but I don't think fraud is the way to go here."

"Oh, you always say that." Now he was munching *and* pouting, which was off-putting and hilarious.

"And I always will." Her phone twitched, and when Ava pulled it away from her ear, she saw "Yummy" pop up on her caller ID. "Gotta go."

"Okay, but remember: FedEx will ship my urine to you anywhere in the—"

She cut him off, and not a second too soon. "Hi, Blake. Did you finally find my bra?"

"That bra is gone into the ether, and you well know it."

"I like how you talk like it's 1535."

"I'm not, actually. Listen, I had a few minutes and saw the news. I know you didn't like to discuss it, but that *was* your friend's memorial that was vandalized, yes?"

"Yeah."

"That is rather unbelievable." He sighed. "I know we aren't . . . anything. Anymore. I just wanted to reach out and let you know I was thinking of you."

"Thanks, but I'm fine." Well, not quite. Blake's kindness right on the heels of G.B.'s was making her eyes water. Stupid allergies! *Change the subject, quick!* "Hey, Blake? You sound tired." In point of fact, Blake sounded like hell on toast:

exhausted and faint, like he was calling from Mars. His baritone rumble was barely sexy, which she hadn't thought possible. *Please don't be my fault. Please be something totally unrelated to me breaking up with him a few days ago. Not that we were ever officially going out.* "Are you okay?"

"My mother and brother are trying to kill me," he reported calmly.

"Huh." Okay, so, a good news / bad news scenario. Whatever was wrong, it was nothing to do with her. But his family might be trying to kill him, which was less great. "How's that going?"

"Like the Wars of the Roses: unspeakable property damage, vicious infighting, betrayal, and a horrifying body count. A figurative body count, but still."

"That sucks."

"It does indeed suck. And I've been charged with saving Sweetheart, North Dakota, from destitution and ruin. And the dry cleaner misplaced my best slacks."

"Sorry to hear it." Soooooo in the few days since she'd heard from him, Blake had fled to the plains of North Dakota and gone clinically insane.* *This shouldn't comfort me, but it does, a little. Nice of him to check in, too.* "Gotta say, you're helping me put a few problems in perspective."

"Delighted to serve."

"So . . . good luck with all of that." Inadequate, but it wasn't like Blake actually wanted her help. This was a controlled Blakevent.™ He wanted to talk and then jump back into whatever he was neck-deep in. "And thanks for reaching out."

———————

* To find out what Blake Tarbell has been enduring, check out *Danger, Sweetheart*. It's problematic. He's barely exaggerating.

"Of course. And good luck dealing with your, ah, situation."

Situation, she thought as she hung up. Yeah, that was one word for it. *Disaster* also fit. As did *nightmare*.

And on that thought, she dozed off. No surprise; she'd gotten little sleep the night before. But she should have held off on her nap until she was thinking of something pleasant, like a perfectly ripe golden kiwi. Instead, she was thinking of nightmares, and got one.

A bad one.

Eighteen

Haven't you ever wanted to disappear?

"You're going to be murdered tomorrow. I think we should talk about that."

Yawn. Nothing very interesting ever happens around here. Which is the point. It's why everyone was so surprised. Bad things happen, sure, but not interesting bad things.

"Again: you're going to be murdered tomorrow. Believe me, it'll be plenty interesting. Cops and news vans up the wazoo. Your mom's gonna alternately hate and love the cameras."

And for what? For nothing. Because WRONG.

"You don't sound like yourself."

Right! And why would I? I'm WRONG.

"Okay. I still feel like you're not internalizing this—"

Yawn.

"—so I'm gonna go over it again: you're about to be the murder victim of a grisly murder because you'll be murdered."

Redundant.

"Well, yeah, for sarcastic effect."

Grisly murder is redundant.

"No, murder isn't always grisly."

Sure it is.

"What's grisly about, I dunno, slipping someone forty Ambien in their milkshake? They'll just doze off and peacefully die and, oh my God, I can't believe we're actually arguing about this. Your grisly murder will be ultragrisly, get it? Grisly in spades. It's gonna look like the killer redecorated in your bodily fluids."

WRONG.

"Your poor mother will lose her goddamned mind."

Sure, but will anyone notice?

"Ouch."

Too many variables. That's going to be the problem. Not the murder.

"Also, you'll be dead, and my folks will die, and I'll get hooked on prescription sleeping pills and fly away and—wait, what? Variables?"

Too many variables, which is why it's going to be WRONG.

"Danielle—"

You're the only one who calls me that. Everyone else sticks with Dani. Even though they know I hate it. Maybe because they know I hate it. I was always part of a crowd, but it didn't save me. It did save you, though. So that's something.

"What are you talking about? What are you trying to say? Dammit, I hate cryptic bullshit!"

Wrong.

"I don't—"

Wrong.

"Danielle—"

Wrong. Wrong. Wrong. Wrong. Wrong. Wrong. Wrong. Wrong. Wrong. Wrong. Wrong. Wrong-wrong-wrong-wrong—

Nineteen

"Jesus!"

She was sitting up and the strange room smelled wrong and the comforter felt wrong and the light looked wrong and it was too chilly and the blanket was too thin and where the fucking fuck was she?

Shivering, Ava took in the subtle-to-the-point-of-bland décor, the anonymously pleasing print on the wall, her carry-on propped in the far corner, the channel list and room service menu and four of her nineteen lip balms on the bedside table.

Right. The Hyatt. Nestled in the hell on earth that was Bloomington, Minnesota. It wasn't ten years ago, it was now. Danielle had been dead ten years; the memorial was yesterday. The ME was a broad-shouldered odd duck who had wonderful dark eyes, a genius niece, a yellow lab, and a maybe-friend named Abe, and Danielle had known something was going to happen.

She knew. And you blew it off as teen angst.

Ava swung her legs around until her feet were on the floor

but didn't trust herself to stand just yet. Danielle's face on that last day haunted her, simultaneously knowing and bored.

But not afraid.

Resigned.

She dug her fingers into the furrows of her forehead and bent at the waist. *You're reading into it*, she thought, staring at the dark blue carpet. *The conversation didn't go like that. You came over to hang out and scarf pizza and figure out the schedule and when the pizza was gone, you were, too.*

No . . . that wasn't exactly . . . wait, was it?

You're trying to feel useful because, back then, you weren't useful to anyone. So your subconscious served up version 2.0 of that last talk to trick you into thinking you know something that you don't.

That's all.

(That wasn't all.)

No, that wasn't all. Danielle had been waiting for something, had given off an air of palpable doom.

Oh, come on. What teenager isn't convinced at one time or another that dire forces are aligned against them?

Right. Except . . . her friend had been dreading something that last day. And because neither she nor Danielle knew it was the last day together, they'd done what they always did: talked about everything and nothing. The killer might be somewhere in the midst of all their babble. Or if not him, then his motive.

Ava realized she was on her feet but had no memory of standing. She had to tell someone. No. No need to be coy: she had to tell Tom Baker. If nothing else, she owed him a follow-up.

Why? Because you had a dream about a conversation that never took place? And because he's got shoulders for days and a

narrow waist and a wonderful rumbly deep voice and kisses the
way gourmets cook, you voice-kink floozy?

Well, yes.

So call and leave a message. If he thinks it's worth a follow-up,
he'll reach out.

Not good enough. She'd promised to help and, dammit, may well have information that could be helpful, dammit, and she needed to find Tom and bring him up to speed, dammit! (Also, she had seventy-two hours to kill, no pun intended.)

Not because he was interesting, although he was. But because once he knew what she

(dreamed)

did, they might be able to get something done. This time she wouldn't wonder if she could have done more because she *had* done more.

So she'd go see Tom. And would respect his efficiency by offering to buy him an early dinner in the process. Because he'd probably like a meeting/eating combo. Because of the efficiency!

But you don't give a shit about eff—

Efficiency!

Twenty

THE LIST
Update Tom
Call union rep back
Order black dress
~~Lotion~~
Stay up late to avoid faux-prophetic dreams about Danielle

"Well, hiya!"

Ava blinked. Apparently when you came to the morgue during reasonable hours (as opposed to following the coroner like an easily distracted stalker having an ice-cream-truck flashback), you were greeted by a pleasant young woman who exuded positivity and favored pastels.

"What can I do for ya?" Argh, so much bright-eyed enthusiasm! And pink! She was wearing a pale pink silk T-shirt beneath a darker pink blazer, which should have made her look like an inverted tulip, but instead the contrast with her dark skin was striking in all the best ways. She was the picture of health, too, with blueish corneas, dark eyes, and a bright smile. She looked like she spent her spare time shooting commercials touting the benefits of drinking milk.

"Hi. My name's Ava Capp. I'm hoping to see Dr. Baker." Before the assistant could chirp the inevitable question, she added, "I don't have an appointment. But it'll only take a minute." *Unless I take him to an early supper, in which case it could take hours. Maybe days! Wait, what's my endgame here?*

"Actually, Doc Baker's just finishing up some paperwork before heading out. Let me just check in and see—aaiiee!"

"Hello, Ava."

The assistant, Darla Tran if the nameplate was accurate, had twisted around in her chair to glare up at Tom. "Swear to God, Doc, I'm putting a bell around your neck!"

"No, thank you. I would find that intensely irritating."

"Ya know what *else* is intensely irritating?"

"You did sort of loom up out of nowhere," Ava pointed out. "I didn't even hear you walk over."

"It's my footwear." Tom smiled down at his feet. "These particular soles muffle my footsteps."

"Oh. That's great, I guess. If gliding noiselessly through the morgue is the goal."

"It's like working for a cat," Darla declared. "A clumsy one." Ava made a great effort and did *not* snicker. "No offense, boss."

"None taken. Ava, you wished to see me?"

"Yeah, if you're not busy. Or at least not too busy. I thought of something that might be useful."

He tilted his head and studied her. She must have been downwind (did you still call it "downwind" when there was no discernible wind?), because she realized all over again how good he smelled, like soap and clean skin. And how the hell did he manage that, given his day job?

Darla must have been wondering the same, because she tilted her head to one side and asked, "You napped in one of the drawers again, didn't you, Doc?"

"Abe maintains he can effectively cool our home by simply closing all the curtains. This is false. The air-conditioning unit arrives the day after tomorrow."

Slept . . . in one of the drawers. Slept in one of the drawers? THE DRAWERS? Oh my God, he's so weird and cool. Literally.

"How . . . how does that work?" Did he keep pajamas at work, too? And a toothbrush? Did he set an alarm? Had someone ever mistaken him for a dead body? So many questions.

He blinked. "I get sleepy. I lie down. I rest. I rise."

It's aliiiiiiiive! "Yep, sounds about right," Ava lied, because it sounded deeply screwed.

"I'd say it isn't as weird as it sounds," Darla said, "but that would be a big fat fib."

"Ava, you have information you think might be useful?"

"Huh? Oh. Sorry. Distracted by the reveal of your nap habits. But yeah, I had some thoughts."

"I'd like to hear them."

"Oh. Yes. Well . . ." *Do I just blurt out my dream right here in front of Darla? See if I can damage her positive outlook? Although if her boss snoozing with the cadavers didn't damage it, what the hell would? An audit? Plague?* "Did you want to grab a bite? And talk it over?"

"Oooooh!" From Darla. "A meal *and* a meeting. Together! So efficient! She's got your number, boss."

"Literally," Ava added, holding up her phone. She'd already put Doc Baker in her contacts. "Darla, did you call him Doc Baker? That's awesome."

"Right? My grandma's a huge *Little House on the Prairie* fan."

"Which makes no sense," Tom pointed out. "Dr. Baker worked on the living." Before Ava could ask: "Darla has regaled me at length about the fictional characters—"

"Hey! Some of them were real people, ya know!"

"—of Walnut Grove, Minnesota."

"I'm sure Doc Baker did all kinds of things, including pathology. Walnut Grove wasn't exactly a thriving metropolis."

"Yes, that's true."

Oh my God, now we're talking about shows that have been off the air for forty years and then I'm taking him out for a meal and to figuratively show him my dream journal and a normal person would find this incredibly weird and off-putting so just WHAT THE HELL IS WRONG WITH ME that I think it's intriguing?

"Tell ya what," Darla said. "You seem like a nice lady and the boss here has done me a few favors—"

"Nothing out of the ordinary," Tom interrupted. "I don't understand why you're assigning more weight to this than it's worth."

"He got my abusive ex to skedaddle out of town," Darla explained, which wasn't any of Ava's business but which she loved hearing about regardless. "And when I was about to get kicked out of my apartment, he got me a loan. And remember when you let Billy crash on your couch for a week?" To Ava: "Billy's the night guy. Nasty divorce."

"She's right," Ava said. "That's above and beyond standard boss stuff."

Tom shrugged and looked down, and it was adorable to see such a big guy behaving like a bashful kid embarrassed by praise.

"Check out Konichi-ha," Darla suggested, oblivious to

Ava's sudden, internal screaming. "It's that sushi place / comedy club on University."

"Hard pass." Nothing against Darla, or sushi, but Ava knew she'd rather do PCP, weed, cocaine, ecstasy, benzos, oxy, and PCP than sit through amateur hour at any comedy club. It wasn't the up-and-coming entertainers who depressed her, it was the hecklers. They were brutal and always made Ava feel like she should go up and give the performer a hug. It made enjoying the meal next to impossible. It made belly landings seem like an effortless task. "No offense."

"Dixie's on Grand?"

"That'll do."

Tom nodded. "Excellent. It may interest you to know that in 2014, a body was—"

"No-no-no-no!" Darla had clapped her hands over her ears. "Please. Boss. I'm beggin' ya. Don't ruin another restaurant for me."

"It wasn't the restaurant; it was the parking lot," he explained with long-suffering patience. "And the victim had no connection to the restaurant."

"Tell me on the way," Ava said. "I'd love to hear it. I know that sounds deeply strange."

"It's the only thing about this job I don't love," Darla said.

"Really?" Ava couldn't help asking. "The only thing?"

"Yup."

"The *only* thing?"

"Yes."

"Darla, I'm leaving for the day. Once you've finished that clinic note, the remainder of the day is yours."

"Don't have to tell me twice."

"That's why I hired you," he replied. "I never have to repeat myself."

"Have I ever told you, you're the most literal person I've ever worked for?"

"Many times, Darla, including twice this week."

"Well, you kids have fun. Nice to meet ya, Ava." Darla turned back to her computer with a flourish and was immediately engrossed in whatever-it-was.

"Dixie's, then?"

"Dixie's then."

Twenty-One

Dixie's was a cheerful restaurant on Grand Avenue in Saint Paul, specializing in Southern cuisine and, to use the colloquialism, comfort food. Although what was comforting about carb overload and rising cholesterol levels had always escaped him.

After minimal discussion, Ava led them to the farthest, quietest corner, though it was a beautiful day and Dixie's had outdoor seating. Since she did not strike him as the type content to lurk in corners (at least not during meals), he briefly wondered if she had done it to accommodate him.

This was confusing, which he did not appreciate. Was Ava Capp genuinely thoughtful and charming and funny and a lovely kisser or was she a machine who could perfectly mimic being thoughtful, charming, and funny and a lovely kisser? And how does one mimic being funny?

"So your assistant is a ray of sunshine." Ava said this between wolfing down slices of fried green tomatoes. "And I say that with total sincerity."

"Isn't she?" When he thought about it, Tom felt downright gleeful. "She is surrounded by the dead—"

"Right?"

"—and works for a man frequently elbow-deep in corpses—"

"Gross."

"—and to the best of my knowledge, has never caught so much as a cold or been unhappy on shift."

"Wait, never?"

"It's the incongruity that pleases me," Tom explained.

"Yep. Lots of incongruity going on there." She took a gulp of lemonade, paused, then swigged down more and set the glass down with a decisive thump. "Could I ask you something?"

Do not say it. Do not say it. Do not say it. "You realize you just have, yes?" *Dang.*

"Fair enough. It's none of my business, but did you really put the smackdown on her ex?"

"I did not. I merely inserted myself between That Boy and Darla." And broke his jaw, when That Boy had the abysmally bad idea to reach around Tom to hurt Darla.

"That Boy?"

"True men do not hit their loved ones. And they certainly don't follow them to their place of employment and shout and grab and knock things over."

"Scumbag," she agreed.

He hadn't thought his actions were at all unusual, so Darla's tearful thanks had come as a surprise. So had the pans of apple crisp she started bringing him every couple of weeks. (He had a lethal affinity for fruit crumbles of all kind.)

To Tom, the situation could be distilled to an equation. Abusive significant other + tearful employee = forcibly remove abusive significant other + help tearful employee with restraining order paperwork. Although he no longer thought of Darla as an employee. He'd discussed the situation with Abe, who had explained the concept of "work friend," which was therefore how he now categorized Darla.

"So the reason I stopped by, Tom. I had a dream. A bad one." She helped herself to some catfish but was now devouring appetizers with a more pensive, uneasy air. If it was an act, it was outstanding. "And it made me remember something. I think Danielle knew she was in big trouble. I think she knew she had a killer sniffing up her back trail."

"Oh?" He gave himself a few seconds to mull over her words. "The police asked her friends, family, teachers, and the like if she had any enemies. They all—you included—denied it."

"I know. Because she didn't. Besides, if anyone *had* said otherwise, you would have remembered reading about it. Because you can't let Danielle go, which means way too much to me to be able to explain."

"That is . . . kind of you." It was absurd, *absurd*, how much that comment warmed him. He had decided years ago that conforming and complimenting was not as valuable as gaining knowledge, and for the most part that still held true.

But. It was Ava.

Again: absurd. You've known her less than a week. But as his late sister had once explained, an absurdity didn't mean it wasn't actually happening. Just that it was difficult to believe.

Ava seemed content to let him think, or she was happy devouring the rest of the catfish basket. After another minute, he asked, "Why would you tell me this?"

"Huh?" The waitress had topped off her lemonade, and Ava paused midgulp. "You kidding?"

"Almost never."

She stared back, perplexed. "Why *wouldn't* I tell you? It wasn't in your files because you only had my original statement. Ten years ago, I was as blindsided as anyone."

"Were you?"

Her dark blond brows arched. "Yeah. Sorry, did I not make that clear? About the blindsiding? We were all shocked and horrified and I threw up a little at the crime scene. The techs were really nice about it." *Trying too hard.* That's what one of the techs said, unfortunately, while she was in earshot. Like the killer had watched too many cop shows. It was that thought—the possibility that Danielle was a prop in her own murder—as much as the smell of wet iron that brought her pizza back up. "So, yeah: blindsided."

WRONG. Something about the word sketched from Danielle's ashes, coupled with *trying too hard*, was stuck in her brain like a fish hook. It was wrong because someone tried too hard? Or someone tried too hard and it was . . . for a moment she felt like she was on the verge of putting it together.

Nope. Gone, like her knowledge of most of her passwords, because companies constantly made her change them.

"We recommend P3623ii6247DF29697mn17 for your new passcode."

"See you in hell, Wells Fargo."

"Do you know what I would like, Ava?"

She brought her brain back online to focus on the present. "I can honestly say I haven't the vaguest clue," she replied. "But I can't wait to hear it."

He smiled before he could stop himself. She was refreshing, no question. And she seemed genuinely interested in the things he said, even when they were gruesome things or blunt things. If she wasn't a sociopathic murderer, he could be halfway in love with her by now, which was—he hated to overuse a word but this one was apt—absurd.

("Yeah, but absurd doesn't mean impossible, big bro.")

He silently told the ghost of his sister to hush. "I would like to go to Danielle's memorial tomorrow."

"Oh. Yeah. Day two, I forgot." She scrubbed her hands through her hair, then grimaced when she remembered she had greasy catfish fingers. "Well. Forgot on purpose. Going the first time was bad enough."

"It's unfortunate you have to go back to work. I had rather hoped we could get together. Ah. At the memorial. To *attend* the memorial," he corrected himself, internally wincing.

"Well, it's your lucky night, pal, because it turns out I'm here for a couple more days."

"You are? But that's excellent."

She shrugged.

"Will you attend with me?"

"Sure, but why d'you want to go? Are you hoping to interview family members there? Because, not to tell you your job, doing that at a funeral is gonna piss people off. And there's nothing worse than being thrown out of a funeral. I wish I didn't know that from personal experience, by the way."

He almost laughed. "Noted. But my intention is otherwise. Killers often attend their victim's memorial. And if, in this case, the vandal isn't the killer—"

"What, a run-of-the-mill vandal? Just passing by and figured he'd trash a funeral home?"

"—I would imagine he or she wouldn't be able to stay away regardless. They'll want visual confirmation that their actions upset the family. They'll want to see how the cleanup went. They'll be looking everywhere for something the crew missed."

"Creepy *and* inconsiderate."

"Indeed."

"I mean, would they at least bring a side dish for the pot-luck after the service?"

This time he *did* laugh. "Who can know the depths of the funeral-crashing killer's mind?"

"Depraved bastard," she agreed.

"Regardless, it happens an astonishing amount of the time. It strikes me as unfathomably risky, which is why it's part of their pathology. They need the adrenaline surge. They love looking at the chaos they wreaked and the family members they've devastated. They want to see the mess they made, and then they want to walk away without cleaning it up."

"This goes back to your theory, doesn't it? That Danielle's killer was at her memorial. You think they'd come back a second time?" Ava looked visibly distressed at the thought, and he fought down the urge to comfort her. "Well, why not? *I'm* going back a second time, which in itself is unfathomable to me."

"There's a chance, which is another reason why I wished to attend. But I fear my attendance as a medical examiner would be viewed by the family as inappropriate, in particular since this is not my case and I was a teenager when she died."

"I'll get you in." Ava tried a smile, but it looked wrong on her face. "You'll be my plus one."

He snorted.

"Right? Awful. All of it. But we could make something up. We don't have to tell them who you are."

"I don't understand."

"Well, we could lie," she suggested. "You don't have to be the ME. You could be . . . um . . . someone passing themselves off as my coworker?"

"I can't."

"Oh. It's against your, uh, coroner's oath? That's okay," she assured him. "I wouldn't want you to do something against your—"

"No, I mean I cannot lie. I'm awful at it. Watch." He looked her straight in the face and announced, "Your hair looks foolish and unattractive."

Her hand rose instinctively to her curls. "Huh. Is it the catfish grease? Or the texture?"

"Neither. See? I was unable to pull that off. I *like* your hair."

What are you DOING? Making a bigger idiot of myself than usual, he thought glumly.

"Okay, so you're a bad liar, and on an unrelated note, I need a shampoo. But come with me tonight; one way or the other, I'll get you in."

Which sounded downright dire, depending on where you were on the "Is Ava the killer?" debate.

"It might work," he said. "There weren't many family members at the scene this morning. Only Mrs. Monahan and Dennis, I believe. If they even remember me—"

"They'll remember you," Ava said quickly. "Believe it."

"—it would have only been a glimpse." He cleared his throat. *Was that a compliment? Did she think I was memorable in a positive context? Or because I'm a freak, even by coroner standards? And why do I care?*

"See? Easy. Your niece is awesome, by the way," she added out of nowhere.

Careful. He tightened up, then forced himself to relax. He was still furious with himself that he had (possibly) exposed his family to a (possible) murderess. "Thank you. We think so as well."

"It's none of my business, but—"

"Automobile accident when Hannah was two." Smashed at a red light by a distracted driver with a BAC of .117. The driver never so much as tapped his brakes. A careless wave, a quick trip to Target to buy Hannah some baby food, and then . . . gone.

Ava nodded sympathetically. "Yeah, my folks, too. Happens all the time—everyone knows someone who was hurt or killed in their car. But sure: let's put the focus on keeping marijuana illegal."

He couldn't follow the non sequitur and didn't try. "We did not . . . Hannah's father made himself unavailable roughly twenty minutes after conception. Even now, no one knows where he is. And Abe's wife had died of cancer just after Hannah was born. We were . . ." Distraught. Dismayed. Clueless and afraid and overwhelmed. "It was Abe's idea to raise her together."

Abraham Simon, who spoke nine languages and told everyone he had been an accountant before retirement, a lie going by the calluses on his palms alone. Abraham Simon, who had been kindness personified to his sister and her family and never qualified that affection but showed over time that it was unconditional.

Tom had not planned on making a best friend out of the tragedy, never mind one in his fifties. And darn it to heck, he still didn't know how to introduce the man to people.

But as the cat was out of the bag, so to speak, he deduced further discussion wouldn't put his family in any more danger than they already were from his dog-park blunder. "Hannah's IQ is immeasurable," he ~~bragged~~ announced.

"Well, yeah. Listen, when she's ruling the world, try to put in a good word for me, will ya?"

"No promises." He brightened, thinking about Hannah's

milestones. First word: "Unacceptable." First full sentence: "Broccoli is unacceptable." And she refused to crawl. Went from sitting to walking, which had been amazing to see. One day she had simply gotten up and done it. His sister had been simultaneously proud and amused to see her daughter and her brother had so many traits in common.

He thought about mentioning Hannah's upcoming trip to the MAGE conference in Boston—Hannah was the youngest invitee in years—but had been careless with too many personal details already. "Hannah and Abe thought you were very nice," he summed up, which was true. Though he'd made sure to take Abe aside to warn him Ava could well be considered a person of interest in the near future. *Well, sure,* Abe had said, amused. *It's always the quiet ones. Except when it isn't.*

"Well, I thought they were nice, too. As well as your giant dog with a wrecking ball for a tail. And now that I've said my piece . . . and you've said yours"—Ava looked up at the waitress, who had appeared to whisk away their dishes—"I'd like to close this meeting-meal by ordering bread pudding."

He shrugged. "If you wish to consume wet bread, I have no objections."

She rolled her eyes, which was as irritating as it was charming. "Oh, you're one of those guys. And it's adorable that you thought I was asking permission to eat dessert."

"Did you know bread pudding was invented as a way to use up inedible stale bread and was often combined with suet?" he asked pleasantly.

"Yes, Tom, I knew that. Well. Most of that." She wrinkled her nose. "Suet?"

"Bread pudding, stuffing, french toast, *casse-croûte, panzanella, ribollita* . . . you are essentially consuming garbage. You are paying restaurant prices to consume garbage."

"And an extra order to go!" she called after the waitress while glaring in his direction. "In case I want to consume stale bread at midnight. Because there is nothing more delicious at midnight than stale bread. So there."

There was nothing for it; he laughed and hoped, again, that she wasn't a killer.

Twenty-Two

THE LIST

Smuggle Doc Baker into memorial for dead friend
Sleuth while not looking like we're sleuthing at memorial for dead friend
Find out if hotel restaurant serves bread pudding
Calamine lotion?

Oh, this is so fucked up.

Yep. Mere days ago, she'd been breaking up with Blake and clip-clopping through her perfectly placid life, and now she was at another memorial on a fake date with a medical examiner who couldn't lie but told the best gross stories, and their mission was to find out if a killer vandal was in attendance. And to *not* get drunk. Probably. Well, Tom wouldn't get drunk. Ava preferred to keep her options open.

Fortunately, she had moisturized heavily before leaving to meet him. She'd needed it, too; her arms and legs were itching like crazy and she felt like an animated piece of bark. Her SPF 35 BB lotion was her armor against harmful rays and passive-aggressive mourners. In Minnesota, they were equally dangerous.

She hopped out of her rental car, the same silver Mitsubishi Mirage that bore a strong resemblance to an electric shaver, waved to Tom (who was climbing out of a practical, navy blue minivan), then took his elbow as they crossed the parking lot to the Crisp and Gross Funeral Home.

"Relatively speaking, are you all right?" Tom murmured, and she realized she was dragging her feet and probably showing too much of the whites of her eyes, like a spooked donkey who just got a whiff of fire.

"Yeah," she managed. "Just thinking how silly it is to see a Tudor-style building in a Saint Paul suburb."

"Sure you were," he said, and patted the hand clutching his elbow, and they headed in. He tripped on the curb, then steadied himself with the air of a man who did it every day. Probably because he was a man who did it every day.

Okay, this isn't so bad. Same people and same setup, but it's not so . . . nope, spoke too soon, here comes the déjà vu.

Yep. Same mourners, same subdued air, same setup, same everything.

A few people turned when they entered, and she found herself the recipient of unsettling stares. She looked down to make sure she hadn't accidentally tucked her skirt into the back of her panties again. *Whew! All clear.*

"Okay, focus up . . . first I want to introduce you to Pat, the head geezer of the Monahan clan who might also be Satan because he can talk anyone into anything."

"Don't tease," Tom replied in a low voice. "I would love to meet Satan. So many questions."

Wow. Okay, focus. "My parents had three cars when there were only two drivers, and he talked them into a fourth." *So silly*, as eleven-year-old Ava had pointed out. *Yeah, he kinda wore us down*, her father had replied with an abashed grin. When they died, she inherited all four cars and promptly sold three of them to pay for rehab. Hazelden was wonderful, but expensive, and with her parents' death, she was off their insurance plan.

"Hello, Ava. You're looking . . . prepared."

Ava blinked. "Thank you?" The speaker was Mrs. Monahan, with Xenia right behind her, glaring at Ava with red-rimmed eyes. "I wish we didn't have to keep meeting under the same circumstances."

"Yes, yes." She was doing that thing with her hands again, like she didn't know what to do with them. They looked like bony sparrows looking for a place to land. "How convenient that you happened to have more funeral-appropriate clothing in your bag."

Huh? She looked down at herself: black, A-line, knee-length, short-sleeved dress, black stockings, black flats, a pair of gold studs in her ears—about as much jewelry as she ever wore. "I didn't, actually. I had the outfit I wore to the first memorial . . ." Like anyone who flew for a living, she always had her toiletries and at least two changes of clothes in a bag near her at all times, one a perfectly serviceable dark suit, but she didn't make a habit of planning for memorials. Her life wasn't *that* bad. Well. Until recently. "And last night, I online-ordered a few things from J.Jill." She wasn't the only pilot to love their clothes: they were comfortable and stylish, and you could wad one of their dresses or skirts in a ball, throw it into a suitcase, and when you got to the hotel, hang it up in the bathroom with a hot shower running. Took about two minutes to steam out the wrinkles. Done. Easy. A little cha-ching, but worth it.

"Oh, you just happened to be able to order a completely new wardrobe at a moment's notice and have it here within hours?"

"Nooooo," Ava replied, puzzlement deepening to unease. She knew Xenia and Mrs. Monahan were mourning and on the lookout for a scapegoat—she'd been the same way when her folks died—but why the hostility over her wardrobe and finances? "I ordered a black dress for overnight shipping to my hotel and got pantyhose at the drug store. I already had the flats. And the bra. And the underwear. And before you ask, I didn't just happen to be walking around with wads of cash. I used a credit card. Which is not an unusual thing. At all."

"Really."

"Yep." Why were they acting like this was a magic trick?

Tom abruptly stuck out a hand, which neatly distracted Dennis's mom from her oral audit of Ava's spending habits. "Hello. I am sorry for your loss."

"Yes, thank you." She looked from Tom to Ava and back. "And you are . . . ?"

Tom opened his mouth, and then locked up. Just stood there. You could almost see *01010101 does not compute 01010101* behind his eyes.

Holy shit, he wasn't kidding about being a bad liar. Actual deer in actual headlights don't freeze up like this.

"He's my podiatrist!" *Oh my God. And it was the best I could come up with. Why didn't we work this out beforehand? We both suck.*

"Your . . . what?"

"Yes. Podiatrist. I doctor feet." He cleared his throat, which didn't sound like he was caught off-guard *at all*. "Extensively.

They are my passion. The metatarsals, you know. And the phalanges distalis. The calcaneus and the talus and the subtalar joint. I simply cannot get enough of them."

In ninety-six hours of bad ideas, we have a new winner. "He's completely devoted to my feet so he's here for . . . for . . ."

"Longitudinal arch support," Tom suggested.

"Yep, that's it." Tom winced and she realized she'd clamped onto his arm a bit too hard. She made a conscious effort to loosen her claws. "Where's Pat? I wanted to give him my condolences."

"The first memorial was too much for him. He's been hospitalized, and the doctors didn't think him coming was a good idea."

"Oh. I'm very sorry." If it was any other family, she'd have added something lame like, "But he'll bounce back!" Except it was almost obscene that Dennis and Danielle's grandfather was still alive while Danielle wasn't. And speaking of Dennis, where was he? Was it rude to ask? Did she care?

"That's why Dennis isn't here, either." Xenia sniffed. "He couldn't take another day of you."

"He said that?" she asked, appalled.

"He didn't have to!"

"So he *didn't* say that. I feel like you might be projecting just . . ." Ava held up her thumb and forefinger. ". . . a smidge." She couldn't blame Dennis for skipping memorial 2.0, but doubted it had anything to do with her.

"Ava?" A new voice, and out of a face she didn't immediately recognize. Jack? Jerry? One of the cousins, for sure. "I can't believe you came."

"Of course I came." Jim? Jeff?

"No." The man, another brunette, this one in his midthirties, had the Monahan eyes and the sleek look of a lawyer who never bought his own lunch. "I meant, I can't believe you had the goddamned nerve to show up."

"The . . . goddamned nerve?"

"Jon, we agreed," Xenia began, still sniffling and glaring.

"Jon! Yes!" *Shit. That was out loud.* "I knew it was something like that." *And so was that.* "Agreed to what, exactly?" She looked around at the faces, most of which wore an expression of stunned dislike.

She said you looked prepared. She said it was "convenient" that you happened to have funeral-appropriate clothing in your bag.

"Oh, Christ." She looked around at the grim faces. Had she stumbled into Shirley Jackson's "The Lottery"? She definitely felt surrounded, though a few couldn't meet her gaze and scowled at the carpet. "You guys don't think I had anything to do with any of this . . . right?"

Dead (so to speak) silence.

"Oh, come on!" She was so upset she could actually feel her eyes bulge. "I was just a kid when Danielle was killed! And I certainly didn't come back and redecorate with her ashes! Besides, I was talking to Mrs. Monahan the whole time! We debated the merits of various hotdishes! Tuna won, but only the kind where you crumble up potato chips for the topping!" *Oh my God, I just said all that at a funeral.*

"You could have had a partner. Then *and* now."

"My podiatrist didn't kill her, either! He was even younger back then."

"That is a certainty," Tom replied, because (Ava almost had to laugh) it wasn't a lie.

"You guys. Think this through." She made a conscious effort to lower her voice and project calm. "Again, I was just a kid myself when Danielle was murdered."

"You could have had help," Jon repeated stubbornly.

"You did find the body," someone said from the back.

"You *did* get the hell out of town as soon as you could," Jon pointed out. "And I'll bet you're getting ready to leave again."

"Because I don't live here anymore! And it's literally my job to get the hell out of town. Daily."

"See?" Xenia said, triumph ringing through her tone.

"Why would I have killed her? I loved her like a sister. I know people say that all the time, but I really did—" She heard her voice crack and steadied it. "I really did. Love her like that, I mean."

"Oh, please. You just glommed onto her because your parents couldn't be bothered with you."

"Well, yeah." She looked around at the circle of judgment. "What? You thought I'd deny it? I barely knew them, and they were, y'know . . . my *parents*. I loved hanging out with Danielle. She remembered my birthday, at least. Sometimes . . ."

Sometimes I wished I was her. Sometimes I deeply envied her. Sometimes I took a class just because she did. Sometimes I dressed like her and we got our hair done at the same place and she never laughed and she never judged so you can all fuck right off.

She couldn't argue with these people. So she just scratched her arms

(oh, sure, furtively scratching and being unable to keep still and avoiding eye contact isn't shady AT ALL)

while her mind emptied itself of any useful rebuttal. *Say something, Tom! Tell a horrible story or come up with a spirited defense. Just say anything!*

"*Post hoc ergo propter hoc.*"

Ava swallowed a groan. *It's my own fault. I did say "anything."*

"It's a logical fallacy," Tom explained, looking earnest and yummy. "After this, therefore because of this. There were many reasons for Ava to leave town. It's hardly definitive."

Well, not the impassioned defense of her honor she was hoping to hear, but "hardly definitive" still beat "we think you're a well-moisturized killer with good taste in clothes."

"If you think I killed her, why haven't you said anything to the police? Then *or* now? I've had more conversations with my union rep in the last three days than any of the local cops." And surely Tom would have said something if she was a—a suspect? Person of interest? Would-be psycho of interest?

Dennis's mother ignored the question. "As soon as I saw you," she said in a thready voice, "it was the nightmare all over again. You don't come back for ten years—"

"I'm in Minneapolis all the time!" she protested. "I hate it! The goddamn runway always forces me to crosswind taxi!"

"—and within hours someone snatches Dani's ashes and desecrates the place and nothing—not the police, not prayers—nothing, *nothing* will bring her back. But you, *you're* back. You brought all that with you. You brought it back on all of us. *Again.*"

"Wait, so am I bad luck or a harbinger of doom or a vandal or a killer?"

"You're the angel of motherfuckin' death!" Xenia shrilled.

At last, Ava thought, still having trouble believing this was happening. *A title for my autobiography.*

"We should go," Tom murmured into her ear, and truer words were never etcetera.

Ava tried to gather her tattered dignity around her, drew herself up, and took a firmer grip

"Ouch."

on Tom's arm. "If you'll all excuse me, I'd like to go back

to my hotel room and burst into tears and then maybe eat more bread pudding. Come on, Tom."

"Excellent. That will give me a chance to check your feet for plantar fasciitis."

"Great, Tom." Still scratching, she led him out.

Twenty-Three

THE LIST
Kill everybody who thinks I'm a killer
Prove I'm not a killer
Rinse
Repeat

"I don't believe it," she snarled, stomping toward her car. "I don't *believe* it."

"Nonsense. We pulled it off perfectly. All those people actually think I have a doctorate in podiatric medicine!" Adding an extra surreal touch to the evening, Tom sounded downright giddy. "I know this isn't an appropriate reaction given what just happened, but I've never successfully portrayed a podiatrist before."

"So you've *un*successfully portrayed podiatrists before now? Congrats. Make sure to update your résumé accordingly. Meanwhile, all the living Monahans think I murdered the dead one. This is why I don't go to memorials, Tom!"

"Understandable."

That was vague enough to give her pause. Did he mean it was understandable that the Monahans put her in their burn book by implying she was a murderess vandal

(Wait, that would be murderous vandal, right?)

or was it understandable that she was annoyed about the (theoretical) burn-book placement?

Never mind. Back to the rant. "How, how can they think that about me?" Ava, too worked up to get behind the wheel, began pacing back and forth while Tom tracked her like he was watching a slow tennis match. Back . . . and forth. Back . . . and forth. "Have they been stewing over this for a decade? What the hell just happened in there?"

"If I were to guess, the Monahans may be wondering at the coincidence of you running into Dennis all these years later."

"Oh, please. The planet only *looks* big. People run into old friends and neighbors all the time—I see it almost every week in every airport."

"Yes, but . . . on a significant anniversary? And just in time to attend a significant event?"

"Yeah, well, as you said: a coincidence." But a horrid thought struck her: if she hadn't gone to Danielle's memorial, would someone still have trashed the place?

That way lies nuttiness.

"A terrible, shitty coincidence," she continued. "And they must *know* that, or they'd have told the cops they suspect me." She stopped in midpace. "Have the cops said anything to you about me being a psycho of interest? And before you play more devil's advocate, that's something an innocent person would want to know."

"The police are pursuing all leads."

"Great, you sound like a press release."

"The lead detective believes your version of events—"

"My *version*?"

"—partly because Mrs. Monahan did not indicate, then or back then, that she thought you killed Danielle. But I believe some of them wondered if you might have guilty knowledge."

Guilty knowledge. A phrase that never failed to make her shiver.

"Partly, huh?" She threw up her hands. "Well, I'll take what I can get. So why would they spring this on me? Why even let me come back here tonight? Why not disinvite me, or stop me from going inside? There's enough of them; they could have posted a guard at every entrance. And at my hotel. And in every parking lot between here and my hotel."

"Perhaps for the same reason you and I attended: to see if we could spot a killer."

"Yeah, except we know it's not me."

Silence.

She turned to face him full-on. "Uh. Tom? We know it's not me. Right? We know that? That's not the royal we, by the way. That's the plural we, as in the you-and-me we."

"Anyone looking at you for this would have to admit any evidence is entirely circumstantial."

Good thing she'd stopped pacing, because she would have walked right into a car: bam! Instant bruises. Instead, she stared at him in his immaculate dark suit, his immaculate face, his immaculate skull, his immaculate brain, which she didn't understand but liked enormously.

"You . . . think I'm the killer, too?"

"Well—"

"Not cool, Doc Baker!" God *damn* her arms itched. She groaned and scratched as the pieces started to fall into place with near-audible clicks. "You knew it was me following you, but you still let me walk right into the morgue." A new thought struck her, one almost as staggering as the realization that everyone in the Crisp and Gross Funeral Home thought she killed her friend, then went to town on a bunch of folding chairs a decade later. "Jesus, no wonder you lost your shit when we ran into your family at the dog park! You weren't worried about how it upset your routine; you were worried that you'd introduced your niece to a psychopath!"

"In this case, I think sociopath would be more—"

"Not now, Tom!" She stared at him, panting a little because the rant had left her out of breath. She now had to re-examine every moment they'd spent together and . . . it didn't look good. "Is that why you haven't tried to kiss me again?"

"No," he replied quietly. "I haven't tried to kiss you again because, one way or the other, you're just passing through. Because that's all you do: pass through."

She decided to brush that aside for now and ponder it later, when she couldn't sleep. "So all of it—meeting me for breakfast and then dinner and coming with me here . . . telling me those stories to keep my interest and pretending you liked me a little—"

"Not just a little," he replied quietly. "And not pretending."

"Shut. Up. All that . . . so did it work? Did you find out I killed her?"

"Inconclusive."

She just looked at him until his gaze dropped. "Inconclusive. Okay. Well. For the record—since that's all this is—I've never killed anyone. Not once. Not ever." She groped in her purse, found the car key which wasn't a key

(Ugh, I miss keys.)

and randomly pressed the thing until her door unlocked itself. She started to climb in and paused for a last look back.

"It was nice to meet you, and I wish I never had. You have a lovely family, and I felt privileged to meet them. Now go fuck yourself."

"Ava . . ."

"Captain Capp."

That gave him pause, she saw at once, and his expression was that of an unhappy man being yanked in two directions.

"It's my own fault," she told him. "I read too much into it." Way, way too much.

"Cap—"

"Good night, Dr. Baker."

She was in such a hurry to slam the car door (mostly to get away from the Crisp and Gross Funeral Home but also to get the last word) she almost closed it on her leg. She withdrew her limb like a startled tortoise (but faster), started the car, resisted the urge to run over Tom, and got the holy fuck out of there.

Twenty-Four

THE LIST
Fuck it
Fuck everything

Once she'd gotten a good cry out of the way, Ava wasted no (more) time returning her union rep's call. To her relief, Jan answered on the first ring. "Oh, hey, Jan. Didn't think you'd be in this late."

"How is it that you never remember I'm in California?"

"Because I don't care about you, or your work, or anything you do."

A gusty sigh over the connection. *"Finally* one of you ungrateful jerks admits it. How are you, Ava?"

Jan's warm sarcasm was already making her feel better. "PCP-free and ready to get back. What's the scoop?"

"Passed with flying colors. That last test was seriously whiffed. Even the vitamin C deficiency was a false positive."

Relief made her knees buckle. Not that she'd worried a lab test would show anything harder than Advil. But once upon a time, that was *all* she worried about—whether she could pass a piss test—so it had stirred up some dark memories.

"You know, it's strange," Jan was saying. "I've never seen a test come back with hits like that before. The lab's trying to figure out if it's the actual test or if it's a computer glitch."

"Like someone entering the wrong results under my name?"

"Exactly. But that's not your problem, it's theirs. And as of 0700, you're clean and cleared."

The magic words. Not for nothing had she made the trip from teenage traumatized murder witness to valuable employee and pilot, even before the belly landing. She knew her time and skill sets were assets, and she enjoyed working for a company that valued them. She could be in New York tomorrow, or Seattle or L.A. or Dallas or Portland. She could be gone from here in no time at all. And if any of those flights took her through MSP, she'd just stay on the fucking plane next time.

That's not very practical, what if you have to—

Shut it, inner voice. And pay attention. "Sorry, Jan, didn't catch that."

"That's okay. Inattention is a quality we prize in our pilots."

"Hilarious." It was, though—Ava giggled in spite of herself.

"Yuk it up, honey. See how you like it on the ground for a month."

"I'll call that bluff, Jan. I know you guys are short-handed."

"You saw through me." The banter dispensed with, Jan got back to it. "Can you take the four-twenty to Boston tomorrow? Eleven thirty A.M.?"

Fly away, Ava. Again.

Are you mocking me, inner voice? Because it's not working.

Because: why shouldn't she? She'd done what she could here, and the sky was waiting for her. She had a wonderful job and a wonderful union and wonderful coworkers and a wonderful life and she needed to get back to all the wonderfulness. Dead was dead, she wasn't a TV detective, and she was done with Tom Baker, who showed her only yesterday where a fast-food employee had been drowned in room temperature cooking oil.

"I'll take it," she said. "Up, up, and etcetera."

Twenty-Five

An hour later, Ava was so busy throwing up she didn't care about the welts blooming all over her arms.

The illness—flu, food poisoning, non-food poisoning, a visceral reaction to all the evil in the world, whatever it was— had snuck up on her. In less than an hour, she'd gone from giddily thrilled about being cleared to calm to vaguely nauseated to nauseated to *oh shit go-go-go* and, as G.B. once put it, "shoutin' at the floor."

Adding to her woes:

"I feel strongly we parted on bad terms and would like further discussion on the matter, please!"

Tom Baker was knocking on her hotel room door and hollering from the hallway.

"Get bent!" she managed, before vomiting again.

"There is a better than average chance you are in danger!"

"Get. Bent!"

Ava didn't often envy the dead, but at the moment Danielle's fate sounded, if not appealing, then at least not completely horrible. Wherever she was in the afterlife, Ava doubted anyone was pounding on Danielle's door as she ejected half a pound of bread pudding and devoutly wished for all the toothpaste in the world.

"I am sorry to trouble you! But I respectfully demand entrance!"

Good God, is this going to go on all night?

"Buzz off or I'll call the main desk." She fought her gorge and lost. "Bbblluurrgghh! And they'll ream you a new one before or after they call the cops!"

"Yes! The police! Summon them immediately! Your life may be at stake!"

It is. It is going to go on all night. Shivering, she flushed, got to her feet, got to the sink

"Have you called the authorities? Shall I?"

"Will you give me *five seconds*?"

washed her face, brushed her teeth, went to the door, took a breath, opened it.

Tom greeted her with a gasp that could only be described as horrified.

"What's the matter?" she snapped. "Have I lost my youthful glow? A barf session will do that."

"Why are you still here?" he demanded.

"Annnnnnd I'm shutting the door now." She scratched her arms and glared. "Can you slam the door in your own face? I've got a lot going on right now . . . no, no, from the *other* side of the door . . . goddammit!"

"Please." Tom had his hands up like he was being arrested. Which was still in the cards for the evening as far as she was concerned. "Please answer my question. Why are you still here? Why were you grounded?"

She stomped to the minifridge and grabbed a ginger ale. "Why are you assuming I was grounded? Maybe I just love all this tropical Midwest weather."

"Because the only reason you would have remained is if you could not leave."

Fair. "If I answer, you'll go away forever?"

"No."

She almost smiled, but it turned into a grimace as her stomach roiled. "Points for—uurrggh—candor. I flunked a drug test. Actually, *I* didn't flunk the test; the test flunked me." That made sense, right? Right. "Took them a day or so to get it straightened out. But I'm flying the mostly friendly skies as of tomorrow morning."

He reached out sloooowly and she watched, bemused, as he did a pretty good imitation of molasses. He gently grasped her arm, turned it over, and studied the welts rising on the pale underside. "And this?"

"No idea. I've been itching like crazy."

"Yes, I saw you were scratching earlier; this looks like textbook irritant contact dermatitis."

"Of course," she deadpanned. "Exactly what I was thinking."

"And you're ill." He inclined his head toward the bathroom, where the toilet was still running and all the lights were on. He reached up, put the back of his hand on her forehead, touched her cheeks. "But no fever."

"Thanks for the update."

"You're being sabotaged," he said flatly, and the moment he said it, she realized he might be on to something.

"By the killer?"

"Very possible."

"But some people think *I'm* the killer."

"Which works out nicely for the real killer, don't you think?"

She sighed. "You'd better come in."

"I am in."

"Oh. Right. Stay put. Don't snoop through my stuff."

Five minutes later, she was reasonably certain the barf party was over—for a while, at least. Tom, meanwhile, had taken a seat at the small desk in the corner and was on his phone, but set it aside the moment he saw her.

"Would you like me to get an antinauseant?"

"Why? Are you sick?"

"Ava. This is serious."

She sighed and perched on the end of the bed. "I know. I'm just a little numb right now. To this and . . . everything."

"Will you tell me about your drug test?"

"It flagged me for PCP, ecstasy, weed, coke, benzos, oxy, and PCP."

"You said PCP twice."

"Apparently there was a lot of it. A lot of fake PCP."

"But the test was wrong."

"Of course. Wait, why do you know that? We've known each other less than a week. Who are you to say I'm not a raging cokehead?" *Wait. Am I actually offended that he assumed I'm clean?*

"Point. However, it's difficult to picture you breaking the law and jeopardizing your health *and* your license for something as oddly specific and ultimately mercurial as a benzodiazepine-PCP-cocaine-MDMA-marijuana-oxycontin high."

"Well. Yeah, that's mostly true. But." She cleared her throat. Took a sip of ginger ale. Coughed again. Good God, she'd told this story to any number of counselors, employers, and coworkers. Why was it difficult *now*? "Uh. Back in the day, after Danielle and my folks were killed, I started having trouble sleeping."

"Having trouble sleeping" was code for lying in bed night after night after night after night, staring at the ceiling with gritty eyes and seeing Danielle's corpse and the demolished wreck that had swallowed her parents (she'd talked the insurance agent into letting her look at the pictures, an action they both immediately regretted), and wondering if anyone would care—or at least notice—if she OD'd. Over-the-counter Unisom turned into booze, but she had to drink too much of it to get numb and disliked the taste of just about all of it. Or, as she told her T-group, "I failed as a drunk. Just couldn't get it done."

So she turned to Ambien, which turned into scamming prescriptions from just about every doctor within a 120-mile radius, which turned into buying loads of it online, which turned into popping six to eight Ambien a night to sleep, then being a zombie during daylight hours, only to gulp down another half-dozen Ambien to force herself under again, and somewhere in there she lost track of a year.

"I ended up in a Minnesota slough—Hazelden—for just under a month, and they helped me get my shit together," she explained. "I've been clean for close to a decade. But hearing I'd flunked a routine screening brought back bad memories."

"Of course it did." He didn't sound judgmental, just upset on her behalf. "It would be unpleasant for anyone, never mind someone with your history. Which makes for an extra sadistic touch, don't you agree?"

Yikes. When he put it that way, it seemed a *lot* more

ominous—and personal. It suggested the killer didn't just know her but had kept up with her post-Danielle history. Could it be?

Dumb question. Of course he or she kept up—they managed to reach out from wherever and fuck up my drug test. Among other things.

"Tell me about the irritant."

"He's sitting about eight feet away."

Tom chuckled. "I suppose I earned that. When did the symptoms start?"

"Late yesterday. I didn't think much of the itching at first, because I'd misplaced my damned moisturizer, so I figured it was just my skin crying out for more Eucerin."

"And then you found it again."

"Yes." On the driver's-side floor of her rental car, as a matter of fact . . . she'd looked down and seen the top of the bottle sticking out. At the time, she'd wondered how she had missed it when she ransacked the car earlier.

"Which you then immediately, and generously, applied."

"Oh my God. What the hell did that shithead put in my lotion?" Poison? Bodily fluids? *Please, please let it be poison . . .*

"I mean to find out." He reached into his pocket and shook out . . . a gallon-sized Ziploc bag? "May I have it, please? I'll have the lab take a look."

"Absolutely. And good fucking riddance." She got up, went to the dresser, opened the top drawer, and pulled out the bottle, using a pair of clean panties as a glove. She let it plop into Tom's bag. And let the panties plop into the garbage can. "That applies to the bottle *and* you, in case you were wondering."

Tom sealed and tucked the bag away somewhere. "Someone has done their research. Which is why I'm here. I have to help you. *Please* let me help you."

This made her pulse pick up, which was annoying. *Down, girl.* "How do you know I'm not self-sabotaging?"

"If you were, you would still need help," he pointed out. "Just of a different kind. But, again: you love flying too much. I can't see you risking your license, health, and freedom in order to gain misplaced sympathy when it's inevitable your deception would be discovered. And given what we know about the drug test and the lotion, I don't think your illness is a coincidence. But I cannot fathom how someone has been able to salt your food with a regurgitant. You're in a hotel, you're not dining in a private home, and you likely haven't eaten at the same place twice."

"I like variety," she agreed. "And bread pudding."

"Nevertheless, we need to proceed as if someone *has* poisoned you and behave accordingly."

"We, huh?"

"Yes, we. I—ah." In half a second, Tom had gone from confident to diffident. "I thought we might join forces."

She studied him. "Why?"

He just sat there for a few torturous seconds, then replied, "Because I cordially despise the thought of *anyone* sabotaging you, never mind a murderer. And . . . I regret doubting you."

"Oh. So it's a guilt team-up."

"If you like."

"I don't like anything about this. Not one thing."

"Understandable. And you won't like this, either: I need to remain by your side."

"Huh?"

"You're being targeted by a clever killer who knows your routine and how to strike at what you love most while simultaneously stirring up your worst fears and regrets of the past, and we have no idea who it is or what, precisely, they hope to gain from this. And so I'm not inclined to let you out of my sight."

"Well, you're gonna have to," she said, equally startled and, it must be said, a smidge thrilled by his determination. "I've got work tomorrow."

"But you're ill," he exclaimed. "You should be resting right *now*. And all of tomorrow. You've been through a great deal in a shockingly short time."

Mental note: never tell Tom how much those words meant to me. "But I'm getting better. I'm pretty much empty now, and I won't eat anything out of a vending machine—or *any* solids—until I get to the airport tomorrow. I'll just push fluids tonight." He opened his mouth and she cut him off. "Listen, if I'm not much improved in the morning, or if I think whatever-this-is will impact my flying, I'll ask for a reassign. I'd *never* put my passengers and crew at risk. If you know anything about me, you know that, at least. But I hope I don't have to."

"As it happens, I was flying out tomorrow as well," he admitted, "though I had planned to ask Abe to forgive my absence in favor of staying close to you."

She shrugged. "If this was a movie, I'd be assigned to pilot your flight, but . . ."

"It's flight 420 to BOS at eleven thirty A.M."

"Oh my God." She groaned, and had to laugh. "So . . . we're in a movie, apparently."

"Really?" The man's face lit up like someone had dumped an unusual death on one of his tables. "I'll get to see you work?"

"You'll get to keep out of my way while I work," she warned him. "Captain Capp and Ava are entirely different people. This is going to get weird, I think. Well. Weird*er*."

"Or it's a sign we're fated to stay close to one another."

"Let's not get carried away."

"It's settled, then." Tom stood, banged his upper thighs on the underside of the desk, sat, pushed the chair farther back, managed to stand again without hurting himself. She managed—barely—to trap her giggle before it escaped.

This hunky klutz wants to guard my body? Pretty sure he's solid bruises from thighs to ankles. Argh, don't think about his thighs . . . or his ankles . . .

"I will remain with you the rest of the evening and take you to the airport," he pronounced, which was annoying, but she was tired and let it slide. "Your rental car may be compromised."

Her annoyance disappeared. "Jesus. I didn't even think of that."

"We'll all fly to Boston—"

"All?"

"Abe and my niece are traveling with me."

"Ah. No longer horrified at the thought of exposing your family to me?"

"I apologize," he said seriously. "I behaved foolishly."

She sighed. The apology was sweet, but she couldn't fault him for listening to his instincts. "Forget about it. It's better to err on the side of 'whoops, my bad' when it comes to family, anyway."

"Thank you." Then he just looked at her. Just when the silence started to skew from charged to awkward, he added, "You require antihistamines, an antinauseant, and I wish to drop off your moisturizer for testing. Please remain in your room and leave it locked and dead-bolted until I return. *Do not let anyone in.* Not even room service."

"A first in my life, but okay."

"And you have to shower."

"Rude."

"A cold shower."

She shivered. "Pass."

"It's the first step toward recovery," he explained, looking earnest and adorable. "Get rid of the irritant. Do you have any diphenhydramine?"

Eh? "Not on me, no."

"Or calamine?"

"Yeah, I grabbed some of that yesterday."

"All right. I will be back within sixty minutes. Please take all precautions until then."

"While showering."

He laughed. "Yes. A cautious shower."

Am I really going along with this? Looks like. And it's nothing to do with the man's essential hotness. Well. That's not the main reason.

If she was honest with herself—and post-Hazelden, she tried to be—it was mostly fear. Someone had her in their crosshairs and she didn't care for that in the slightest. And while Tom appointing himself bodyguard was presumptuous and possibly problematic, he was also the one who put it together and who seemed determined to get to the bottom of . . . well . . . everything.

That she could understand, even if it was the only thing about this she understood.

Sighing, she got up, flipped the lock and the dead bolt, and went to run the

(warm, thank you very much, Tom)

shower.

.   ..   .

Twenty-Six

"This isn't how I pictured this." This in a low voice as he smeared medication all over her arms.

"You're blind to the erotic qualities of calamine lotion, Dr. Baker?"

He snorted. True to his word, he'd returned within the hour in time to hand her a robe, politely look away as she dropped the towel to slip into it, then got her to sit down and briskly rubbed her hair with another towel. After she'd gone to the bathroom to comb out the mess he made, he politely hectored her into downing a couple of Benadryl, gave her sugared ginger to chew on

(Where the hell did he find that? And where has it been all my life? It's roughly a zillion times better than Pepto!)

and then got out the calamine lotion.

He cleared his throat as he dabbed more lotion until she looked like someone with vitiligo. And not someone beautifully cool, like Winnie Harlow. More like Michael Jackson just before the autopsy. "I . . . think about you all the time."

"Yeah? Well, I definitely haven't thought of you more than

several times an hour for the last few days, so don't get your hopes up."

He smiled and dabbed.

"Like what?" she persisted. "When you think of me?"

"I think about the night we met." Dab. "And about what it might have been like . . ." Dab-dab. Dab. ". . . if you'd invited me up that first night."

She could feel her face getting warm, because she'd be lying if she claimed the thought hadn't crossed her mind, either. "Well. It wouldn't be like *this*. I'm pretty sure. Is the calamine doing anything for you?"

"Not really," he confessed, and they both giggled.

Twenty-Seven

THE LIST
Check-in MSP
More calamine lotion
*Brand new moisturizer THANKS TO THE PSYCHO WHO
    HAUNTS MY NIGHTMARES AND ALSO MY LOTION*
Never come back
Ever

The door had no sooner closed behind her than someone came from somewhere and flung his arms around her.

"G.B.?" She was so startled she nearly dropped her tea. "Oh. We're doing . . . whatever this is."

"It's so good to have you back, though you were technically only off the boards for a day or so," he declared into her shoulder. He smelled like coffee and oranges and (faintly) sarcasm. "Are you okay?"

"Thank you, G.B. And yeah." She reached up and patted the back of his arm. "Uh. How long are we doing this?"

"Just shut up and let me comfort you."

"No problem," she replied, stealing a glance at the clock over his shoulder. Plenty of time to put up with whatever-this-was before check-in. And she was feeling immeasurably better than last night, so she didn't have to worry about barfing all over his crisp uniformed shirt front. Or back. "Take your time. But not really."

"Fine, I'm done." He drew back and squinted at her. "Well. You look great, for what it's worth. Hardly traumatized at all."

"You should have seen me yesterday." For a few seconds, she wondered if G.B. could be her saboteur and then realized that until the psycho was caught, she could look forward to doubting absolutely everyone in her life. Not that she'd let many people in after Danielle. But still, it hurt to wonder about G.B.'s motives. "Doesn't matter," she added. "I mean—it's good. To be back! At work. Very good to be back. Y'know, at work."

"The mind of a poet, the speech of a concussed cheerleader."

"Hey! Leave cheerleaders alone."

By now other crew members had come up to them and were offering congratulations. The new attendant, Becka Miller, looked particularly curious. For a "private" drug test, a shocking number of people knew all about it. She made a mental note to discuss the matter with her union rep and resisted the urge to blast a whistle to force instant dispersal. "Thanks, everyone, but I'm fine and I just want to get back to work."

"What work?" G.B. asked, smirking. "Admit it: your biggest challenge is to stay awake while the autopilot does ninety percent of the work."

"Don't talk about Captain Bellyflopper that way," India mock scolded, gently plowing through the forest of crew members that had sprung up around her. Cripes, she hadn't even hung up her suit jacket.

"Oh, shut up. Both of you." Pause. "Well, G.B. might have a point. If it's a really long run. Regardless, I'm ready to work."

"We could tell," India said. "What with how you're back to work and all. No way you're here unless you want to be, not with all the hours you've got in your bank."

"Exactly. Nice to be flying with you again, India."

"Well, I *am* terrific. Seriously, how are you?"

"Seriously, let's get to work."

Ava freshened her tea, scored a croissant—her stomach was audibly goinging and boinging at the sight of it; apparently her bout of whatever-it-was was over—and counted her blessings. For many airlines, it was rare for the same pilot to keep flying with the same crew, but Northeastern Southwest paid big bucks for studies that showed familiar crews worked better together.

Duh, G.B. had scoffed at the time. *Can you imagine office drones who had to work for a new boss every day?*

"Drones" seems unnecessarily mean, she'd pointed out.

He'd ignored her, as was his wont. *You go to your cubicle or whatever and the HR rep is new every day, the company president is new, and the receptionist is new. And they're all different each day. Can you imagine? The world would be in flames, Ava. FLAMES.*

So she wasn't at all surprised to see the familiar faces, which in this case

"Forget about my wife's cousin," India said as he handed

over her paperwork. "My wife's *other* cousin is a cop, and now he's dying to meet you."

was a mixed blessing.

"All of you stop bugging me and go straight to hell," she commanded. "Not you, Becka. You're fine. What's our load, India?"

"Full flight, eight oversold. Weather's good, should be a straight shot to Logan. And no live animals this trip, thank God." To Becka, who had been a flight attendant less than a month: "Much less stressful. For everyone, really. Especially now they're cracking down on fake service animals."

"It's why we can't have nice things," G.B. added. "Also, how dumb do the geese* think we are?" It wasn't a rhetorical question. The answer: extremely dumb. "Who ever heard of a service boa constrictor? What the *hell* would a service snake even do?" To India: "Make *one Snakes on a Plane* joke. See what happens."

India, wise for his years, raised his hands and took a step back.

"To be fair, it was little. Barely three feet long," Ava pointed out while G.B. shuddered so hard it looked like a brief seizure. "And it didn't bite anyone. Just wanted to keep under the guy's sleeve. I think it was cold."

"That checks out," Becka announced, looking up from her phone. "Also, there's no such thing as a snake service animal."

"Oh my *God*." G.B. breathed, staring at her. Becka looked up and was startled to see several people giving her the "slash across the throat" sign. "Scourge!" he declared.

---

* Slang for "passengers."

"You're holding the scourge of mankind right there in your palm."

"Uh," Becka replied, slipping the phone in her pocket.

"You really aren't," Ava assured her. "And it's a sliding scale anyway. Last month the scourge of mankind was Net-flix."

"Do not get me started on Netflix!"

"Next month it'll probably be the uniforms again," India added.

"Never!" G.B. actually backed away from them, as if Ava and India were going to strip off his uniform then and there. "They finally don't suck. I'm happy, relatively speaking. My mom's letting me put in a gym!"

"Hey, that's great! And the uniforms weren't that bad," Ava said, looking up from her preflight lists. "At least we don't have to wear high heels anymore."

That snapped him out of it. "Of course not. Management isn't entirely insane, and they don't think it's 1955, either. But you have to admit, the old reds were a disaster. Bad design, bad material, bad color, bad execution, bad everything, just all around bad, a boatload of bad."

G.B. had a point, though the big lug looked good in any-thing. The old uniforms were bright, screaming-red, with screaming-red flared pants for the men and screaming red A-line, knee-length skirts for the women and bright white dress shirts—totally impractical for flight attendants, who by the end of a shift were nearly always decorated with coffee *at best*. These were paired with screaming-red box-cut jack-ets that swallowed figures and flared sleeves that swallowed wrists and anything the person wearing the jacket was trying to pick up. Entire cans of ginger ale had disappeared up those cuffs. The white belt and white scarf were mandatory.

We looked like walking stop signs. Angry, self-aware stop signs.

The new ones, designed by Wisconsin native Lisa Hack-with, with final sketches voted on by employees, weren't just an improvement, they were stylish *and* practical: comfortable khaki pants and skirts (elastic waists and loads of pockets). Short-sleeved button-up tops in navy blue or cream—dealer's choice. Short-sleeved button-up empire dress in navy blue. Reversible fitted jacket—navy on one side, khaki on the other—and through some sort of dark sorcery Ava didn't understand, even more pockets than the pants. The khaki and navy blue sashes and scarves were optional; the belt, mandatory. No one really knew why, but they didn't fight management on the belt issue, as they'd gotten more than they'd asked for.

"Um, I know it sounds dumb and shallow," Becka began.

"Ooooooh!"

"You have our attention," India prompted. "Let your pettiness out."

". . . but I didn't apply here until I knew the uniforms were gonna change." She patted her bright, bright red hair self-consciously. "I mean—my God. Can you imagine?"

"Well, it's shallow," G.B. said, "but not dumb. So that's okay."

"You're one to talk," Ava teased. To Becka: "G.B. led the revolt. Give us khakis or give us death! That was literally one of the signs he made." Oh. Lord. So many signs. She'd fallen over stacks of them on more than one occasion.

"Damn right. D'you know how hard it is to meet women who aren't disappointed when they find out I'm not a pilot? When on top of that I'm dressed head to toe in an uncomfortable outfit that makes me look like a mobile blood bag?"

"Is this the part where we pretend to believe you have *any* trouble getting laid, you flaming man-slut?"

"Hey, I'm good, but that was a major drawback even for me." Ignoring Becka's grimace and India's fake throwing-up noises, he added, "But I gotta give you guys credit. If the pilots hadn't gotten on board—"

"I see what you did there."

"—it would have been a lot harder to get management's attention."

Ava waved that away. "If you guys have a problem—with the uniforms, a company policy, what have you, then I have a problem. I have a *huge* problem." As the giggles started, she added, "That came out wrong. I meant to say I'll back you."

"You *do* have huge problems and you *did* back us, so no complaints on my—shit."

As G.B. bent to retrieve the sugar packets he'd accidentally spilled, Ava saw the bulge in his trouser pocket, grabbed her clipboard, and whacked him in the hip.

"Ow!" G.B. straightened and managed to simultaneously glare *and* look guilty.

"What have I said about bringing Tasers on board?"

". . . not to?"

"Not to," she replied firmly. "With your luck, it'll fail at a critical moment or you'll tase the wrong person. And who's going to mess with someone your size?"

"That's right," India put in.

"If anything, a mugger will go for someone small and slender and unassuming, like India here."

"Hey! Makes sense, though."

"But it also charges my phone," he whined, clutching his pocket and backing away.

"Okay, that's definitely not true—"

"Dammit."

"—but imagine if it could? Why hasn't someone invented this? *No.* Don't distract me. Check it in your luggage—"

Now he was backing away while looking deeply affronted, like she'd spit in his coffee. "Like a *goose?* Never!"

"—with your ice axe and pepper spray."

From Becka: "Whoa."

"Hey, I used to be a Boy Scout. Be Prepared."

"Wow. I could actually hear the capital letters when you did that. G.B., let's play a game where we pretend I'm your captain and just gave you an order and you have to comply: check that thing already."

"Dammit."

Ava looked around at the small group. "So now that we've gotten my eventful weekend out of the way and are happy with the uniforms and G.B. won't accidentally electrocute one of us—"

"That was one time!"

"—let's get to it. Where—"

"—are we flying today?" they chorused.

"You all suck. I don't say that *every* time."

But she was awfully glad to be back regardless. And she hadn't thought about Tom Baker in the last hour.

Nope. Not once. While she slept, he'd worked through the night, made sure she was feeling well enough to fly, helped her pack, then dropped her off at the airport in time to return for check-in. It was an oddly domestic scene . . . she'd rarely spent the night with a man in a hotel room and *not* had sex, so she had no idea how to behave the morning after.

Anyway, she wasn't thinking about him. This particular moment didn't count.

Totally out of my mind. Tom, that is. Yep.

So.

Twenty-Eight

"Why is there a tiny hole in all the windows?"

"That's a breather hole. See how there are actually two windows? The breather hole regulates pressure between both so the outside window takes most of the pressure in case of an accident."

"But why are all the windows round?"

"Because corners are inherently weak, and air pressure increases that weakness. Round or oval windows spread out the stress and are fundamentally stronger if there's a pressure drop."

"Oh. So the likelihood of a fatal catastrophe is lessened?"

"Yes."

There was a low cough behind him and Tom turned to see a flight attendant with a name tag that read G.B. "Love all the science, but maybe a little less fatal catastrophe chit-chat?"

"I apologize. I didn't mean to make the other passengers uneasy."

"Yeah, I don't care about that. You're making *me* uneasy."

But he smiled, a perfectly friendly grin that Hannah cautiously returned. G.B. was such a large man—a lifter, clearly, and quite tall—Tom briefly wondered if he had to turn sideways before going through doorways. "Let me guess—the MAGE conference?"

"What gave it away?" Tom deadpanned. MAGE, the Massachusetts Association for Gifted Education, was having their annual conference in Boston tomorrow. This was Hannah's first year. Tom had had to make sustained efforts not to boast about that at work.

G.B. bent to speak to Hannah directly. "Y'know, our captain would be glad to let you come up and see the cockpit once we're at the appropriate altitude."

"We don't want to interrupt her work." Tom said this with some reluctance, as he would have liked a peek at the cockpit of an Airbus A319. And a private chat with the crew. They were bound to have interesting stories about death in the sky. And of course, it would be wonderful to speak with Ava again, this time wearing her captain hat. Literally.

He forced his mind back on track in time to hear Hannah. "Because distractions increase the potential of a fatal catas—of a thing you don't want us to talk about," she added anxiously.

G.B. smiled. "It really doesn't. And she does it all the time. Let me know if you want to take a look later."

"Really?" Hannah looked delighted. "Thank you, Flight Attendant G.B."

"You're welcome, passenger 22B. Why don't you guys have a seat and get buckled in?"

"All right." There was a decisive "snap" as Hannah complied, then got back to business. "Uncle Tom, why do we have to board the plane on the left? I don't think that's very efficient. And for the jumbo planes, why not board both sides at the same time?"

Nuts. He had tried to anticipate all Hannah's questions and researched accordingly. Alas. But G.B., who had been moving past them, replied over his shoulder, "It keeps you bums out of the way of the ground crew. They always fuel on the right."

"I like flying," Hannah replied, wriggling in her seat a little. "It's so interesting. And even if something looks inefficient, it isn't."

"Wait until we're actually flying," Tom said. Meanwhile, Abe had gotten himself buckled in and had handed Hannah a tablet with which she immediately busied herself. Tom leaned back and caught his eye over her bent head. "Thank you again for coming."

"You kiddin'? Who'd miss it? It's my first genius conference."

Hannah made a noise that sounded suspiciously like "well, duh," but kept her gaze on the screen.

"And I haven't been back to Boston for years. I'm gonna show you all my old stomping grounds when the kiddo isn't dazzling geniuses with her supergeniusness."

Hannah stopped midswipe to look up at him. "Grandpa, a lot of people there are going to be smarter than I am. You should be resigned."

"I'll decide when to be resigned," Abe retorted. "And yeah. In theory there will be bigger geniuses there. *Maybe.* But I won't believe it until I see it."

"Not very scientific," she observed. "Besides, Uncle Tom has an ulterior motive. *That's* what you should be wondering about."

That got Tom's attention, because his thoughts had begun

to wander back to Ava, which was bad, and worse if Hannah had somehow picked up on that.

He'd been appalled to find her so ill the previous evening, which, coupled with her drug test and doctored moisturizer, was alarming. Once he'd talked her into letting him stay close, he'd contacted his supervisor and requested the next two weeks off. Because he rarely took time off (Hannah's bout with chicken pox fourteen months ago had been the last time), he had loads of vacation and family leave time accumulated; his employer accommodated him with nary a murmur of protest.

But none of that mattered now, because Hannah's comment demanded his full attention. "Did you say I have an ulterior motive?"

"Yes. MAGE isn't the only reason we're here."

"You are always my top priority," he replied, because it was the truth, the whole truth, and nothing but. It had been that way since Hannah took her first breath.

"This is a working trip for you. Well, for me too, if my 'job' is to be a genius, but also for you."

"MAGE is the priority," he said again.

"Which doesn't make my previous statement untrue."

Abe had been leaning forward to catch his eye, then looked down at Hannah. "If you have a point, darlin', make it."

"Uncle Tom thinks Danielle Monahan's killer might be targeting Captain Capp. He's going to bodyguard her."

"It is impossible—and inappropriate—for you to know that," he said sharply.

"You probably shouldn't have downloaded the Monahan file into your phone then."

"Hannah—"

"Or your approved family leave request."

"*Hannah.*"

She threw up her hands, flashing the Cone of Shame bandage across her palm.* Hannah's two favorite movies were *UP* and the documentary *Jiro Dreams of Sushi*. "I can't be blamed if you make it so easy to guess your password."

"My password this week is *follicle*," he protested.

"See? Easy. You shaved your head earlier this week, you've been reminding me I'm overdue for a trim, and you've mentioned Ava's curly hair twice. I can only assume you *wanted* me to hack your phone."

His late sister's teasing came back to him

(*"Why has God punished me by making my kiddo exactly like you, big brother? Shouldn't he have made* your *kid exactly like you?"*

Dead four months eight days seven hours later.)

and he only *just* managed to avoid smiling. Instead, he thought of dead puppies. An unbreakable cell phone contract. Ava murdering Danielle Monahan. When he was sure he had affected an appropriately stern mien, he said, "You know perfectly well I would not want you looking at files pertaining to my work."

"Also, you seemed tense when you came home and I wanted to find out why," she added in a small voice.

"Oh." He sat there, at a loss, until Abe cleared his throat.

"There were other ways to get to the bottom of that, Hannah. I know your intentions were good, but that doesn't make it okay to snoop."

"I wasn't—"

"Definition of 'snoop,' please."

---

* These bandages exist! These are a real thing! www.perpetualkid.com/bandages/

She sighed and brushed her bangs out of her eyes. "It's a verb. It means to pry or sneak."

"I know when you get curious about something, it won't let go of your brain 'til you're satisfied," Abe continued, "and I know you've been smarter than me for two years. But some things I know more than you, even so, and snooping on someone you love is not okay."

Another sigh, this one sounding more than a little put-upon, and Hannah turned back to him. "I apologize for hacking your phone. I was concerned, but that's no excuse."

"Thank you."

"Is it Ava? Is that why you were worried?"

". . . partly." Anyone else would have just assumed he was in a quiet mood, or tired. Leave it to Hannah to suss out the emotion behind the fatigue. "But it's nothing either of us need concern ourselves with."

"We'll see," was the mysterious reply, and not for the first time, Tom realized he was in over his head.

Before he could comment further, he heard the brief chime that preceded an announcement. And then an unmistakable voice came over the intercom: "Good morning! This is Captain Capp chiming in to welcome you to flight 420 on Northeastern Southwest—we fly everywhere! We're departing on time, but don't worry; we'll do everything we can to unnecessarily delay you and then refuse to explain why.

"The weather in Boston is partly cloudy and seventy-five degrees, and also I hope you're okay with going to Boston. If not, speak up now, since it'll be a lot harder to deplane once the wheels are up. In a minute, the cabin crew will get into the safety speech fully three quarters of you will ignore, and to that I'd like to suggest you be very, very nice to them since they're CPR-certified and also experts in how best to evacuate the aircraft. I'm not saying they're vindictive, but don't make them throw away half-full cans of soda and don't treat them like truck-stop waitresses. And I say that as a former truck-stop waitress.

"I also want to add that in case the oxygen masks drop, put yours on first, *then* the kid's. I know that seems like something out of *The Hunger Games*, but there's a method to that madness. Anyway, sit back, relax, take the miracle of flight for granted, and we'll be taking off shortly."

His face hurt, and he realized he was grinning like a fool. Which Hannah, who was the polar opposite of a fool, picked up on.

"You liiiiiiiike her," she sang, which got Abe chuckling. Tom knew perfectly well denial was a waste of time, so he said and did nothing . . . including wiping the smile off his face.

Twenty-Nine

Flight deck
27,000 miles over Lake Michigan

"You're out of your mind."

"Saw it with my own two eyeballs."

"There is *no way* a tarantula defeated a rat in spider-to-rodent combat behind the New York Public Library."

"I saw the whole thing!"

"Why were you even behind the library in the first place? Did they try to lock you out? Were you sneaking in? Were you ambushing people who were late returning books? Tell me if you were ambushing people who had late fees, Ava. You tell me that right now."

"Irrelevant to the story. I pity you, India, with your closed mind and refusal to embrace the weird."

"I embrace the weird every time I climb into the cockpit with you."

Before she could retort (good one, though!), they heard G.B.'s distinctive "shut up, there's a passenger in tow" knock.

"To be continued," she told her copilot, then turned to greet the newcomers.

"Captain Ava Capp, First Officer India James, this is—"

"Holy sh . . . out, it's Hannah!"

"Hi, Ava!"

G.B. smothered his laugh into his fist. "Did you just say 'holy shout,' Captain?"

Ava smiled to see them. There was G.B., taking up half the flight deck, cute-as-a-bug Hannah wearing a MAGE T-shirt, and, hovering uncertainly in the doorway: Doc Baker. She'd known they had boarded, of course, but preflight had kept her busy.

The girl put out a hand and, bemused, Ava shook it. "Uncle Tom's glad you're the captain."

"Oh?"

He was glancing around the cockpit and at India, and Ava realized that he was wondering if her copilot was the saboteur. Just as she had wondered about G.B. Tom was also looking exceptionally striking, which was irrelevant. And, it must be said, a little irritating. *Why is he tan? He's a nerd who hangs out in morgues; he should be sickly pale like a fish belly. And why is his gaze so direct and captivating? And why isn't he wearing something wildly unflattering like almost every other person on this flight?*

And why do I give a shit about any of it?

"It's nice to see you again, Captain Capp."

So that's how they were doing it. Okay, then. "Thank you, Dr. Baker." To India, who was staring at the child like she was an oracle come to life (an oracle with shaggy bangs and a missing front tooth and . . . was that a Cone of Shame bandage?), she added, "Hannah's one of a kind. I know that's technically true for everyone on the planet, but it's really, *really* true for her. And there are too many people on my flight deck. G.B., please escort Dr. Baker to his seat. I'll walk Hannah back when we're finished here. If that's okay with you, Tom."

"It is, Ava, thank you." With that, he turned and left with G.B.

"Oh-ho." This from India, but she declined to engage.

"I'm glad you're friends again," Hannah said.

"Huh? We weren't really friends before. I've known him less than a week. It was never going to . . . y'know. Go anywhere." *Why am I having this conversation with a child?*

"Exactly."

"What?"

"That's the point. He liked you *so* much after less than a week. Even when he thought you might have killed someone. Or had guilty knowledge of killing someone. Or made a mess with the dead girl's ashes."

India's mouth dropped open. "Excuse me, *what*?"

"Think how Uncle Tom will feel in a month!" She turned to India. "May I ask a personal question?"

"I have no idea."

"Were you named after India the peninsula, India the country ruled by the British until 1947, India the republic, or India ink?"

"I was named after my uncle."

"Oh." She blinked. "Tradition. I hadn't considered that. Which was foolish now that I think about it. I'll need to re-calculate the variables . . ."

"Did you have any questions about the flight deck?" Ava gestured to the dizzying array of instruments and screens, often incomprehensible to passengers. "Or flying in general? Or about becoming a pilot? Or your plans to eventually conquer the Northern Hemisphere?"

"Mmmmm." Hannah was looking at the instruments with a small frown, eyes moving back and forth as she scanned the array in a way that definitely didn't remind Ava of a terminator *at all*. "No, I've got it now, and I can research more tonight. I just came up so you and Uncle Tom could see and talk to each other."

Ava stared. "You are *terrifying*."

She grinned. "Thank you!"

Thirty

"I've returned her safe and sound," she announced unnecessarily.

Abe smiled and tried to courteously rise, but had forgotten his seat belt and thumped back down. "Hello again, young lady!"

"Two lies. I'm pushing thirty, but thanks."

"What are the odds that we're flying on one of your planes?"

"Technically, it's the airline's plane."

"Thousands to one, actually," Tom said. "Particularly when you factor in all Northeastern Southwest flights and every city to which they fly." He stood so Hannah could take her place in the middle and looked at Ava. "I hope you thanked the captain for letting you into the cockpit, Hannah."

"That's not necessary," Ava put in hastily. "It was a pleasure to have her up there." An intimidating, terrifying pleasure. "She probably gets this all the time, but she's gonna—"

"Do great things," Abe finished. "Yeah."

"At this point, I consider it more a dare than anything

else," Hannah said. "As well as something to cross off my bucket list by the time I'm driving age."

I don't even want to think about what this teeny genius would do on a dare. "You're way too young to have a bucket list." She looked around their small family and decided the niceties had been handled. "Well, it was good seeing you, but I should probably check to make sure the autopilot hasn't burned out . . ."

"I have some time after we land. Have dinner with me," Tom blurted out of nowhere.

She hesitated. "I don't want to get in the way of your family plans."

"Don't worry about us," Abe put in. "The conference doesn't start until tomorrow, and we were just gonna take the Blue Line to our hotel and goof off 'til supper."

"The hotel has a pool!" Hannah added. "That's where we'll do most of the goofing off."

"Tom can take you to an early dinner and meet up with us later," Abe added, and seemed way too pleased about all of it.

"You could go to Legal Seafood," Hannah suggested. When Ava raised her eyebrows, the girl added, "What? You love seafood. I read it on your Facebook page. Also, vampire movies, popcorn, and tailwinds out of the Midwest."

Well, at least she isn't telepathic. Probably.

"All right," she said, and grinned at how happy Tom looked. "But you're paying."

"Of course."

"No, wait. That's not very twenty-first century." She stuck a finger in his face. "*I'm* paying. Don't try to talk me out of it."

"Of course."

"Oh, no you don't! Wait. You know what? Let's just split the bill."

"Whatever you want."

Good plan. And let's not pretend this has anything to do with solving a murder. You like him and you want him to like you back. That's all it is.

Well, that and the fact that you literally have nothing else going on right now. Blake's out of the picture, Dennis was never in the picture—where the hell has he disappeared to, anyway?—and Doc Baker has wonderful eyes.

True enough. Although that last bit was irrelevant. That said, it would be easier for Tom to guard her bad bod if they were having dinner together. Time to chow down a boatload of chowder!

Well, maybe not chowder.

Thirty-One

". . . please remain seated with your seat belts on until the aircraft comes to a complete stop. *Complete. Stop.* Thank you for flying with Northeastern Southwest and remember: nobody loves you or your money more than we do. And, as always, the last person off the plane has to clean it. So thanks in advance, mystery passenger!"

Tom was already on his feet despite Abe's eye roll and Hannah's "Uncle Tom, Ava *just said* not to do that until we stopped." He hit his head on the overhead bin, but such things happened so often, he barely noticed.

"I'm sure she was only joking about how the last person off has to clean the plane, son."

Tom grunted in response, but felt his cheeks warm a little. He would be embarrassed to admit how much he loved it when Abe slipped and called him son. It meant nothing, of course. Abe was a nice man who was nice to the people around him. But he liked that Abe was comfortable enough around him to make those slips.

And it was no surprise to him that Ava was relaxed enough

to make jokes during flight announcements; one thing the woman never seemed to lack was confidence. Well, until he almost broke her spirit by implying she might have killed her best friend, took a ten-year vacation, then trashed that same friend's memorial.

He got their bags sorted, double-checked to make sure Abe had all the details for their lodging

("This isn't my first jaunt out of the neighborhood, Tom. I know how hotels work. And airports. And the subway. And e-mail confirmations.")

shook Abe's hand, hugged Hannah, enjoined them to take every care, then planted himself like a redwood in the waiting area and waited. (Always nice to find an area appropriately named.)

He heard her before he saw her; she was scolding her first officer—fortunate bum!—as they came up the carpeted ramp.

"—with the cousins already!"

"No, no. You've got this all wrong, Ava. He's not a cousin."

"Oh."

"He's a stepbrother."

"Dammit!"

"Why are you fighting me on this? When have I steered you wrong?"

"Chicago. Honolulu. Los Angeles. Anchorage. Portland. The other Portland. Dallas. San Fr—"

"You have to trust me. I'm literally your wingman."

She groaned and rubbed her forehead. "First, this isn't a movie. Or a *Top Gun* remake. Or a rom-com. Well, maybe that last. Eventually."

"Don't you *ever* make fun of *Top Gun*. You know it's the reason I'm a commercial pilot."

"Yeah, about that—if *Top Gun*, the gayest nongay movie ever, inspired you, why didn't you join the navy?"

"Huh. That's exactly what my mom said."

Ava glanced up, spotted him, and Tom hoped the look of relief was more about real pleasure in seeing him rather than escaping the conversation. "Hi, Tom. Thanks for waiting. India, you remember Tom Baker, Hannah's uncle. Tom here is my . . . uh . . ."

This he could handle. "Her podiatrist."

"What? No, we're not doing that anymore. Tell him who you really are."

"Oh, apologies. I thought we were still using that subterfuge." He extended a hand to First Officer James. "I'm the medical examiner for Ramsey County in Minnesota."

"Sure you are." India turned back to Ava. "Come on, you guys can't even keep your stories straight. There's clearly nothing happening here."

"Ouch," Tom said mildly.

"All I'm saying is give my guy a call. If you don't like him, case closed."

"Your wife has, at rough count, two thousand cousins and at least one stepsibling. The case will *never* be closed. But speaking of closing cases . . ." She paused and gave Tom an expectant look.

No worries; he still had this handled. "I'm *not* a podiatrist. I'm a medical examiner."

"Oh my God. I gave you the perfect opening to talk about the—never mind." She shook her head and took his arm, which he supposed some might have found inappropriately proprietary. "Let's go. Chowder beckons. Well, maybe shrimp cocktail beckons. See you on the next leg, India, you annoying male version of Emma Woodhouse."

"Hey, you finally watched it!"

"I read it, you troglodyte." Then, under her breath to Tom: "Okay, I might have watched it, *then* read it. Still means I read it."

"I heard that!"

"Run," she told him, and they both broke into a jog.

Thirty-Two

Thanks to their timely sprint, they were able to beat a small crowd traveling together and snagged a decent table toward the back. Ava eschewed the justly famous chowder for a bucket of steamers, and Tom went with the grilled salmon. The waitress left, and they got down to business.

"What's on your mind? Besides murder and bodyguarding?"

"I was wondering if you had heard from Dennis."

"Uh . . ." She paused, thinking. "Not since I took him to see the disaster the vandal left. Haven't heard from him since, and as you saw, he wasn't at the second night of the memorial. Why? Do you think he's in trouble?"

". . . no."

"You're killing me with the pauses." She heard herself and nearly choked. "Not literally."

"Did he have an alibi ten years ago?"

"You know he didn't," she replied slowly, watching Tom's face. Guy was probably an ace poker player; he might be concerned about Dennis, concerned *for* Dennis, or wondering where the salt was. "You've read the file. He was out of town to check out some colleges, but nobody could put him at the U of M or anywhere else he said he'd been. Which isn't proof, by the way." She leaned forward. "He's a goofball with a flair for drama who might be an alcoholic, but he didn't kill his own twin. They weren't alike at all, but he'd never have hurt her."

"Try and call him," he urged. "Right now."

"Okay, rude, but . . ." She hated when people played with their phones in restaurants, but this could be a literal matter of life or death. Which she would tell the first person who tried to give her any side-eye. She hit his number and it went straight to voice mail. "Not there. Or not where his phone is. Or his phone is off." *Or he's dead, killed by the guy who just can't let this shit go.* "Should I report him as a missing person? Or . . ." She shivered, but it had to be said. ". . . reach out to his mother?"

Tom shook his head. "It's too soon. But it's something else to think about. Wouldn't you say? Identifying all the variables is always a positive."

"Argh, science. You really can't help yourself, can you?"

"I cannot," he admitted, looking simultaneously stoic and embarrassed, which was quite a trick. "Has anything else happened since last night?"

"No. I haven't gotten sick again, none of my belongings have disappeared, nobody fiddled with my last drug test. Except . . ."

"Tell me. Please."

"Everyone seems to know all about it," she explained. "Which was odd. The only people who should have been privy to the details were me, my union rep, HR, and my direct supervisor. But my crew had heard."

"Not surprising, given the nature of the tampered drug test."

"Sorry, what? Elaborate for the clueless layman, please."

"That's only half right," he said, smiling. "I researched the test favored by that particular lab. Their protocols are exacting—"

"Well, yeah. The FAA's like that. And they tend to be pretty detail-oriented. They wouldn't farm that particular lab work out to amateurs."

"Precisely. It would have been much easier for the killer/vandal to crack their server and change the numbers as opposed to sabotaging your urine."

"Well, if there's anything I hate, it's people sabotaging my urine."

"And if he or she can do that, perhaps they can hack into other servers. Or your company's intranet."

"Oh."

"Yes."

"Shit."

"Quite."

"I gotta think about what that means," Ava said. "Right now, I'm thinking it's nothing good."

"And this is speculation on my part. I have no proof. And perhaps your union representative is a heartless gossip." At Ava's snort, he continued. "But I think you should proceed by assuming the killer has access to your e-mails and anything Ava-related on the company servers, and plan accordingly."

"Fucking great."

"And . . . may I ask an unrelated question?"

"Hit me."

"I was researching the articles about your belly landing and got to wondering . . . your fellow pilot's aneurysm aside, how often do such things happen?" He leaned forward. "Statistically speaking, it's bound to happen, if infrequently. But . . . how often? Not murder, perhaps, but a passenger succumbing to a myocardial infarction or the like and dying in the air?"

"Well, first, we don't call it 'dying in the air,' because yikes, think of the other passengers. It's classified as a 'catastrophic incident.' And besides the belly landing, it only happened twice on my shift, and only once when I was the pilot. Poor guy keeled over in First, total cliché: overweight business guy in a nice suit fretting about important meetings and refusing to put his laptop away."

"But that's insane. It could become a projectile."

She nearly threw up her hands in victory. "Thank you! We're not *trying* to ruin their good time. It's just we're prejudiced against pesky details like a passenger getting beaned in the brain by a laptop going 150 miles an hour. Or not hearing the safety lecture because of their headphones, then losing their shit when there's an emergency landing. 'Wait, *who* gets the oxygen mask first? My dog?'"

Tom laughed. "It would depend on the dog, I think."

"Don't get me wrong. I love my job. Except for, y'know, the daily contact with people.

"So anyway, my crew knew CPR and how to use the defib, so they did their best while I landed. We had to stop on the runway so the ambulance had a clear path to the plane; the paramedics boarded, did their best, whisked him away; and the other passengers were really nice about it. There were a lot of 'wow, that puts being mad about my layover in perspective' observations. He was pronounced at the hospital, but to be honest, given that three billion people are in the air every year, I'm amazed it doesn't happen more often. Yes!"

This to the waitress who was laden with clams and salmon. Delighted, Ava put the sexy plastic bib around her neck, the better to avoid clam spatter as the waitress set down the bucket of steamers. "Ohhhhhh, I love these little buggers so much. What? It's not wet bread."

"Bottom feeder."

"That doesn't mean they only eat bottoms, just that they eat *near* the bottom. And back off with the judgment."

"I wouldn't dream of it. My focus is keeping you safe and remaining in your good graces. Everything else pales."

She stripped three steamers out of their shells, rinsed them, dipped them, ate them. "You're not fooling me. I can tell you're dying to comment. So go ahead and criticize these delightful little fruits of the sea."

"Clams are mud dwellers that will eat anything, including particles of deceased animals." He sighed and slumped back. "Thank you for letting me get that off my chest."

"If you're angling to get me to share some, you're going about it the wrong way."

She almost laughed to see him visibly shudder. "I'm not angling for that at all. At. All."

"Sure. So, what? You're here for MAGE but wanted to bodyguard on the side?"

"That's exactly right. I'm officially on vacation for the next few days, so this won't cut into my other duties."

"You're kidding!" She stared at him. "That's so great. Above and beyond, Tom. Truly."

He shrugged, but she had the impression he was pleased. "I'm fortunate that my supervisor allowed me access to the relevant files, given that Danielle's is a cold case and that my investigation isn't necessarily in an official capacity."

"Right. I mean—you're not exactly Kay Scarpetta."

"Pardon?" He'd begun to eat his salmon and paused to swallow. "Who?"

"The heroine of all those Patricia Cornwell novels? She's an ME who teams up with the cops and solves murders while being a great cook and a supportive aunt. The books always hit the bestseller list. You're an ME who has never heard of Kay Scarpetta?"

"It's possible to be one," he pointed out dryly.

"Right. Well, in the books and movies, coroners always team up with cops and catch killers—"

"Like in *Bones*! It inspired me to study forensics."

"Wait, you've heard of *Bones* but not Cornwell?"

"Yes, David Boreanaz is my favorite actor."

"David Boreanaz is your favorite actor," she parroted. "You must have loved *Buffy the Vampire Slayer*. And *Angel*, though I've gotta say, *Buffy* was the superior show."

"Mmmmm . . . I don't believe so. I don't care for paranormal shows."

"David Boreanaz is your favorite actor but only because he played a cop in *Bones*, which made you want to be a medical examiner?"

"Now that I hear it out loud, I understand your surprise. It *does* seem odd."

"Yeah, just a smidge. Hey, do you mind? Because it smells incredible." He nodded at once and let her stab a chunk of salmon with her fork. "Great, thanks—anyway, my point is, in the real world, to the best of my knowledge—MEs don't actually—"

"I see your point. I spend ninety-five percent of my time in a lab, which I imagine could make for dull television."

"Good call."

"For other people, not me . . . I would watch a show about

someone who spends ninety-five percent of their time in a lab environment."

"Of course you would. Well, what do you think?"

"I think you are a lovely, passionate, intelligent woman who eats garbage."

"I meant, where do we go from here? And you're wrong about that." She left it vague so he could wonder which attribute she had a problem with. "I'm in the same boat you are, by the way. Actually, my boat's much leakier—you're at least part of the criminal justice system. I've got no official responsibilities and no training in forensics or law enforcement. But fuck it. The killer chased me away last time.

"Well, not again. Not this time. This would normally be the part where I proclaim that I never make the same mistake twice, except I do that all the time. But I'm owning it now. I'm not running away. And I'm in the game now, Doc Baker! Not that this is a game." *Stop talking. Eat your bottom-feeder dinner.*

Nope. Her inner voice was denied; turned out she had more to say. "I'm still using the playbook from ten years ago, is what I'm trying to stay. And it got me exactly where it did before: flying away and pretending nothing ever happened, or if it did, that it was so long ago it didn't bother me anymore. But the hell with that playbook and the hell with the killer. You're coming with me and we're going to actually do something."

"Technically, *you're* coming with *m*—"

"Don't wreck my self-actualization, Tom!"

"Right. Sorry."

"Okay then."

"Yes."

"Glad we're on the same page," she added.

"As am I. Also, I suspect I am coming to adore you, which I can't explain."

"Probably just some bad fish."

He laughed and made a show of gobbling the rest of his salmon.

Nice speech, her eternally snarky inner voice piped up. *But for someone who keeps saying this isn't the movies, you're making lots of movie-heroine mistakes.*

Maybe so. But at least she wasn't hiding. She'd face her fuckups head-on, and nothing was going to stop her.

Probably.

Thirty-Three

"You're *grounding* me?"

"Yes, Ava. I'm very sorry."

"But my follow-up test was clean! Everyone agreed the first test was deeply screwed!"

"It's not a punishment, Ava. But someone blasted past our firewalls and e-mailed half the company your fraudulent test results."

"Good God!" And on the heels of that: *holy shit, Tom was right!* On the bright side, this latest unwelcome announcement saved her the "why does my entire crew know I flunked a piss test?" phone call to HR.

"You're still getting occasional press about the belly landing, which means this has the potential to become a major news story. And while you've done nothing wrong, what do people usually assume when they hear a celebrity—"

"What? Ridiculous."

"—flunked a drug test?"

Ava sighed. "People usually assume the subject lied, not the test."

"Exactly. We need to find the leak, plug the leak, and make sure something like that can't happen again. All of which will take time. And meanwhile . . ."

"This sucks, Jan."

"I know," the rep replied quietly. "Again, I'm sorry. It's not a punishment; it won't cut into your sick leave or vacation time. It's a literal paid vacation from us to you."

"Well, golly, when you put it that way, I should be *thankful.*"

"Well, no," Jan replied in a meek voice utterly unlike her normal briskly sarcastic tone. "Just that it won't cost you anything."

"You mean in terms of money," Ava said flatly.

"Well. Yes."

She sighed. "Anything else?"

"For now, no."

"You'll keep me posted."

"I note that wasn't a question—"

"Picked up on that, didja?"

"—and yes, absolutely, Ava. I will keep you posted."

"All right. I'll talk to you later."

"Goodbye. And again, I'm v—"

Childish, she knew, but she couldn't handle one more apology from Jan, and ended the call with a stab of her index finger.

Grounded.

Indefinitely.

Fuck.

Thirty-Four

Ava hopped off the Green Line at the Kenmore station and thought, not for the first time, that for a city whose streets were paved cow paths, it wasn't *that* hard to navigate. Or maybe all pilots felt that way. Maybe any transit system was a piece of cake once you had to land at Nepal's Lukla Airport. (Mountains + short runway + no lights × no air traffic controllers = brace for impact.)

It was a relief to be off the subway; she'd fumed from State to Cleveland Circle. But when she'd boarded after the meeting, she felt . . . not better, exactly, but less out of control and impulsive. Even better, it wasn't hard to find Geniuscon; she followed the signs, several of which offered lectures she didn't understand (EULER DIAGRAM YOUR DISJOINT SETS!), Solutions to problems she didn't have (HOW TO ENUNCIATE WHEN YOU STILL HAVE DECIDUOUS TEETH), and programs she'd never heard of (EXTRAORDINARY DAVIDSON* FELLOWS CHECK-IN

---

* No relation, alas.

HERE!). Were there ordinary Davidson Fellows? Did they check in somewhere else?

Finding Tom and the little family he'd made wasn't difficult, either.

(Family he made*? Are you jealous?)*

Well. Maybe. She'd been a family of one for close to a decade. By choice! Entirely by choice. It wasn't like she lost a bet or was cursed by an evil fairy ("Never shalt thou marry or bring forth children; thou art condemned to Lean Cuisine and *Cooking for One* cookbooks! Forever! Ahhh-ha-ha-ha!").

Anyway. Hannah, Tom, and Abe were clustered just outside the entrance leading to a hall that, she assumed, contained any number of genius inventions: time-traveling toilets, a gun that shot Twizzlers, maybe an app that knew to automatically swipe right when you were horny. (Well. Maybe not that last one.) Appropriately enough, the sign directly over Hannah's head read, WE'RE NOT FAMOUS . . . YET.

"Ava!"

"Hi, Hannah. Hi, guys. Sorry to be late."

"We're running late, too." Abe shook her hand. "So don't fret." He was wearing spotless jeans, sneakers, a dark blue T-shirt that read, I'M ONLY HERE BECAUSE THE SERVER IS DOWN, and a bemused expression. "Aren't you a sight!"

"Yeah, I don't know what that means."

Tom, whose face had lit up (*gratifying!*) when he spotted her, picked up on her mood. "What's happened? Are you all right? Did someone give you some trouble? Is that why you're behind schedule?"

"Nothing like that. Turns out my fake drug test results got e-mailed to a few hundred people. I'm grounded while the IT department looks for the crack in the wall."

"Well, shoot, that's not fair," Abe said, and she resisted the urge to throw her arms around him in sheer gratitude.

Hannah reached up and gave her hand a solemn pat. "I'm sorry you're grounded." To Tom: "So you were right about the cybersecurity issue."

"How did you even—you're weren't supposed to be listening."

"We're all in the same hotel room, Uncle Tom."

"It's a suite!" he protested.

"Yes, one with exceptionally thin walls, with all the connecting doors wide open so I won't fall down in the night if I need to pee." She glanced up at Ava. "I did that *once*. Two years ago! I was just little then!"

"It probably seems like an eon ago, huh?"

"Well," Hannah pouted, "it does."

"On the upside, now you've got more time to spend with Tom."

"Abe, you know you're not subtle, right? You're actually winking at us."

"Something in my eye," Abe replied. Then, shamelessly: "You two go off and have fun. We're gonna go see about some supper, hopefully by way of several food trucks. I've been craving cotton candy with a tomato juice chaser all morning."

"Ye *gods*. What is wrong with you?"

"Too many things to list just now, Captain. We'll see you two later."

"Bye, Uncle Tom. Bye, Ava!"

With that, Tom took her elbow while the rest of his family disappeared into the exhibition hall. "You're truly all right? This must have been a blow."

"Would've been a harder one if you hadn't warned me.

And I made time to take a meeting to get my mind serene. And just to get it on the record—"

"I'm not the killer, or the vandal, or the hacker."

"Got it. Thanks. But now I—hey." They'd been walking toward the street when Ava stopped, took another look, and—yep, she'd know that improbably red hair anywhere, a gorgeous mass that looked like grenadine syrup set on fire. "Becka?"

Becka turned, and the moment she saw Ava her eyes got big. She didn't say anything or move as they approached. Frozen, the way India froze when he realized she'd bought a Christmas gift for him but he didn't have one for her.

"Well, hey there. Tom, this is—"

"Flight Attendant Becka. She was helping your man G.B. on the flight to Boston. Hello again."

"G.B. isn't 'my' anything, unless it's 'my God, did you get caught in a rowing machine'? Nobody's that ripped outside of slick magazines and action flicks. Well." She gave him a critical up-and-down glance. "Besides you."

"It's far more efficient to have a muscle-to-fat ratio of seven percent, which puts me at a BMI of twenty-two point five, give or take."

"Oh, sure. For the ratio. Very logical."

"Well, it is," he replied, sounding not unlike his niece. "And I make efficient use of the time in terms of transcribing and paperwork and the like."

"Because of course you do." Ava was trying to picture Tom squat thrusting or what have you while dryly dictating the autopsy of a guy who suffocated in a crate of tinsel. And failing. "Sounds totally normal. But we're getting a smidge offtrack."

"Yes, I agree. To return to the subject under discussion,

your colleague, G.B., did seem exceptionally fit," Tom said. "I'd wager his interior and superior venea cavae are pristine."

"What a coincidence. That is *exactly* what I was thinking: pristine veins! But the topic under discussion was how we just now ran into Becka." To Becka: "So! What's up?"

"Nothing!"

Ava blinked and, when neither of them said anything, Becka elaborated. "I mean, my brother. He's a teacher here. Gifted students. *I'm* not gifted. But I'm from Boston, so . . ." She tried a shrug, but it looked more like she was twitching her shoulders the way horses do to shoo flies. "Here I am."

"Oh. Well, I'm not sure if you heard but I'm taking a couple of days off for personal—"

"Oh my God, did you flunk another drug test?"

That gave her pause. "No, just the one. Which was a false positive. That was the only one I flunked. Except I didn't, not really."

"A number of false positives," Tom added, because he thought he was being helpful. "Apparently, PCP hit twice."

Ava forced brisk cheerfulness into her tone. "It shouldn't take long to straighten out. I'm sure I'll see you at work later in the month."

"Yes! Okay!"

Jesus. She's almost vibrating. That's how badly she wants to get away from me. Or this conversation. Or both. Probably both. "Well, nice seeing you again."

"Yes! Nice! Okay. Bye!"

They watched as she practically sprinted away, and Tom broke the silence with, "How well do you know her?"

"Barely. She just started less than a month ago."

"Hmmm."

"Yeah, that about sums it up. Let's catch up to Hannah

and Abe. And on the way, you can tell me which of my colleagues might have murdered my friend and then came back to wreck my life."

"Your wish," Tom replied, still watching Becka beat her not-at-all-suspicious hasty retreat.

Thirty-Five

"Govahment Centah!"

They were on the T's Green Line,* on their way to meet Abe and Hannah. She liked Boston's subways, especially the way the conductor blared the names of the stops (piercing by necessity; the car was a sea of bent heads and smartphones) over the PA system in a full-on Boston accent. She knew generalizing was lazy thinking at best, but she'd never run into someone with a Boston accent who at the *least* didn't have a ton of common sense.

From the Baker family's hotel, Ava would hop a train back to her own hotel, where she'd get some sleep and then . . . then she'd . . . um . . .

"So what's our next move? Since we're both on vacation?"

"Keep trying to reach Dennis. Do whatever research we can on Becka. See if this person left an IT trail. Eat garbage."

---

* MBTA (Massachusetts Bay Transit Authority), the city's subway system, is, from personal experience, pretty great.

"Pahk Street!"

She snorted and, as the train took a sharp curve, clutched the nearest pole but was thrown against his side anyway. This didn't bother him at all, if the way he took her hand and held it was any indication. She was on board, too (no pun intended), if her accelerating pulse was any indication.

It's holding hands on the subway, not a marriage proposal. All you know at this point is that he thinks holding your hand is less disgusting than clutching a subway pole anyone might have licked.

"You're joining us for dinner."

"Is this a date thing or a bodyguard thing or a just-being-polite thing?"

"Yes."

"Oh. I." *Wow. Are you seriously having heart palpitations over this? Could you stop acting like you're hard up? CALM. DOWN.* "I wouldn't want to intrude."

"Accepting a sincere invitation is the opposite of intruding."

"Your niece and your—your Abe—might disagree."

"*Thank* you." He let out a sigh. "I do *not* know what to call him. And I never know how to introduce him."

"Ahlington Station!"

"Yeah, I noticed. That's not a criticism, though. I thought it was pretty cute."

He groaned. "Exactly what a grown man wants to hear."

"Adorkable?"

"I'm too old to be adorkable."

"Nobody's too old to be adorkable. That's just a straight fact. You have to accept my wisdom on this issue because I'm decades older than you in maturity and life experience."

"You're barely five years older than I am."

"But, again—decades mentally."

"I'm reasonably certain that I, in fact, am older than you mentally."

"I'll put my Inver Hills Community College degree up against your lame-ass medical school—"

"Harvard."

"Ha! Couldn't get into Yale, huh? Well, number two tries harder. Also, I know you are, but what am I? See? You've got no comeback for that devastating riposte."

"I concede." Tom rubbed his scalp, and his mood shifted from playful to fretful in half a second. "Abe's old enough to be my father, but he isn't. He was a member of my sister's family, but not mine. And it feels distinctly odd to introduce him as a friend. It seems wholly inadequate."

"Cawpley!"

"Well, what does your father figure / best friend / in-law think?"

Tom shrugged.

Ah. You haven't discussed it with him. Well, it's a tricky subject. "Abe, I think you're dreamy. Will you wear the other half of this best-friend necklace I bought from a mall kiosk?"

"I have . . . difficulty navigating social scenarios like this. I don't always understand what's appropriate. And when I ask, sometimes I make things worse."

"You're talking to someone who almost had a giggle fit at her own parents' double funeral. Trust me—you're fine."

His smile was so warm she practically felt it. "You're very kind."

"Uh, no. No, I am not. I can present a number of witnesses who will back that up, if you need it."

"I prefer to make up my own mind. And Abe and Hannah will not mind if you join us. Frankly, the addition of a non-family member could be helpful. I cannot bear the thought of another argument with Abe over the pullout sofa. I need very little sleep—"

"Plus, that hotel suite isn't a luxurious morgue drawer. How could you possibly be expected to get any sleep?"

"—and he has arthritis! But he insists that I take the gigantic bed, which is ridiculous."

"Oh, well. In that case, I'll definitely come to dinner." A Tom/Abe slapfight could be fun. "You wanna tag-team him? We could do that. Or Hannah could invent some kind of hypnotic that tastes like cotton candy and use it to drug him into avoiding pullout couches for the rest of his life. Hell, she probably wouldn't even need the drug. She could just hypnotize him with her geniusness."

"That's not how hypnosis works. Or genius."

"Oh, look at the hypnosis expert. You hypno-snobs are all the same."

"Hynes Convention Centah!"

"What is happening right now? What are we talking about?"

"I could tell you, but then I'd just have to hypnotize you into forgetting."

He laughed at her. "I don't always understand you."

"Noted."

"Which is charming. But also out of character for me."

"Aw." She looked down at her fingers entwined with his. For some reason, it made her think of Dennis and Xenia, who were supposedly a couple but who hadn't touched each other during the memorial. Where could he be? She hoped he'd fled and was sleeping it off somewhere, because the alternatives

(Is he dead?)

(Is he the killer?)

were awful. Worse, she wasn't sure which one she wanted to be true.

"It's none of my business, but I would like clarification. Earlier, you said you 'needed a meeting to get your mind serene.' Were you referring to a twelve-step meeting?"

"Sure. I needed one after my rep told me I was grounded. And Boston has lots. I went to one for AA because there wasn't one for NA* until seven o'clock. But I'm not picky. It's not the specifics—for me, anyway. It's the ritual. It's the Serenity Prayer and listening without judgment and talking without judgment and knowing everyone in the room gets it and maybe the cookies."

"May I ask you a question about the Center City drug treatment facility?"

"Hazelden? Sure. Fire away."

"What was the strangest—"

"Circus Day."†

"I beg your pardon?"

"They had a Circus Day. And for some unfathomable reason, they didn't warn—I mean tell—any of the patients. So picture any number of addicts in active recovery waking up one morning and going to breakfast and finding all the cooks are dressed like clowns. And several counselors. And the grounds people. And the gift shop people. For no reason that we could immediately surmise."

Tom, she could see, was trying (and failing) not to laugh.

"Yeah, sure, yuk it up. But it freaked a few of us out. One of my roommates actually grabbed my arm and hissed, 'Am I high right now?'"

"And?"

---

* Narcotics Anonymous. For more info, check this: www.na.org.
† This really happened when I was there!

"I told her that I wasn't sure the truth would make her feel better, and no, she wasn't high." Over Tom's chuckles, she added, "I mean, I give them top marks for literally everything else, but that always seemed like a spectacular blunder to me. Freaking addicts out en masse is just a terrible idea. We're in a treatment program, we're *already* . . . oh, stop laughing." But she smiled to remove the sting.

"I apologize. Truly. It's just . . . it's equal parts funny and appalling."

"Yep, that sums it up perfectly."

"I'm glad you got help," he added.

"Yeah, me too. And the years have slowly rid me of my fear of counselors dressed as clowns running a T-group."

"Courageous," he said with a straight face.

"Anything else you want to know?"

"Just this," he replied, and kissed her.

Thirty-Six

The first time hadn't been a fluke powered by loneliness and booze; Dr. Tom Baker *was* an excellent kisser. Given his occasional verbal fumbling and general klutziness, this was an exhilarating surprise.

Oh my God that mouth THAT MOUTH. Oh, and he's not trying to choke me with his tongue and he smells terrific, which is a good trick in a subway car, and even if nothing comes of this the day has been so strange that I will remember this kiss forever, even if I live to be an old lady, and how everything about it

"Kenmah Station!"

was perfect.

Tom pulled back, scanned her face, smiled. "That's us."

"Whuh?"

"Our stop."

"You're a really good kisser."

"Thank you." He stood and she realized he hadn't let go of her hand, had taken it and kissed her and was leading her out, and following wasn't really her style unless an ice cream truck was involved but what the fuck, it was that kind of day/week.

The entrance to the hotel lobby was just a few steps, and they pushed past the revolving doors to be enveloped in the guilty

(bad for the environment)

bliss

(soooo cooooool)

of the hotel's central air-conditioning system.

"Y'know, when I asked about your next move, I have to admit I was talking about the case. This is fine, though," she said, indicating their clasped hands. "But we're being pulled into Hannah's tractor beam, so this is your last chance to play the 'strictly work-related' card."

"Noted," was the dry reply as Hannah jumped up and down and waved at them from the other end of the lobby; Abe, holding her other hand, waved, too.

"Oh, man, look at that smirk on Abe's face."

"He spends an inordinate amount of time fretting over my dearth of female companionship."

"Well, everybody needs a hobby. Hi, guys."

"Captain Ava."

"Hi, Ava! Are you hungry? Grandpa and I are famished. We're going to dine. Will you dine? And if so, will you do it with us?"

"I am, I know, I will, and yes."

"Productive day?" Abe asked, and he definitely wasn't staring at their clasped hands. Nope. Not at all.

"Depends on how you define productive."

"I asked Ava to join us for dinner. Suggestions?"

There were several. But one clear winner: Bertucci's, just a short hop from the hotel. The minute they walked in, Ava took an appreciative whiff. Hand-tossed pizza, house-made tomato sauce, fresh cheese, wood-fired ovens. They found a table in short order—something of a miracle on a Saturday night—ordered, drank, talked.

"Stanford and MIT *and* Princeton all talked to you?"

"More like glommed on, Tom," Abe said. He was slouched back in his chair, fingers curled around a beer, and looked as content with life as anyone she'd ever seen. Hannah was clearly feeling the day, too, yawning while she scribbled anagrams on the kids' menu. "I was worried I'd have to set a fire or something, distract them so we could get some distance."

"A fire," Hannah said, switching out crayons, "would have been a bad plan. It could have become a blaze. A conflagration!"

"No one's saying there'd be no downside to setting a fire, Hannah."

"She's far too young to be talking to recruiters," Tom protested. "It's inappropriate!"

"She also loathes it when grown-ups talk about her like she isn't sitting right here and hearing every word while she colors."

"Ava's creeped out by people who refer to themselves in the third person. See? I know some smart stuff, too. Stop smirking," she added, giving the girl a poke in the ribs, which elicited a giggle.

"Besides, it was a waste of time. I was—Ava!—happy to talk to them but—don't poke!—I'm going to be a forensic pathologist, like Uncle Tom." Ava relented while Hannah straightened her bangs. "And once I get my juris doctorate, I'll do autopsies to catch killers, then prosecute them."

"Then maybe invest in private prisons, so you can also keep an eye on the killers you exposed, prosecuted, and incarcerated?"

"I *think* you're being sarcastic, but it's not a terrible plan."

"I was, Hannah. And it is." Ava shrugged. "But what do I know? I only ever wanted to be one thing."

Well. Mostly. Once upon a time, she and Danielle were going to travel the world buying eclectic nonsense for their online store, AvaDan ("AW-vuh-dawn", because pretension and their teenage selves went hand in hand). The plan was to first run it out of Danielle's basement and, once they were internationally famous and profitable—which they assumed would take no longer than thirty-six months—they'd move their headquarters to Paris, expanding to London and San Francisco as required.

It was a measure of how much she still missed her friend that, even now, the online-store idea didn't sound completely ridiculous. Even if she had only kept to one part of their plan.

"You're missing your friend."

"All right, Hannah, how'd you do that?" She probably should have been annoyed, but dammit, the kid was impressive. Ava wasn't too proud to learn new tricks. "I could have been thinking about anything. Pizza. Climate change. How I'm ordering the tiramisu just to gross out your uncle." *Also your uncle's mouth, which is goddamned sinful.*

"Incorrigible," Tom commented, smiling.

"You were smiling and happy until you talked about only wanting to be one thing. Then you looked down and went very quiet, and you snuck peeks at Uncle Tom, who's helping you catch the killer. So the only thing would be flying—were you going to fly together?"

"Something like that."

"Hannah," Tom began, but Ava reached out and touched his wrist.

"It's fine. Yes, I was thinking of her. Yes, I still miss her."

"That's okay. I'm not laughing at you," she said, sounding solemn for her years. "I miss my mother. I think about her sometimes. A lot, today. She would have thought the MAGE conference was hilarious. Right, Grandpa?"

"That's just right, hon."

"She would have teased my uncle because I'm more like him than I'm like her. And the oatmeal bottles."

"I'm sure she would have—what?"

"When I was a baby, Mom would make the holes in the nipples of my bottles a little bigger and put oatmeal and pureed fruit in with my formula."

"Helped her sleep all night," Abe added.

"Peach was my favorite."

"You remember being bottle-fed?"

"Yes. It wasn't boring, though," she added, as if she thought Ava was going to accuse her of being a lazy baby who contributed nothing to society while she sucked down bottles stuffed with oatmeal. "If I tried it now, I'd be tremendously bored. But back then, I didn't mind just being there. That's what I remember best. Just being there. And the taste."

"Remarkable. You're remarkable. That's—wow." Ava shook her head. *Outclassed, outgunned, outsmarted by a kid younger than my favorite bra.* "My first memory is getting my hands on a tube of cookie dough, gobbling it down in front of the fridge, then throwing up, also in front of the fridge."

"Eeee-yuck!" Hannah giggled. "But I didn't say it was my first memory. Just that I remember my bottle phase."

"Holy sh . . . shawarma."

"I know the word 'shit,' you guys."

"That's enough," Abe said mildly.

"It's just, I'm not sure why you're doing that. I know profanity is socially unacceptable in children, especially in public places. Which is why *I* don't swear. But whether you say 'shit' or 'shawarma' doesn't change that knowledge, or even reinforce it."

"Hannah, what have we said?"

A put-upon sigh, followed by, "That when I'm running the world, I get to make the rules. But for now, you and Uncle Tom are the bosses of me."

"Right. So that gives us at least ten years where we're the boss."

"Five," Ava said. "Tops." And at Hannah's delighted beam, she thought, *Wow, she smiles just like Tom!* Which was good, because it was one of the last pleasant evenings she was going to have for a good while.

Hindsight: always a bitch.

Thirty-Seven

"Just a heads-up, I'm not going to bang you tonight."

"I'll update my schedule accordingly."

"I know there's a stereotype about pilots having a girl and/
or guy in every port, but I've never had girls in any port, and
only seven guys. Wait . . . six. And I haven't seen two of them
in over a year."

"You cannot scare me off with your sex statistics."

"Who's trying to scare you off? Also, I've just decided that
Sex Statistics is going to be the title of my autobiography."

He laughed, then gasped as his hip banged into the side of
the check-in desk and he almost went sprawling. She had to
plant her feet to keep him from dragging her down as well.

"Luckily for you, I've decided your rampant klutziness is
endearing."

"I have *several* things to keep track of," he said with faux
haughtiness. "Where parts of my body are in relation to random large objects is not high on my list."

"I like that you're embracing it, too."

He had insisted on walking her home, which in this case

meant walking her to the nearest T station and taking the Blue Line to Airport Station, then walking her to her hotel.

"I don't have anyone in any port," he confided as they stepped into the elevator. "I trust that isn't a mark against me."

"Nope. Just the opposite." *Argh, cards!* Was no one allowed to use an elevator without jamming a card somewhere? And it couldn't be a random credit card. (She'd tried.) Had to be the room's key card. Not to pull a *Pretty Woman* (for any number of reasons), but she liked keys better.

Once they were off the elevator, she fumbled for five or six hundred hours until the thing was plucked from her fingers by more nimble fingers (nimbler fingers?), inserted, green light, click, in. "Show-off."

"Mmmm . . . no. This is not a rare skill set."

"Speaking of skill sets, you're a first-rate kisser."

"Where am I on your list of six? That's rhetorical," he added, as if worried she had a ranking system and was about to show him graphs she'd made to chart his abilities or the lack thereof.

"Right now, you're number one on a list of one: people I really, really need to kiss right now." The door swung closed behind him and he was on her at once, his mouth slanting over hers, his left hand gently cupping the back of her neck. His right arm went firmly around her waist as he pressed her against him, and he shivered a little when her tongue gently sought his. This went on for five seconds. Or years. Who cared? What, she was a referee who had to keep an eye on the clock?

He sighed, pulled back, went in for another kiss, this one more chaste, then pulled back again, his dark eyes filling her world for those few seconds. "When can I see you again?"

"In what capacity? Are we talking about more murder

research? Because I'm okay with that. But if we're talking about . . . what? A one-night stand? A series of one-night stands? Dating? Friends with benefits? I know I blew you off the night we met, but a lot's happened since then and . . ." He'd leaned in again and was nuzzling her neck, which made everything (heh) harder. "Erm. What were we talking about?"

"Whether I would see you in your self-appointed capacity as my murder clerk—"

"Oh my God. Never refer to me like that again. It's co-murder clerk or nothing."

"—or my self-appointed bodyguard, or in the profoundly to-be-hoped-for capacity of a couple exploring social inter-actions to hopefully embark on a relationship." He'd been gently backing her into the room until she could feel the bed just behind her. "It's both, I hope. But if I had to choose one, I would choose the latter."

"Aw, you're sweet. I'm not being sarcastic, by the way— that's really nice." *I don't share that exact sentiment just now, but it's still sweet.* "As it happens, I'm on board for most of it, too. But . . . we don't know each other very well. Are you sure you want—it's just, long-distance relationships are tricky." *Careful. Don't get ahead of yourself.* "Not—not that we're in one. I meant in general. Y'know, statistically speaking, long-distance rela-tionships are tricky. I'm sure there's a study somewhere that's gonna back me up."

He grinned and shook his head. "I cannot understand why you're single."

"Well, I'm grumpy, I like having my own way, I used to gobble down sleeping pills like Tic Tacs, I hate my home state, I use humor and sarcasm to hide, and the miasma of death follows me around."

"Nonsense."

"Yeah, that last one was just dumb. You have to put up with way more death miasma than I do."

He laughed. "You're charming, intelligent, lovely to look at and listen to—"

"Aw."

"—and you have an exciting and demanding job that only 0.002 percent of the population are qualified for."

"You looked up what percentage of the population are pilots?"

"Of course," he said, because . . . well . . . it was Tom. So: *of course*. "Further, you make self-deprecating jokes about being unintelligent or unkind, when neither of those things are true. Your flight crew holds you in high esteem. My niece, who does not take well to strangers, adores you. So does my bud, Abe."

"Ooooh, are you trying that? Bud? Is it because I called you his bud and Abe didn't burst out laughing or throw up?"

"Trial run," he admitted. "My point: I feel extremely fortunate to have met you. I wish to see you again—and again and again and again—in a socioromantic capacity."

"All right, I've got questions about what constitutes 'socioromantic' which we'll circle back to later. But you're okay with this, even though we're both weirdos who live fifteen hundred miles apart?"

"You're a pilot. Who better to be in a long-distance relationship with?"

"You have won me over with your practical outlook and gold medal make-out skills. Let's do it—let's see if we can something-something socio-something. I'm not seeing a downside at the moment. Not a bad omen in sight."

Tom started to say something when the room instantly went dark. "Whoa."

Too late, she remembered the room was set up so that if

the key card *wasn't* in the slot by the light switch, the lights would go off after a couple of minutes.

"We're not reading into that," she said in the dark.

"Absolutely not."

"It's meaningless."

"Laughably so."

"All right. Just making sure we're on the same page." She gripped his arms and fell back onto the bed, pulling him with her. "And on the same bed. I meant what I said earlier. I never fuck on the first whatever-this-is. But I love kissing and I love your mouth and your hands and how you smell like clean cotton, so let's do terrific above-the-waist things to each other for a while and then get ice cream."

"I think you might be a genius."

"That's how low you've set the bar now? Hey! Ahhhhh!"

As it happened, in addition to being a Gold Star kisser, Tom Baker was also a devastating tickler.

Thirty-Eight

Terminal C
Logan International Airport

THE LIST
~~Sign suspension paperwork~~
Return texts
New vibrator

"Sherry!"

"No. Oh, no. Not you. Not again." But she was smiling. "Seek professional help, Ava, and I say that as a pseudo-friend."

"Back atcha. Gimmee."

Sherry sighed, feigned reluctance for a few seconds, then grinned and unfolded her cane with a snap of her wrist.

"That always looks cool. You're like Hela in *Ragnarok*."

Sherry, fake sighing, held it out as Ava put her sunglasses on. "Once again you've drawn me into one of your dark schemes."

"Oh, please. Like anyone has ever drawn you anywhere you didn't want to go. Tell it like it is: we're copranksters who occasionally team up when all the astrological signs align." She let Sherry take her elbow and began tap-tap-tapping her way to gate C34. "There's no way you can pin this on me. Well, not entirely. This prank literally doesn't work unless you're in. And you're always in."

Meanwhile, various passengers were staring at Ava's uniform and the white cane and looking degrees of shocked, worried, flabbergasted, freaked, amazed, dumbfounded.

"Wait, she's—"

"Is that a—"

"Oh my God."

"Yeah, but . . . she's a flight attendant. Right? I mean, it's still weird, but at least she's not *flying* the—"

Sherry giggled. "You're a cruel fuck, Captain Capp."

"Again: back atcha. Three gates to go."

"This is literally the blind leading the blind. Except for the part where you have twenty-twenty vision. Did I just hear two people smack into each other because they were so busy staring at you?"

"Us. They're staring at us." She raised her voice. "I'm so excited about my first flight!" Tap-tap-tap. "The simulator was great but nothing compares to the real thing."

"Hell. Straight to hell for you, no waiting."

"Us, Sherry. We'll burn together."

"Again with this, you sick idiots?" Before she could turn, G.B. gave her a light smack on the back of her head. For a large man, he moved like a cat in socks. "What is wrong with you? That's not rhetorical, by the way. I'm genuinely wondering what the hell your damage is. And Sherry! Complicit

again! I'm disgusted by both of you, but you, Sherry . . .
Ava's hopeless, but you're better than this."

"She's really not."

"I'm really not," Sherry agreed.

"I can barely *look* at you."

"I feel the same way," Sherry deadpanned.

"Oh my God, this is hell." He moaned.

"Pretty sure we're all going to hell," Ava observed, handing back Sherry's cane and taking off her sunglasses to the
relieved sighs of various onlookers.

"Yeah, you've got a point." He focused on Sherry. "Are you
getting off in Minnesota or going all the way to L.A.?"

"The latter."

"Want to get a drink after we land? I've got nothing on at
LAX until 0500 tomorrow."

"Are you going to pay this time?"

"This time *and* next time."

Sherry shrugged. "Sure."

"Yes!"

"He just did an actual fist pump, Sherry. In front of God
and everybody. I'm appalled. Jeez, G.B. Play it cool." The way
she wasn't with Tom. Hopefully G.B. wouldn't pick up on the
hypocrisy.

"Why? It's Sherry!"

Sherry Lupe didn't wear sunglasses and her eyes were
the color of whiskey; she handled her cane like a ninja, and
anyone who tried to fuck with her was in for an unpleasant
day. Blinded at age ten, confident with or without the cane,
a lawyer (per gossip from G.B., several defense attorneys
were terrified of her) who did the BOS/LAX hop twice a
week, long black hair, tip-tilted eyes, designer suit, killer

heels, and if you didn't know she was blind, you wouldn't know.

Which reminded her. "I'm going out with this guy

(it's official, then?)

who's a bit of a klutz. Got any tips?"

"Yeah, tell him to break up with you. G.B., would you make yourself useful and have a screwdriver ready when I board?"

"I will, but only because it's my job and I have to. It's not because of anything you said."

"Sure it isn't." Sherry saluted her with the cane in a motion that, ironically, could put someone's eye out. "Always a pleasure, Captain."

"I know that's a cliché, but it *is* always a pleasure." To G.B.: "So that's exciting."

"What are you even doing here? You told me you're grounded."

"I'm just deadheading. I wore my uniform to make a point." Said point: *This is me now, and yesterday, and tomorrow: Captain Capp. CAPTAIN Capp. Captain Fucking Capp.*

"Captain Capp?"

"Agh!" Apparently, it was sneak-up-on-Ava day, because she'd had no idea Becka was there until she turned around. "Good morning! How'd it go with your brother at MAGE?"

For some reason, Becka chose that moment to look terrified. "Fine! It was fine! Everything is fine!"

Okaaaaay. "You seemed a bit weirded out. Like when you're a kid and you see one of your teachers at the grocery store. It's out of context, right?" *Is that the problem? Or is it something else?*

"I enjoyed seeing you!"

G.B. coughed. "Yeah, I don't know what all this is, but I'm not standing around while the gate lice* gather. Plus, I gotta get going on Sherry's screwdriver."

"Sure. See you on b—annnnd he's sprinting down the ramp." She turned back to Becka, who had closed the distance and was now standing less than half a foot away. "You were say—uh, hello."

"Hello. I'm sorry about the murder." Becka was close enough for Ava to tell she'd had coffee and some kind of pastry for breakfast. She'd also gone from shouting to whispering, and Ava was having trouble keeping up with . . . well. All of it.

"What?"

"And your drug test."

"Because . . . ?"

She blinked. "Because you keep getting—I mean, it's not *you*. But—it's you. I mean, your thing. To be in the middle of all this bad shit."

"My thing?" *Bad shit?*

"Well. Yes. I know you can't help it, though," Becka hurriedly assured her.

It's not what you think. It CAN'T be what you think.

Well, I think there's a possibility she might be having a mini-stroke . . .

"You're standing really close for this conversation."

"S-sorry." Becka audibly gulped and stepped back three

---

* Flight-crew slang. The ones who cluster around the gate right before boarding, inadvertently blocking everyone's way so they can be first on the plane. I have been guilty of this many times over. #noregrets

inches. "You—why were *you* there? At MAGE? You weren't supposed to be there."

"Where was I supposed to be?"

"Somewhere else."

"Can't argue with that."

"You don't live in Boston."

And you know this how, exactly? "That's correct. I do not live in Boston. I was not at the MAGE conference in the capacity of a local checking out the visiting geniuses."

"But you were there. Which makes sense! I'm here because of you!"

"You—okay."

"But why? Why were you there?"

"Well, Becka, as a matter of fact—and you're still standing really close for a conversation between colleagues who haven't known each other long—I was in Boston at the request of a new friend who thinks Danielle Monahan's killer might be targeting me."

"Oh! Oh. But why would the killer even do that?"

"Excellent question, Becka. Anything else? Because you should have been on board twenty minutes ago."

"On board what?"

"The *plane*, Becka. The Boeing 757 the airline puts into service as a gigantic flying Uber. C'mon."

It's probably not what I think. And even if it is, I can't just bar her from the flight and tell HQ that they should take my word that she might be a killer, a vandal, or a killer-vandal, even though I've got nothing to base that on.

But there's no question she's behaving strangely. I haven't known her long, it's true, but—weird. That was the cold truth. Less cold, but still true: she was dying to call Tom and give him the latest on Becka Miller. Yay, an excuse! Not that she needed one. They agreed they'd see each other.

But she had Becka to thank for one thing: whether the scattered flight attendant had guilty knowledge or not, it meant she'd be seeing Tom sooner than she thought.

Thirty-Nine

"My favorite MAGE exhibits were the disaster-recovery drones and the empathetic AI, Uncle Tom."

"Because?"

"It's one thing to ask an Echo to order pizza, but one that can tell when you're angry or sad and counsel you appropriately? I can't think how Marcus got the algorithms right." Hannah shrugged. "Well, he's old. Prob'ly took years."

"I believe Marcus just turned nineteen."

"Which doesn't disprove my last sentence."

"No." Tom smiled at her. "It does not." They'd packed for the trip home; Tom was inspecting the room to make sure nothing would be left behind, and his niece was perched on the end of the bed, sneakered feet swinging as she chattered. Abe had wanted the indulgence of another trip through the decadent food courts of Faneuil Hall

("Smoothies *and* raw oysters *and* éclairs *and* roast beef *and* spaghetti . . . c'mon, bud! I'll bring ya back a doggy bag.")

and would meet them at Logan.

"The empathetic robot was impressive," he agreed. Laptop,

check. Toiletries out of the bathroom, check. Tiny hotel conditioner that he did not need but that gave him a silly thrill to take, check. (Ditto the shower cap.)

"'Impressive' is Uncle Tom—ese for 'this is a startling technological advance, which I can barely understand much less embrace,'" she teased.

"You are correct." He thought about the AI in question. It had resembled a large plastic light bulb, and he could imagine it scooting around the house dispensing empathy, therapy, and the occasional monoamine oxidase inhibitor. *Good morning, your serotonin levels are low and you are sad. Would you like an antidepressant or to discuss your childhood?*

"He'll be *rich*," Hannah said with satisfaction. At his curious gaze—he hadn't been aware Hannah cared about such things—she added, "Don't worry, Uncle Tom. I'll be rich, too, and I'll take care of you and Grandpa the way you're taking care of me now."

"It's not a trade, Hannah."

She snorted. "Of course it is. And it's important for all parties to keep to such an agreement. Just ask anyone ensconced in a nursing home."

"And that's important? Taking care of elderly parents simply because there's a social contract?"

She gave him the same look he got when she realized they were out of Cocoa Pebbles. "That's not why I would take care of you."

"I adore you," he said, zipping the carry-on closed.

"Thanks!"

"What is that?"

She looked where he was pointing. She was wearing shorts, and just above her kneecap she had what looked like a cloud sticker.

"It's a temporary tattoo, the kind they give children," the child explained. "See?" She rubbed her fingers across it, but nothing smeared.

"But what *is* it?"

"It's a lamb. See?"

Tom squinted and could make out little black legs on the clou—the lamb. "Why?"

"They were handing them out at the sleep clinic. You know—'counting sheep'? That's why it's shushing you. So you quiet your mind and sleep."

"There's not a temporary tattoo in the world that can effectively shush me."

"All right. But as I was saying, you could have done something like Marcus did."

"I could never have done such a thing," he said. "Even now, I couldn't. Your fellow MAGE is far more intelligent than I am."

"But it's not about intelligence, Uncle Tom. Well, it is, but in this particular case it's also about parsing emotions. Like when you tried to help that boy when you were younger."

Yes. That. His father had been a psychiatrist who frequently consulted for adolescent treatment programs. This included examining teenagers accused of violent crimes and testifying in court. Tom occasionally came along.

He had been waiting for his father in the processing area of Hennepin County Juvenile Detention. (Processing area = customer service with armed guards and the more disgruntled customers in handcuffs.) His father was late (a not uncommon occurrence), he had finished his book (also not uncommon), and after twenty minutes of boredom Tom struck up a conversation with the youth sitting across from him.

"Does that bother you?" Indicating the handcuffs.

"Naw."

"Why?"

"Not the first time."

"What happened?"

The other boy blinked slowly, but was also bored, so he answered. "They think I killed some guy I never met. Can't kill someone you never saw."

"Oh. Maybe your lack of affect was off-putting."

"What?"

"The next time someone thinks you killed a person you never met, you have to convince them that you care, but not too much."

"What?"

"Like this: you know Jenny through a friend."

"Never met Jenny."

"Jenny is hypothetical. So someone tells you Jenny's husband is dead. It's unfortunate when someone dies, right?" When he didn't get an answer, Tom added, "Well, theoretically it is. So you should be sad. But not *too* sad, because you never knew Jenny's husband and you barely know Jenny. So while it's *technically* sad, it won't have any real impact on your life and it doesn't necessarily make *you* sad. So how to react to that news?"

There was a long silence, and then the other boy leaned forward and said, "How?"

"You want to project a kind of vague sorrow. It's mildly sad when someone dies . . ."

"Even if you don't know 'em," the youth repeated. "It's *technically* sad."

"Right! So even if you don't care about Jenny's dead husband, you can be a little sad for *her*. So that's what you put across: vague sorrow."

"Huh." The boy leaned back. "Still doesn't make a lot of sense."

"Well, you're no worse off if you try, right?"

"Yeah. Right. Thanks, man."

(Tom's father was equal parts horrified and impressed when one of the guards told him what happened. "Just so you know, Tommy, that boy killed two people and was carving up a third when he got caught. Vague sorrow indeed.")

"I am better at such things now," Tom admitted, "though I struggled when I was younger."

"You struggled last month when you tried to explain short-term gain versus long-term gain to Mr. Herbekker."

"I should have factored his Alzheimer's into the discussion," Tom admitted. "So we'll change 'I am better at it' to 'I have improved but there's room for more.' Do you know how I've improved, Hannah?"

"I . . . think so."

"Proximity to you."

She nodded and tucked her tongue up into the slot where her permanent tooth would come in. "There's something to that, I think. Remember my first birthday party? You were the only one I wanted to talk to." And then, abruptly: "Are you worried I'm on the spectrum?"

"No. I'm curious about it."

"Okay. When can—"

Tom's phone had clicked at him, and he reached for the thing at once, hoping Abe wasn't delayed or otherwise in trouble.

Not Abe. Better: Ava.

CAPTAIN AVA CAPP: Just had the WEIRDEST run-in with Becka, the new crewmember we met Saturday.

TBMD: Are you all right?

CAPTAIN AVA CAPP: Fine. Definitely not murdered. But she's squirrelly and weird and talked about death. And not in a fun way, like we do.

TBMD: Police?

CAPTAIN AVA CAPP: For what? Creeping me out and being a close-talker?

TBMD: A what?

CAPTAIN AVA CAPP: OMG. We'll go over pop culture later. Are we still on for Thursday?

TBMD: Of course.

CAPTAIN AVA CAPP: Want to make it tomorrow?

TBMD: Of course.

CAPTAIN AVA CAPP: Let's do more amateur sleuthing after you get off. Heh.

TBMD: Technically only one of us is an amateur.

CAPTAIN AVA CAPP: Technically that's a good way to get smacked.

TBMD: Noted.

CAPTAIN AVA CAPP: You know what's weird? We both text in complete sentences.

TBMD: Anyone who doesn't is a savage.

TBMD: A SAVAGE.

CAPTAIN AVA CAPP: Yow! Noted. Say hi to Hannah and the bud for me. Cool name for a band BTW. "And now, for your polka pleasure, HANNAH AND THE BUD!"

TBMD: Never while I live.

CAPTAIN AVA CAPP: ☺

CAPTAIN AVA CAPP: Yeah. I'm one of those. I'll never apologize for gratuitous emoji use, either. Be resigned.

TBMD: Noted.

"You have the *silliest* grin on your face, Uncle Tom."

"Irrelevant. Ava says hello. Ready?"

"Yes. It was nice of her to think of me, especially since she had new information about your case." Before he could ask, she added, "You tensed up when you first started reading her texts—your shoulders got *super* tight and you were frowning. But toward the end you loosened up and were smiling. So she must have told you something about the case and then, I'm guessing—"

"Deducing."

"It sounds less cold-blooded when I say I'm guessing."

"Point." He personally adored the way random passersby reacted to Hannah's towering intellect. Especially since she often "turned it off" and sounded like a typical child immediately afterward . . . until something new teased her intellect. "You needn't do that on my account."

"Thank you. Anyway. I'm guessing that after the case update, she moved up your timetable for social interactions. Which made you smile."

"So it did. Right on all counts." He swung both bags off the bed. "Shall we?"

"Obviously. I like Boston, but I miss our house."

"Those are my exact sentiments as well."

"Uncle Tom, I don't want to know what happened to that boy you tried to teach empathy, do I?"

"You do not."

"Ah."

Forty

Hilton Boston Logan Airport

"What can I do for you, Ava?"

"Well, Jan, first I'd like props for remembering you're in California. It wasn't easy, because my mind is the opposite of a steel trap."

A snort. "Congratulations. You finally remembered something that you have literally known for years. I'll FedEx you a cookie."

"*Two* cookies."

"I'm sorry to say we're still working on your, uh, problem, so I don't really have an update yet. Is that why you called?"

"That, and to give *you* an update. I know we're supposed to come to HR or a union rep when someone makes us uncomfortable . . ."

"Whoa, whoa. Is this a #MeToo thing? Should I be recording this conversation?"

"No! Nothing like that." If only. Not to belittle the movement, but she'd rather worry about being sexually harassed than a serial killer chatting her up. "Nobody's sexually harassing me. Well, India thinks I should score, so he's trying to fix me up with one of his wife's relatives. Would that be sexual harassment by proxy?"

"I can honestly say I have no idea."

"Besides, if someone ever tried it, G.B. would *devour* them." She paused at the thought and decided it wasn't much of an exaggeration. Two years ago, the new VP cornered one of G.B.'s colleagues when he thought he had the room to himself. For some reason, the gentleman in question thought taking his dick out was an appropriate way to make an introduction. He never heard G.B., who clocked him over the head with a water pitcher. It took him four minutes to regain consciousness, and three hours to file his termination paperwork.

"It's not a #MeToo thing," she reiterated. "But an employee got a bit in my face and was asking me a lot of questions about my personal life and acting incredibly strange and I have to tell you, it made me uneasy."

"Becka Miller."

(??????????????????)

"Ava? Are you there?"

"Okay, how did you know that?"

"She's an admirer. Your name is all over her application paperwork."

"Okay, weird."

"It's not *that* strange. I think," Jan said gently, "and this is off the record and I can't prove any of it and we never had this conversation, which I'm definitely not recording to cover my ass, but I think she has a bit of a crush."

"I . . ." Ava trailed off. The close talking. The shouting. The excitability. The murder talk. Coincidentally running into her in Boston. ". . . I don't think that's it. She was pretty together the first time we met. But she knew I wasn't from Boston, then followed me to Boston, and she didn't start acting weird until we saw each other in Boston."

"Would you like to file a complaint?"

"No."

"Then what can I do for you?"

"I just—look, I get that this is skating right up to the line—"

"Whenever you say that, you're already over the line."

"What can you tell me about her?"

A sigh from the other end. "Ava. I could lose my job."

"I know. I know it's a lot to ask. That's why I made sure to remember you were in California before I called."

A snort. "Look, all I can say is, she sailed through all her paperwork and her psych evaluation looked great." Although not required by the FAA, Northeastern Southwest required psychological screening for all air crew before they could join Team "We fly everywhere!".

"And?"

"And that's it. Honestly. No red flags. She even joked a little about how being an orphan actually helped her choose this line of work—no family to let down when she'd inevitably work during the holidays."

"But . . . she has a family. A brother, at least. That's what she said when we saw each other in Boston and she freaked right out. Because, again, something's up with her."

"Ava, honestly, that's all I can tell you. And I shouldn't have told you even that much. If you don't want to file a complaint, my hands are tied."

"There's nothing to file a complaint *for*," Ava fretted.

"Then I'm ending this conversation by assuring you that I don't think you're in any physical danger from Becka Miller."

"Well, that—wait, just physical danger?"

"I'm hanging up now."

"Am I in emotional danger? Psychological danger? Jan? Hello?" Dammit. One thing about Jan, she was as ruthless as Ava about ending phone calls. When she said she was hanging up (so to speak—did they even have the phone receivers required to hang up over at Human Resources? Or were they all on their smartphones?), she never bluffed.

So Becka's smart, did great on her tests, aced her psych eval, and poses no physical danger to me. But she's also an orphan who may or may not have a creepy brother she may or may not resent and who talked about me to strangers to an extent that the HR rep knew instantly who I was calling about.

Yeah, not convinced this puts her in the clear.

If Ava was a cop, she'd have nothing. But she wasn't a cop, which was the advantage of being a pilot instead of a police officer: she didn't need much more than her intuition to look into something.

She'd lay it out for Tom, see what he thought. Maybe after some kissing. Well, no. This was important. Before the kissing, then. But then *immediately* after she laid out the Becka speculation, on to the kissing.

Always good to have your priorities straight, she figured. *Right?*

Forty-One

Mall of America
South Street Dining Area
Bloomington, MN

She could see at once meeting at the food court had been a bad idea. Tom looked tense, which given his line of work was alarming. What could freak out a guy who carved up corpses for a living? A rubber glove shortage? A zombie apocalypse? (To be fair, that last would upset her, too.)

He didn't even notice her until she was almost on top of him (figuratively). "Hey," she said, reaching out and taking his hand. "It's great to see you." It was. He was in khakis, loafers, and a black polo that set off his build and eyes to wonderful effect. Ava knew she had it bad when she thought how sexy he looked when the decidedly unsexy mall lighting hit his shaved skull. "Are you all right?"

"It's dinnertime," he replied in a low voice, brown eyes almost black in their intensity. "It's . . . very crowded. Hard to focus. And I should be with you more. I can't keep you safe if I'm not with you."

She squeezed his hand, turned at once

"Ava, please don't g—oh."

and started leading him through the food court and back to the entrance to the Radisson Blu a few hundred feet away.

"I'm not going anywhere. Well, I am, but you're coming with me. What, you thought I'd run because you're stressed?" she chided him.

"It's been known to happen. Not with you. Others."

"Every day, you have to wade through the worst people do to each other; it's literally your job description. I'm impressed you're not stressed every *day*. The reason I wanted to meet here is because I'm lazy—my hotel is here—and because I like the Mall of America."

"Why?"

"Because Danielle never came here—utterly refused—and because my folks only went a couple of times. Called it a marketing monstrosity. It's one of the places in this benighted state that doesn't remind me of murder."

"Oh."

"But it's fine if you need to leave. We'll grab dinner at the hotel. In my room if you want—it's nice and quiet and oh my God, people have been murdered in the Mall of America. That's what that look on your face means."

The tension around his eyes had eased, and he looked down and grinned. "Well. Yes."

"In unusual ways, or you probably wouldn't have remembered. The mall's not even in your bailiwick. It's Hennepin County, not Ramsey. Let's go somewhere quiet where I can have a steak and you can tell me about murder." *What have I become?*

"Thank you," he said quietly, and she could sense the weight of feeling behind his words but, because she was an immature idiot, shrugged and looked away. Which is why she didn't notice her would-be muggers until it was close to too late.

She'd led him outside rather than taking the skyway, and they were skirting the edge of the parking ramp when opportunistic thieves made their presence known with, "Give it up."

Oh, swell. This is on me. Tom's probably still freaked out; I should've been paying attention for both of us. An unpleasant experience is nigh. Nigh, I say!

She knew the best and safest option was to meekly hand over her purse

"Man said give it the fuck *up*."

no matter how much she wanted to arm-wrestle them for it. Still, they were both big—almost as tall as Tom. More worrying, they didn't seem especially nervous or edgy—she had the impression they'd done this before. The one on the left was wearing a knitted cap pulled low, which also should have tipped her off, and had one hand stuffed into his pocket

(knife? gun?)

while his empty hand dangled at his side. His partner was shorter and wider, and flashed his knife with disconcerting confidence. Less-than-even odds, in other words.

She started to unsling her purse from her shoulder

(better update my list and get more Tootsie Rolls and also a new wallet)

when Tom struck. Literally. She felt the wind of the blow as his fist shot past her face, which was followed by a "crunch" not unlike the sound of someone wrenching a turkey leg from the thigh.

The tall one made an outraged, bubbly sound as blood

poured down his chin while his partner lunged into Tom's left hook. She was astonished at Tom's speed—she would have expected him to be strong, not swift. Tom made a grab for the first guy, but they had decided to git while the gitting was good, and were around the corner and away not even ten seconds after Tom had thrown his first punch.

"Holy shit! Are you okay?"

"Yes. Are you?"

"Are you kidding? Nobody touched me. I didn't even get my purse all the way off. C'mere, let me see." He held his hands out to her like a kid letting a grown-up see if their hands were clean. One was fine; the other was . . . holding something?

"Oh my God, you lifted his wallet." She stared up at him in amazement. "I thought you just grabbed for him and missed, but you picked his pocket!"

"Yes."

"That is so cool!"

He grinned and ducked his head, affecting a "no biggie" shrug. "I don't believe this attack is related to Danielle's murder or the vandalism, but I'll hold onto this just in case."

"Sure, fine, great plan, and also maybe your bodyguarding idea isn't as craptastic as I assumed."

"Thank you," he replied dryly, as she produced Kleenex and dabbed the blood off his knuckles.

Radisson BLU
Bloomington, MN
Room 263

". . . and the filet mignon with mushrooms."

"Yes."

"And cheddar herb mashed potatoes."

"Yes."

"And a pitcher of iced tea."

"Yes."

"And white chocolate banana cream pie."

"Yes-yes-yes!" For a moment, Tom thought the room service server was in real danger as Ava lunged. No, she was merely in a rush to sign the bill and devour her meal. "Looks great. Thank you. Tom! The food's here."

"Ava, I am six feet away. I'm very aware the food is here."

"Keep up the snark and no dessert for you."

She had brought him back to her one-bedroom suite and ordered their food while he excused himself and fled to the bathroom, washed his hands, then glared at the idiot in the mirror and told him to *calm the hell down—yes, hell, I meant hell and definitely not heck—for God's sake!*

It wasn't the fight. She was fine, he was fine, the threat had been neutralized. It was the other thing. He thought about how best to explain. *Most of the time I would have been fine in such a bustling place. But there were a number of factors that heightened my anxiety and shattered my focus. The first factor: Ava Capp.*

Must I explain? He was surprised by the thought, one his much younger self would have asked plaintively. *Again?*

The sharp rap on the door had splintered his concentration, and a few seconds later he heard a delighted yelp

"Food's here!"

and left the bathroom.

So here they were, eating in companionable silence while he struggled to think of what to say. Ava had wasted no time spreading out the food in the separate dining area; she was a fourth of the way through her steak by the time he pulled his plate of chicken kebobs toward him.

"Thank you. For coming back here."

"Thank *you* for going all Apollo Creed over those two. It's nicer here anyway. Better food and more privacy."

Yes. Privacy. To talk about the killer. And. Perhaps. Something more?

He did not know, and wasn't sure how to broach the subject. So he avoided it with, "I like this carpet. It's incongruously blue."

She looked up from her plate and giggled. "It *is* incongruous, isn't it? Most of these places have tan or brown or gray. Or a pattern. But this is very, very blue."

"Like a moat."

"A fuzzy, deep-blue moat."

A short silence fell, which Ava broke with, "Where'd you learn to fight? Can all medical examiners do that, or just you?"

"I box at Top Team. It's an excellent full-body workout as it's a valuable balance of resistance and cardio. Abe got me into it."

"Please tell me you don't spar with Abe."

"Not anymore."

"Tom! One hit and you'd blast him through the ropes! And possibly the wall behind the ropes."

"Like I said, not anymore."

She groaned, then realized he was teasing and smacked him on the elbow. "Well, I'm officially thanking you for preventing my mugging and subsequent need for a new purse."

"The important thing is that you weren't hurt," he said softly.

"No, the important thing is that neither of us were hurt. And speaking of hurt, will you tell me about the Mall of America murders?"

Never had he been so pleased to talk shop. "Murder, singular. It wasn't murder so much as manslaughter. The restaurant had a new employee who was behaving foolishly with the machine they use to make eggrolls."

"Am I about to be very glad we didn't order egg rolls?"

"Perhaps. During the employee's shenanigans—"

"Oh, man. Gotta give full props to anyone incorporating 'shenanigans' into a story about death by egg-roll machine."

"—one of the blades violently detached and nearly amputated one employee's arm. And while people were panicking over that, a cylinder somehow rolled loose and crushed the first employee. His chest cavity filled with blood and he suffocated."

"Wow."

"Yes."

"Awful."

"Yes."

"So the takeaway here is to keep the shenanigans to a minimum when you're making egg rolls. Got it. Y'know, I love this macabre shit, even though I spent ten years pretending otherwise. I'm sure someone died a horrible-yet-weird death right here in this building."

"A banker had an allergic reaction to someone else's service dog and went into anaphylactic shock. It wasn't murder, but it was interesting."

"It *is* interesting!"

"I'm pleased you're pleased. But if you'll allow me to go off topic—"

"No more carpet and egg-roll chitchat while you work up the nerve to tell me what's really on your mind?"

That took him by surprise, which was foolish. Ava was many things; stupid was nowhere on that list.

"—you checked the peephole before you opened the door, yes?"

"Yep. Don't worry, it definitely wasn't Becka with a crowbar. Though I'm so hungry, I might've let her in if she'd had food."

"Your text alarmed me."

"I didn't mean to scare you. I just wanted to tell you what was going on. I called Jan, my union rep, too. To ask about Becka."

This, too, was alarming. He set down his partially gnawed kebob. "Ava, I do *not* like your exposure here."

"Don't worry, Jan won't say anything. And she didn't give me much, either. Apparently Becka was a big fan of mine even before she started working for the airline."

"Oh?"

"Yeah. Jan knew who I was asking about before I mentioned Becka's name."

He had picked up his kebob, then nearly dropped it. "I don't like that, either."

"Weird, right? But apparently she aced her psych exam. All her exams. And Jan didn't think I was in any 'physical' danger from her."

"That's an interesting way to quantify such a thing."

"That's what I said! Then that rotten bitch hung up on me, which is only fair, but it's still annoying. So what do we—salt, please—what do we know? Becka's young—early twenties."

He took the salt back. "Which could rule her out."

"Except we can't use the 'she's too young' rule because she could have a partner. That's why you suspected me at first."

"Yes, but in her case, she's—what? Eight or nine years younger than you are?"

"Yeah. So if she has a partner, it hasn't been for long, is

that what you're saying? Because it's a good point. And talking about Boston, that's the other thing I wanted to know—how'd she know I was going to Boston and how'd she find me, also in Boston?"

"It is troubling. If you'd never before met, never moved in the same circles, why would a random pilot seize her attention in such a manner?"

"Hey! No, wait. You're right. I *am* a random pilot."

"Perhaps the exposure from the belly landing flagged her attention?"

"Maybe, but that wouldn't explain how she knew all about me months earlier, when she was applying to the airline."

"Point. Fortunately, there's a simple way to get some answers."

"Have Hannah dose her with truth serum? Bug her uniform? Dig a pit and lure her into it, and refuse to let her out until she confesses?"

"Those are all terrible ideas."

"There *are* no terrible ideas in brainstorming, Tom."

"That is a lie." He batted away the mushroom she tossed at him. "Ask her. The two of us. We sit down and we ask her. *We*. As in, the two of us. As in, do not rush off alone, Ava. Do not tackle this without backup. Do not—"

"O-*kay*! Cripes, I get it. And I've got to give you points for the direct approach. I like the idea of inverting a trope."

"What?"

"Or would it be subverting? In the books, the amateur sleuths never just sit down with their suspect. They come up with all these plans to do everything *but* sit down with her, or him. They spy on them or follow them around or bug them somehow . . . everything *but* a sit-down."

"What books are we talking about?"

"Ones you haven't read, apparently. Never mind. It's a good idea. Especially if we do it in a public place. Not a food court," she added quickly.

Do it. Perfect opening. "Ah . . . Ava. About that . . ."

"Uh-uh."

". . . I wish to explain—pardon?"

"You don't have to explain dick."

"I don't have to explain dick," he parroted, bemused.

"You couldn't think there. So we came somewhere you could. And, by happy coincidence, somewhere I could have you all to myself. Win-win. Case closed. Well. *That* case, anyway."

Do not be fooled. It's never this easy.

Yes, but in the past the Ava Capp factor was never in play, either.

"So I'll reach out to Becka and we'll set up a meet. She's probably still doing the MSP-BOS-LAX run. We could probably meet her here in the Cities in the next couple of days. Assuming she wants to even meet with us."

"My advice is to frame it as a meeting with *you*. She needn't know I'm there until it's time."

"Okay. Definitely worth trying. And if she doesn't want to get together, we can—"

"She will," he said at once. "She will not be able to resist."

Ava just looked at him. "Is that a fact?"

"It is."

"So I guess that's what we're doing."

"Very well."

"This is about the time when I'd make a really clumsy innuendo like 'so how do we kill time until then, wink-wink, nudge-nudge?'"

He laughed. "You are dazzling in your subtlety."

"Aren't I?" She rose, circled around the small table, came to him, rested her hands on his shoulders. Smiled down at him and—ridiculous thought—the light behind her lit up her hair like a curly halo. "I really need to kiss you right now, with your kind permission, so you're gonna have to deal with that."

He was already gently pulling her down, slotting her upper lip between his and gently sucking it into his mouth, encouraging her lips to part for him and then

"Oh. Yes."

she was on his lap and wrapping both arms around him. "Oh my God," she murmured, "I love the way you smell."

"I love—" *Every single thing about you. Even the oddities and cavalier approach to death. Especially the cavalier approach to death. Also these feelings are impossible. We only just met.* "—how you taste."

"Like steak and confidence," she declared, and then giggled as he huffed laughter against her neck.

"Ava." He slipped his hands under her shirt, up her back, cupped the smooth warm flesh of her shoulder blades. "I have to tell you something about myself."

"Are you the killer?"

"No."

"The vandal?"

"No. I don't know why anyone vandalizes. So inefficient."

"Planning to kill, fold, spindle, or maim me?"

"Never."

"Do you have a secret family in Canada?"

"Not anymore."

"Don't care, then. More kissing, please."

He obliged, to their mutual delight.

Forty-Two

THE LIST
Bottle Tom's kisses somehow, market to public, make fortune
Moisturizer [sigh]
Corner Becka like a rat and wring a confession out of her
Or clear her
More kissing

She'd just finished shrugging into her sleuthing outfit (tan shorts, red sleeveless blouse, black flats, frizz going every which way because *argh* humidity) when she heard a brisk knock.

Excellent! And right on time, which came as no surprise. She darted across the room and checked the peephole. Nothing.

Disappointing.

She looked again.

Nope.

So she opened the door and craned her neck to check the—

"Are you trying to be the sacrificial lamb?"

"Ack!"

Tom frowned and shouldered his way past her into the room. "I cannot believe you opened the door."

"It's kind of necessary, since I don't actually live here and need to periodically emerge for moisturizer and airport runs and sleuthing. And you said you'd be right back!"

He'd spent the night, at his insistence; she'd let him talk her into it. Something-something danger, something-something not taking any chances with her safety, etcetera. They had another smoking snogging session, then slept apart, her in the king-size in the bedroom, him on the foldout in the small sitting room. She'd regaled him with more Hazelden/airline mishaps; he'd talked about his work, his pride in and worry for Hannah, his friendship with Abe. They'd commiserated over dead loved ones. Probably no one's ideal of a first date—if that's what it was—but it worked for them.

Tom, meanwhile, was still standing with his arms folded across his chest, frowning. "Even if the killer is not affiliated with Becka, he's fixated on *you*, Ava. What you just did is incredibly reckless."

She opened her hand, showed him what was in it, hit the fulcrum lever, and with a flick of her wrist, the blade snapped out.

"Oh."

"Yeah."

"Gravity knife with a 3.25-inch blade. Titanium?"

"Yeah."

The frown eased but didn't disappear. "I still think you took a risk."

"Tom. Honey. I'm a pilot. That doesn't mean I'm reckless, but it doesn't mean I'm risk-averse, either. It's literally my job to manage risks in order to keep my crew and passengers safe. And if you think I'm going to hide behind locked hotel room doors—or in the air—until the killer is stomped, then you don't know me at all." She paused. "Which, given that it's been a week, wouldn't be a mark against you. But either way, that's where it stands. Speech over."

"I liked it when you called me honey."

"Good to know, honey-bunny."

He snorted, then sobered. "I shouldn't have underestimated you. Again."

"You're looking out for me. I've got nothing to complain about. Well, at this particular moment in time, at least. And where's my kiss? Look, I'll put the knife away so a smooch is slightly less dangerous."

"I wouldn't be here if I minded danger," he murmured, stepping close and giving her a kiss that managed to be chaste and delicious at the same time. "Also, when we know each other better, I would not be averse to you relieving me of my virginity."

"Well, I'm here to hel—what?"

He drew back. "You hadn't guessed?"

"Are you kidding?" The word kept reverberating in her brain, turning it into

virginity virginity virginity does not compute virginity virginity BUT ALL THE HOTNESS THO!!!!

a clanging echo chamber. "Have you *seen* you? Have you *kissed* you?"

"No. And no. Obviously."

"Have you—" She gestured to his face, his shoulders, his legs, all of him, every bit of him, each and every yummy part of him. "—seen all this? I wouldn't have guessed in a hundred years."

"I have some experience," he said candidly. "But I identify as demisexual."

"Okay. However you're comfortable. It's all fine."*

He sighed and employed the family mind-reading trick. "Which does not mean I am attracted to demons."

"I wasn't thinking that!"

His hands settled on her shoulders. "It means I'm only aroused by someone I have an emotional connection with. And making such connections was always difficult for me, so I put my focus elsewhere. Work had been my priority until Hannah was born; now my priorities are my family and my work. So finding a partner under those circumstances is . . . difficult."

"I can see that, sure. So you've dated, and you've liked some women enough to try a few things, but no one's ever completely, uh, devirginized you?"

"Good *God*. Please tell me you don't think that's the technical term."

And then. The eureka moment: "That's why you're such a good kisser! It's your go-to move. And when your focus isn't on going all the way, you can get *really* good at the other stuff."

"So this . . . situation . . . poses no difficulty for you?"

"Are you kidding?" One shock was following another, except, for a nice change, they were *good* shocks. "First, I'm flattered that you're willing to share yourself with me, emotionally and physically. So incredibly flattered. To an *insane* level, the flattery. Second, I get to be the first person to do any number of delicious things to you? It's like winning sexual lotto!"

He burst out laughing. "I'm relieved you're pleased. In fact, I don't think anyone has *ever* been so pleased about my condition."

---

* BBC *Sherlock* reference!

"Ew, never call it that again. You don't have the mumps, for God's sake. So now that that's out of the way, what's next?"

"In what way?"

"In the nonsexual way, you virginal perv."

"Already I regret confiding in you. But yes. Absolutely. Except." He gave her another long, sweet kiss, and they were both just a bit out of breath when it was done. "There."

"I can't believe you've been depriving the world of you."

He snorted. "As you would say, 'aw, that's sweet.' Meanwhile, I'm having trouble believing you're real. You really—ouch."

"See?" She pinched him again. "Real. Need more proof?"

"No. I'm relieved—ouch!"

"Yeah, this whole Ava-and-Tom team-up is definitely going to be a mixed blessing for you."

"Intriguing *and* frightening. Perfect."

She was about to retort when her phone vibrated; she reached for her phone and nearly dropped it when she saw who was calling.

"Dennis! Fucking *finally*."

"Excellent."

Forty-Three

Except it wasn't Dennis, and it wasn't excellent.

"What did you do?" Xenia shrilled in her ear at such a pitch, Ava abandoned the idea of putting her phone on speaker.

"Xenia? What are you talking about? Are you okay? Where's Dennis?"

"I'm asking *you*, bitch!"

"Rude. I have no idea where he is. I've been calling his cell for the last couple of days."

"I know!"

"You—well, that would explain why he hasn't called me back. Xenia, I haven't seen him since I drove him to the funeral home to scope the vandal damage. God's truth, not a peep—no texts or calls or messages."

"Liar," she hissed.

"I was starting to get worried."

"*Liar.*"

With an effort, she ignored the redundancy. *Come on. Dennis's cell doesn't just make calls; it has a thesaurus. Just like yours. Dissembler. Falsifier. Deceiver. Mix it up a little!* "But if you haven't seen him and he didn't take his phone—wait, how did you get it?"

"The funeral home called. He left it there."

"Wait, just now? Or it's been there for a couple of days?"

"How should I know?" she shrilled.

"Xenia, I think it's time to call the cops."

"Oh, you'd like that, wouldn't you?"

"Yeah, actually." Beat. "Wouldn't you?"

"So you can play the victim again."

"I have *never*—"

"All anyone at Dani's funeral could talk about was how hard this was on *you*."

"Xenia, you weren't even *at* Danielle's funeral." Wait, was Xenia mad because Dennis was missing, because Ava had been calling Dennis, because Dennis might have been murdered, because Danielle *was* murdered, or because people felt sorry for Ava *and* the Monahans? "And trust me, I wasn't the focus."

Sure, the mourners and the kids at school had thrown a lot of sympathy her way. Which was hardly out of line—she and Danielle had been best friends. They did everything together, shared everything, even the same job. Everyone knew that, from Dennis all the way down to people who barely knew them, like what's-his-name, the funeral home scion.

"Xenia, check with his family to make sure they haven't heard from him—"

"They haven't! They're beside themselves!"

"Then *call* the *police*. And don't go through Missing Persons, call—" She blinked. Tom was holding up his phone so she could read from the screen. "Detective Gary Springer in Major Crimes, 651-266-5500, and tell him Dennis has been missing for four days. Then we—hello?" She stared at the phone, then looked up at Tom. "Silly bitch hung up on me. It's like an epidemic. An epidemic of poor phone etiquette. Started by me," she admitted.

"So then: Dennis is apparently a missing person or a person of interest. Or both."

"She said the funeral home called. And I'll tell you what, if she doesn't call the cops within the hour, I'm going to." Ava stood there and thought, but nothing clarified. "Y'know, I haven't been to a funeral home in almost five days. I might be going into funeral home withdrawal."

"We can fix that."

Forty-Four

Tom pulled up to the funeral home and shut off the engine. When Ava didn't immediately look up, he tapped her knee. "Ava."

She started, then immediately dropped her phone back in her purse. "What? I wasn't googling 'demisexual.'"

"You are the *worst* liar. God forbid you have another engine fail and have to inform your passengers. 'Nobody fret and both engines are definitely functioning, just don't look out any of the port windows.'"

"Ha! You know that's happened to me, and it all worked out fine. Besides, most planes fly just fine with one engine. It's just that engineers are big fans of redundancy, and thank goodness. I've never said 'one of our engines is dead, completely *dead*, so buckle up, l'il *hombres*, you're now one of the flying dead!'"

"Good *God*."

"There *are* things even I wouldn't say. But I've said 'one of the engines is indicating improperly.' And we landed just fine. Honestly, it was just another day. Besides all the paperwork. There's *so much* paperwork if even the tiniest detail—"

"No one in their right mind would consider engine failure a tiny detail. What other emergencies have you dealt with?"

"You really want to hear?"

"Of course I do. How often have you listened to one of my macabre murder stories?"

"Yeah, but those are fun. Horrible, but fun."

"Exactly."

"Remember when I told you I'd seen people have heart attacks on planes twice, once when I was captain? Well, the other time was a year before I made captain. We had an engine fail *and* a heart attack on board. Unrelated, but I was wondering if we were gonna be in the middle of a Michael Crichton–style cascade of events. *Jurassic Park on a Plane* or something just as nightmarish."

"So a millions-to-one event has happened to you in the air . . . twice."

"It's not the mechanical malfunctions that are rare, just the medical emergencies. Ugh, I said 'just,' like medical emergencies are no biggie. Anyway, Captain Vang did the 'engine indicating improperly' speech and we were cleared for an emergency landing. In *Daytona*, ugh."

"Clearly the worst part of the ordeal."

"Tell me. So Captain Vang's got it all under control, which is exactly what I would have expected because he was awesome— he's retired now, and if anyone earned a peaceful retirement, it's him. He got in touch with ground medical services, and we knew there'd be an ambulance waiting when we touched down. So he asked me to go back in case the flight attendants needed another pair of hands—this was before we flew with defib machines, so CPR was manual. And as you probably know, that's quite a workout.

"So I go back and I relieve one of the flight attendants for a couple of minutes, and this poor little kid is crying because her dad's going into cardiac arrest right in front of her, and nobody can calm her down, so I did what I always do—"

"Took refuge in inappropriate humor?"

"Gosh, however did you guess? Anyway, the guy actually comes around, we give him oxygen, he's coherent enough to give his kid a thumbs-up, I talk to her for a couple more minutes and explained that we had the best medical care all lined up for him and he'd be whisked to the hospital—in Daytona, but you know what they say about beggars and choosers—and then I went back to the cockpit to give Vang a sitrep and we landed and the guy turned out fine. And his kid, this adorable little strawberry blonde, just gloms onto me when we're all finally on the tarmac and starts asking what classes you have to take to be a pilot, and I eventually peeled her off me and helped her and her mom into the car the airline provided for them, and away they went."

"Remarkable."

"It was a busy morning," she agreed. "And I guess we'd better get back to ours."

They got out of Tom's van and headed into the funeral home, their idea to kill time while setting up the Becka intervention ("We think you might be in league with a killer, and it's affected our lives in the following ways . . ."). They might not get any closer to finding Dennis, but it was better than waiting around for the next awful thing to be set in motion.

"Hello again, Ava."

Blinking in the sudden gloom—*damn*, it was sunny outside—Ava didn't immediately place him until he came closer.

"Hi, Pete. This—" She started to introduce Tom, who was

inexplicably facedown on the carpet before she could finish with ". . . is my lover, or he will be when I devirginize him."

Taser, she thought, staring. Pete was holding a dull black electroshock weapon little bigger than his hand, from which he'd fired two electrodes and their conductors. Both were now trapped beneath Tom, who had gone over like he'd fallen off a cliff. *He was waiting for me. But he didn't count on Tom.* And, out loud: "Oh, shit."

"Well put," Pete agreed.

Forty-Five

"Wh-wh-why-what-wh-"

"Articulate as ever," Pete said with a thin smile. "Just like when we were in high school."

"We weren't in school together, you cock!"

"*Yes, we were!*" This in a high-pitched scream that was almost as shocking as watching Tom succumb to fifty thousand volts. She didn't dare look down at him; she needed to keep her focus to fill the time.

Meanwhile, Pete had visibly calmed himself. "We were. For two years. I graduated at the end of your sophomore year. You didn't remember me then, just like you didn't remember me at the nursing home or last week or probably next week, if you were still alive next week."

Past tense. Aw, c'mon, spoiler alert! "So it's my fault you're . . ." *Boring? Forgettable? Uninteresting? Inconsequential? The human equivalent of dryer lint?* ". . . introverted?"

"Ah, yes, the new feel-good term for shy people. Sure. Introverted."

"Pete—why?"

His narrow face twisted, and she could see he wanted to shout at her again. When he spoke, his voice was noticeably strained. "Don't do that. You know. Don't pretend otherwise."

"Pete: I promise; I'm clueless. Ask anyone. You and I weren't close and you barely knew Danielle. You haven't even seen me for a decade. Besides, you were so calm at the memorial. Remember? There's—there was nothing there."

"*Wrong*," he said coldly, and she had a flashback to the word written in Danielle's ashes.

"Jesus, you trashed the funeral home, too," she realized. "But why?"

"No, I just finished trashing it."

"Wait, what?"

"It wasn't supposed to be Dani," he muttered, and she made a note to get her hearing checked, because she was having trouble following him. *It's probably not your ears,* her inner self soothed. *It's him, because he's crazy.*

"What are you saying?"

"It was supposed to be you!"

For the first time, she noticed how wretched he looked. The dapper guy in the pricey clothes who lived a nice life abroad was gone. Now he was in faded jeans and an old T-shirt, sneakers, no socks. Ironically, seeing him slouching around in what had essentially been his high school uniform helped a memory click home.

"Is this because of the nursing home?"

"You know it is! Stop pretending otherwise."

"I'm not pretending anything, Pete. I have no idea what you're going on about."

"Why are you doing this to me?"

"Pete, you've got the right script, but you're reading the wrong lines. Why are *you* doing this to *me?*"

"You know, Ava! You even taunted me about it at the memorial. Bad enough to find out you were alive, bad enough to have to come back here and end up face-to-face with my worst fucking nightmare—"

"Hey!"

"—but you just had to get your little digs in."

"I don't know what you're talking—" But then she did.

Did you hear Shady Oaks finally had to shut down?

Shit.

I guess the drug thing—the latest drug thing—was a bridge too far.

"Are you a pharmacist now?" he mimicked. "You fucking well knew I wasn't."

Would the truth—that she had no inkling of his career path—help or hurt?

"You must have figured out why I left by now."

She was still wrestling with her dilemma. Tell the truth? *I didn't notice when you left. I didn't care when you left. I didn't think of you while you were gone. And I barely remembered you when you came back.*

She strove for a reasonable, measured tone. "You said you moved abroad after you got your degree."

"Yes, from Inver."

"An associate's degree," she realized aloud, because Inver was a community college. "Two years. And you're two years older than me. You didn't leave because you got your degree—that was just how the timing worked out. You left because you wanted an ocean between you and your murder. But I still don't know why you killed Da—" He visibly twitched at that, and she rapidly rephrased. "—why you wanted to kill me."

"You found my stash. You sent me an e-mail about it. You were going to report me."

It was finally coming back to her, but in pieces. She might have remembered sooner, if Pete had been the slightest bit memorable and if she had been the slightest bit less self-absorbed. But he wasn't, and she wasn't. Back then she had been too wrapped up in her own grief and, after her parents died, her own need to get far away.

"I only sent it because I didn't know what was going on. I found all this stuff from residents who died, and when I looked up the paperwork, you were on shift each time and . . . shit, I didn't know. Shady Oaks was slacking off even then, and when I asked around, nobody seemed to know what you were doing, or even gave a shit."

"Stop it. Don't pretend you didn't know I was doing something wrong."

"Why would I? Come on—a seventeen-year-old volunteer sent one measly e-mail asking about a Tylenol-Three stash, which you explained. I mean, I know *now* you were lying, but I didn't then. I believed you. I dropped the subject. I didn't even save the e-mail! You couldn't have thought you were in any danger."

But he had. And he'd acted accordingly.

"It was a little more than Tylenol-Three. It was Xanax and Klonopin and Tranxene and benzos and oxy. And that doesn't count the shit that was already in my system. That was just what I boosted from the Oaks that month."

She rubbed her eyes. "And you fucked with my drug test."

"I was sure that would jog your memory."

"There wasn't anything to jog!" Wait. Rephrase. "In your e-mail you said you were . . . God, what was it?"

"Reappropriating."

"Yes! That. You said the patients didn't need their meds anymore but you'd pass them down to ones who did need them. Like residents who didn't have good insurance, or however you put it. And I believed you, Pete! Again: seventeen. Not a medical professional. Stuck in a job I couldn't quit. Resentful and pissy, as only teenagers can be." Well, teenagers and cats.

All of which was why Danielle had her very own Volunteer Aide Ava name tag: so they could share a job she'd come to hate. Back in the day, she assumed they'd gotten away with it because they were just that clever. She was now beginning to realize they got away with it because Shady Oaks was just that shitty.

"Not only was it just the one e-mail, you and I never even talked about it face-to-face," she said slowly, as her rusty brain gave up memories she hadn't sought in years. "I only knew you to say hi to, and I almost never saw you in person. And being constantly doped on all kinds of bad shit didn't help matters, did it? So you panicked and killed the other teenage brunette who answered to Ava." Wrong girl. Wrong job. Wrong life. Wrong choice. "But why now? Why drag all this up a decade later?"

"Unfinished business," he said shortly. "I left and had no intention of returning. I made something of myself. It was all behind me."

"Behind you? So I take it you found a good rehab facility in Scotland? What'd you do when you got to step nine? How did you make amends to the Monahans?"

"I didn't need rehab," was the short (and grotesquely inaccurate) reply. "And then Captain Bellyflopper made the news, and I realized my mistake."

Damn you, Internet. And Tom had guessed right again. He'd speculated that Becka had appeared in Ava's life because she saw the emergency-landing coverage. He was wrong about the person, but right about the impetus.

"So you came back for Danielle's memorial. You knew about it because it's your family business. And to test the waters, or whatever."

"Why are you narrating?"

"It helps me think. So when we talked about Shady Oaks, you assumed I was taunting you. Which is why you sabotaged me. You—" She groaned as another realization hit her. "Computer science. That's how you fucked up my drug test and got into the airline's intranet. And you lifted my purse, didn't you?" She remembered losing track of the thing for a few minutes and then Dennis came from the office and handed it to her. "The night of the memorial?"

"I made copies of everything in your wallet," he confirmed. "You really shouldn't keep your passwords on your person."

"My person is none of your business. And you stole my lotion!" No question, the man was a fucking monster. "Don't," she added when he opened his mouth. "I don't want to know what you put in it. And then you poisoned me."

"What?"

"Knock it off. You know what you did," she snapped. "I spent half the night throwing up. Giving me a skin condition was bad enough, but leave my food alone!"

"No, that wasn't me. Probably something you ate."

"Oh. Well, okay. But the rest of it: not okay, Pete! Why the hell would you do all that? Risk showing your hand like that?"

"To isolate you. To get you alone."

She shook her head. "I was never alone, idiot. Even if it took me years to realize. You killed Danielle for nothing, do you understand? Not only was she *not* going to rat you out, I wasn't, either. Like I said, I believed you."

"I couldn't chance it. Stealing drugs is a felony, even if

you're just robbing the dead and demented to feed your habit. It wouldn't have just been the Department of Health, it would have been the cops and it would have followed me around for the rest of my life. It would have destroyed me."

"So you destroyed Danielle instead. And ran." She hesitated, but took the plunge anyway. "You're pathetic. Oh, what? I'm supposed to be nice to you? I'm supposed to believe you're *not* going to kill me if I flatter you and pretend you don't disgust me? Please. I know you don't want me to leave this room under my own power. Anyone who's ever watched a murder mystery would know that.

"And the worst part, Pete, you fucking piece of shit? I was with Danielle that whole last day! You probably only missed me by an hour or so. And then you showed up and—" It was a day for dawning realizations, apparently. "Trying too hard," she muttered, rubbing her forehead. "That's what the tech said at the crime scene." She looked up. "You stabbed her and she bled out—I'll bet you waited until her back was turned, because you're a cowardly POS. And once she was down, you got creative—but you overdid it. Just like you overdid it with her ashes. And my drug test. You wanted it to look like a random psycho vagrant. Not the local junkie who stole from the dead and then pissed himself when he thought a teenager was going to get him in trouble."

"You should talk," he snapped back.

"Hey: this junkie never robbed a dead nursing home resident, didn't pull an over-the-top murder to cover my theft, and didn't flee like a fucking coward only to skulk back and play petty tricks to lure me into an 'alone with the psycho' moment."

"It wasn't exactly fun times for me, either. I threw up in *two* Ziploc bags."

"Jesus Christ. What'd you do with Dennis?"

"Why is everyone worried about Dennis?" Pete had the gall to sound wounded, which was as offensive as it was hilarious. "I have no idea where that idiot is."

"You—you don't?"

"I needed to get you alone. Why the hell would I want Dennis Monahan hanging around?"

"But you had his cell."

"I *found* his cell. And the whole thing was taking too long, so I used it. I've got a life to get back to, y'know."

Wow. He really thinks that. Unreal. And why hasn't someone walked in or called in the last five minutes?

"So I called his little girlfriend," Pete continued. "He doesn't lock his phone, can you believe it?"

"You're right. This is taking too long. So what now? I'm here. My bodyguard's down for the count."

"Your what?"

"Never mind. Just so we're on the same page, you're going to kill me because you're a nasty, vindictive brat, and also because you don't want anyone finding out you killed Danielle. Do I have that right?"

"That's only two reasons," he snapped. "There are loads more. I know what you're doing, by the way. You're not clever, and I'm not talking because you're tricking me. I'm talking because you deserve to know why. You think I won't get your phone later and wipe whatever recording you're making?"

"What about Tom?"

"Fuck him." But he sounded rattled. Ava wondered when Pete had tipped from vengeful sociopath to clinically insane nutjob. Because he was crazy, she was sure of it. Ten years of looking over his shoulder had taken a toll; even when he thought he was free, he wasn't.

"Fine. Get on with it."

He just looked at her, then at Tom. And she saw what the problem was. He'd tased Tom, who had collapsed facedown. Meaning he was lying on the electrodes embedded in his

(broad, yummy)

chest.

In other words, Pete couldn't tase her from where he was. All he could do was zap Tom again. If that was even how Tasers worked—did the thing need to build up a charge? Could you pull the trigger again if the electrodes hadn't retracted? *Note to self: see G.B. about Taser lessons.*

Did he have a gun? Or a knife? Would he try and strangle her with those scrawny, manicured paws? She almost hoped he would. She'd stick her thumbs in his eyes so deep, he'd spend the rest of the year looking for a service animal.

"Second thoughts?" she asked.

"No." He dropped the Taser, which was great. But he pulled what looked like a .38 from somewhere, which was less great. Had it been tucked in the back of his jeans? Dolt.

"You've been watching too much TV. That's an excellent way to get a bullet up the crack of your ass."

"Shut up."

"Aren't you worried about someone dropping by to coffin shop? What are you going to do with the bodies?"

"Frame Dennis. And the only one who's going to need to shop for a coffin is—nobody, actually. You've got nobody. It's why you always hung out with the Monahans. No one will give a shit when you turn up dead."

"I'd explain how you're wrong, but you'd never get it. Also—whoa."

"Whoa" because Tom's hand had shot out, clamped around Pete's ankle like a fleshy handcuff, and yanked. Pete vanished from her line of sight like he'd dropped through a trapdoor and hit the carpet so hard she saw dust puff up.

Her relief was so great, her knees almost gave way. "Figured you were awake."

"Barely," Tom muttered, then groaned as Pete kicked him in the forehead with the foot Tom didn't have a death grip on.

"*Don't.*" Ava had pulled her knife—she'd been waiting for her moment, and it was hard to picture a better one—and flipped the blade open.

"You shouldn't have come back," he snarled, trying to claw for the gun, which had fallen about two inches out of his reach.

"Finally, we agree. Also, you see I'm armed and will stab you, right? So maybe give up now before everything gets much worse for you?"

Pete finally managed to shake loose, then rolled to his feet, snatched up the Taser, and came for her. Tom's muscles must still be jelly, because to say he was disoriented would be an understatement. She was amazed he'd kept his grip as long as he had and—oh, shit, here was Pete, four feet away and closing.

She could see that he'd ejected a cartridge from the Taser, leaving the electrodes in Tom but still able to zap her with the electric discharge. The arc was the brightest thing in the gloom of the funeral home.

"If you don't step off, I will stab you." She'd had to rush that last bit because she was out of time, sidestepped Pete's lunge, and brought up the blade of her puny little three-incher right under the shelf of his jaw: schump!

And then, horrified, she let go. Because Pete was making a series of low squealing noises as he flailed for the knife sticking under his chin, as blood poured down, as he missed, grabbed again, missed. It took Ava a couple of seconds to realize that she'd managed to stick the blade in hard enough and far enough to puncture Pete's tongue, and oh shit she was gonna barf.

Nope. Just the dry heaves as she watched Pete sink to his knees, still pawing for the blade.

"Ava, my God, are you all right?" Tom had managed to climb to his feet and was swaying slightly.

"Comparatively speaking, yeah." To Pete: "What, my best friend was slaughtered and you didn't think I'd learn self-defense or carry a weapon? How could you be so diabolical and so dumb at the same time?"

Tom staggered, then steadied himself. "Well, that was illuminating."

"Are *you* okay? You were down for so long . . ."

"Because you put yourself at risk to buy time, so I waited for whatever opening you were going to give me. Christ, Ava, you are a lunatic. A formidable one, but nevertheless."

She slung an arm around his waist. "What was it like?"

"Like a full-body muscle cramp magnified by a factor of five." He looked down at Pete, who'd fallen silent save for the occasional wet gargle. A growing red stain was spreading beneath his head. "What about him?"

"Fuck him."

And that was that.

Forty-Six

Two days later, they were having dinner in Ava's minisuite at the Radisson Blu. They'd both been interviewed multiple times by the authorities, and Tom admitted he found it interesting to be on the other side of the desk, so to speak, as opposed to his usual role.

"That wears off," Ava said dryly.

The Monahans had been amazed to finally discover who killed their Danielle, none more so than Dennis, who was alive and well and had checked himself into Twin Town, a mens' live-in treatment center for alcohol abuse. He'd left a message for his mother, who preferred denial to acknowledgment and thus had said nothing. He then abandoned his phone, knowing he wouldn't be able to use it in rehab, and went to see what parts of himself could be salvaged and what needed to be remade.

"Idiot! You had everyone worried sick! Except possibly your mom!"

"*I* was worried sick." She'd been able to see him during visitors' hours, though she wasn't a family member. Apparently when you had to tell an old friend that you killed his sister's killer, exceptions are made. "I had to get the hell gone. I should've realized Mom would be too embarrassed to tell anybody where I went. I'm sorry you were worried, but I had to come. Who gets piss drunk the night of their twin's memorial, sobers up, sneaks back in during the wee hours and trashes a funeral home, and then drinks more?"

"It's a trick question, right?"

The police (and Tom) pieced together the sequence of events: Dennis had taken a cab (somehow), upended tables and broken dishes, failed to notice Pete's presence, then staggered back to his cab and, ultimately, the hotel, where he regained consciousness hours later with only the vaguest memories of what he had done. Pete, meanwhile, had finished the job, taking special pleasure in not only using Danielle's ashes but also knowing Dennis would get the blame.

The past two days had dragged and flown, something she hadn't thought possible. Jan had been dismayed to hear Ava was involved in another murder, this one by her own hand ("Self-defense? But you're okay? Yes? Promise? All right, that's great. *Jesus*, what is it with you?") and had referred her case for final review, one of the last steps before she was cleared to fly again.

"Ava? Are you in there?" Tom teased.

She gave herself a mental shake. "Yeah, sure. Are you still okay with spending the night?" Possibly a dumb question. He'd brought a small suitcase, a sizable toiletries bag, and a suit bag. And showed up at 4:00 p.m. for their 8:00 p.m. meal. *He does know it's just one night, right?*

"I am delighted."

"Good." She was just grazing by now, nibbling at the last few fries simply because they were in front of her, so she put the plates back on the cart and, with Tom's assistance, pushed the thing out into the hall without accidentally locking herself out of her room.*

Once back inside, she went to him and looped her arms around his neck. "I hate that you were there," she said, rubbing her nose back and forth just under his collarbone, which prompted the most adorable noises (ticklish!). "But I'm also really glad you were there."

"My exact sentiments." He cupped the back of her head, ran his fingers through her curls, tipped her head back for a long kiss.

By the time the kiss broke, concentration was getting tricky, but she managed. "And if you don't want to . . . or you'd rather wait . . . or even just cuddle and sleep, or sleep and cuddle, that's okay. I'm not going anywhere. Well. I am. But I'll come back. For you, always."

He smiled as he eased her shirt over her head. "I do want to. I don't wish to wait. And I also want to cuddle and sleep, and then sleep and cuddle."

"Okay. So. We've got that sorted." Jeez, why was *she* nervous? Simple: this mattered. It wasn't a one-off. It wasn't a "see you next time I'm in town maybe but if not, no biggie." When they were done, she wouldn't wish he'd take his leave. When they were done, she'd lie in his arms and think about the future and she wouldn't be afraid of one thing.

And she'd never been anyone's first before. Not even for her first.

They helped each other out of their clothes, stopping to

---

* Don't judge! Happens all the time. It doesn't mean that person is dumb. Just uncoordinated. Or so I've heard. Because that's definitely never happened to me in real life. Not once.

trade kisses and murmurs until they were both nude, and then she toppled them both over onto the bed. She straddled his hips and swooped down for another kiss while his hands roamed over her hips and breasts and his back arched beneath her touch.

"Careful," she teased. "Don't want to go off too soon."

"Ah—no," he gasped. "I masturbated earlier to prevent just such an occurrence."

"Romantic."

"Anything for you," he said, and then chuckled when she poked him.

"Anything you don't want?" she asked gently. "Or don't think you'll like?"

"If you're the one doing it, I won't mind."

"Wow. That's a big blank check you just wrote."

"Yes," he said simply, and reached up to brush her cheekbones with his thumbs. "Have I mentioned my great relief that your ridiculous courage and chronic immaturity didn't get you killed?"

"A few times. Tell me if you don't like something, okay? And I'll stop the second you say."

"And so begin the threats."

She snorted, then leaned down for another kiss and he flipped them, ducking down to nuzzle at her breasts. She sucked in a breath as he pressed kisses to her nipples, then tentatively licked one. She could feel herself stiffening in his mouth, which was pretty damned glorious, really. "Oh, that's—that's lovely. Keep doing that."

"Your wish." He'd shaved that morning—fastidious man!— but his stubble was already blooming along his jaw, and the friction was delightful. She cradled his head as he kissed and nibbled and worked his way lower, as he kissed the tender skin of her inner thighs and spread them open and made himself at home for several minutes. And ohhhhhhh, when your endgame wasn't penetration, the focus on other aspects of lovemaking

"God God God *God God*!"

—was immediately apparent.

"Jesus," she gasped. "I never come that fast. And I have a Hitachi wand."*

"How very kind," he panted, surging up to kiss her, hard. "I need—after that—my *God*, you're responsive. Can we—" He groped blindly for the toiletries bag he'd placed on the bedside table.

"Yes! Let me." She reached over, fumbled with the bulging leather bag, and when she got the zipper down, the bag seemed to blow up. Two boxes of condoms as well as strip after strip popped out; she'd inadvertently made it rain prophylactics. "Jeez, how many condoms did you bring?"

"I, um, wanted to be prepared for any eventuality."

"It's like a clown car! Do you even have room for your toothbrush in here?"

"I don't see how that's relevant."

"Gosh, which one to choose? Such a vast array!"

"Stop it," he groaned.

"Okay, here, I somehow managed to find one." She snatched it up, then ripped the packet open with her teeth.

"Is that supposed to be insanely erotic? Because it is."

"Glddooikeddid,"† she mumbled around the packet. She carefully smoothed it down over Tom's cock and then lay

---

* Ladies: get one. Like, yesterday.
† "Glad you liked it."

back and stretched her arms toward him in warm welcome. "C'mere, gorgeous."

He obliged, catching his weight on his elbows as she pulled her left leg up a bit, and he entered her in one long glorious slide.

"OhmyGod."

"Yeah."

"MyGodmyGodmyGod."

"Perfect. Now move."

He obliged, moving tentatively at first, then gaining confidence as his strokes lengthened. She crossed her ankles behind his back and urged him on with a series of gasps and groans and "Oh Gooooood, that's good . . ." Her orgasm took her by surprise (again!) as she shivered and tightened around him, as he dipped his head for a messy kiss.

"Is it—is this good?" he panted.

"Perfect," she murmured against his mouth. "Oh, you feel *so* good. When you get some practice under your belt—"

He groaned.

"Sorry! Totally unintentional pun. I was just—just saying—ah—that if you're—ah—this good *now*—oh-oh-oh-oh—imagine what—ah—what—Christ, I'm coming again . . ."

"C-can I? Can't wait . . . much longer . . ."

"Yes! I didn't realize you—please, yes, don't hold back. I've got you. And you've got m—ah!"

He shuddered above her and his eyes rolled back and she thought, *you're beautiful and I'm so lucky*, and then he collapsed as gently as he could.

"Oof!"

"Mupolgeez," he mumbled against her neck, which she took for "apologies."

"Naw. You earned that collapse. But if you're still squashing me five minutes from now, that's bad form."

"Noted."

She ran her fingers up and down the long planes of his back as he struggled to get his breath back, still hard inside her (no worries about condom leaking just yet, at least).

"That was wonderful," he said. "You're wonderful."

"It was. And yes. And ditto."

"Do not panic . . ."

"Oh my God."

"I am merely making postcoital conversation—"

"Oh my *God*." What? *What?* What the hell could it be?

"But would you ever consider moving back to Minnesota?"

"Oh." She paused, thought. "Let's just say that's not as off the table as it would have been a month ago. It's not the state. Can't blame Minnesota for the Monahans—and I promise that's the last time I'll say that name tonight."

"Excellent. On all counts. I'm not trying to rush you," he said, propping himself up on an elbow to gaze into her face. "I just hope you would be willing to keep your options open."

"I will. We can talk about it. After my folks died, I always thought home was where my travel bag was. And that's still true." Which was something else Pete got wrong. It's just, maybe soon, home will be where my travel bag and you and your gigantic condom collection are."

"I adore you."

"I—" *Whoa.* Her voice caught, her eyes filled—what was wrong with her? She never got choked up about stuff like this.

You never even talk *about "stuff like this." It's a lot to take in; that's all. Nothing to be scared of.*

"I think you're wonderful," she choked out, and returned

his kiss. "I want to be in your life. Your lives—I like Abe and Hannah, too. The thing is, I see now that it wasn't Minnesota I hated; it was all the collateral damage."

Tom blinked. "Yes. Of course. Are you saying you only now realized that?"

"Uh. No? No. Definitely no. Don't be smug," she scolded, slapping him on the bicep, because that was definitely the beginning of a smirk on his gorgeous face. "And we need to get that condom off before there's a mess."

"Consider me your most attentive pupil."

"Great. Now we—" She froze suddenly, eyes widening in realization, and Tom immediately tensed up.

"Ava? What is it?"

"Oh, shit!" She stared at him, horrified. "We forgot about Becka's intervention!"

Forty-Seven

TBMD: My uncle is on the spectrum.

CAPTAIN AVA CAPP: Thanks for the update, Hannah.

TBMD: Hmmm.

CAPTAIN AVA CAPP: See? I'm smart, too! Sometimes. Does Tom know you've scored his phone?

TBMD: I'm not using his phone.

CAPTAIN AVA CAPP: I sense trouble coming your way. Or at least a lecture.

TBMD: You already knew.

CAPTAIN AVA CAPP: What? That he's blunt and adorably clumsy and doesn't worry himself to death over social niceties and has a strong sense of justice? I guessed and I don't give a sh . . . out.

TBMD: You don't give a shout?

CAPTAIN AVA CAPP: That's right! Not a single shout. Also, this is a conversation I should be having with Tom or no one. You're super-cute, now butt out.

TBMD: Acknowledged.

CAPTAIN AVA CAPP: Also I'm a little afraid of you.

TBMD: ☺

Forty-Eight

THE LIST
Apologize to Becka
Return G.B.'s and India's calls
Pick up dessert for Abe's BBQ
SPF 40 lotion for same
Condoms

"You thought *what?*"

"I'm really sorry," Ava explained. Though she was still grounded, she'd set up a meet with a number of her crew at MSP before they went their separate ways. "I was being paranoid, which wasn't fair to you. But some of your questions were, um, off-putting."

"Like what?" Becka's eyes had gone very wide and she sounded equal parts crushed and horrified, and Ava hoped like hell she wasn't going to cry. She felt bad enough she'd assumed the worst, then stood the poor woman up in favor of devirginizing Tom.

"Well. You were saying some pretty odd things like how you're only here because of me . . ."

"It's true! You're the reason I'm a flight attendant."

"But . . . why? You don't know me. We've never met. Also, I'm not a flight attendant."

"We did meet. Just not officially. My dad had a heart attack on one of your flights. You came back to help the attendants and cheer me up."

"Oh. Oh!" And like that, things made a lot more sense. "But then why ask all those creepy questions about the murder?"

"Because you're my hero! What the hell else would I talk about? My lame girl-crush? The paper I wrote about you in college?"

"There's a *paper*?" G.B., who'd been leaning against the table sipping coffee, looked like Christmas had come early. "I'll be needing to see that. Immediately. Hard copy *and* electronic. There are a few sites I'll need to post it on . . . and a few bathrooms I'll need to strew with hard copies . . . Could you get that to me within the next half hour?"

She flapped her hands at him in irritation, but kept her focus on Becka. "But why did meeting me make you want to be a flight attendant?"

"I wanted to be a Northeastern Southwest employee," Becka clarified. "After you've been on the air crew for three years, they pay for pilot lessons."

"We really do have a great union," India put in.

"Oh. So I'm your hero, which led you to work here to work your way up to pilot?"

"You're right to be skeptical about your hero status, Ava," G.B. put in, looking her up and down. "I mean . . . whyyyyyyyyyy?"

"Jesus," Ava mumbled. "You know, I did manage a belly landing with zero injuries."

"Pfffftt. Call me when the captain's down for the count, the hydraulics are shot, *and* the plane's on fire. Then you can brag."

"I like how you never hesitate to belittle my proudest accomplishments."

"Right? You need more friends like me."

"That's unimaginable," Ava admitted.

"I'm going to assume that's a compliment."

"Are you two done?" India asked. "So, Becka, you didn't sign on because of the uniform change?"

"Well, no." She shrugged, embarrassed. "But I couldn't tell you all the real reason."

"There's a *paper*," G.B. reminded everyone, delighted.

Becka sighed, then added, "I was so freaked out when you wanted to get together. That's why I lost my nerve and canceled at the last minute."

"Don't worry about it. It all worked out. And I definitely didn't forget about it, so it's all good."

"What? You—"

"Nothing! Sorry, you were saying?"

"I just . . . really look up to you." She was blushing now, staring at the floor. "My dad's still with us, y'know. He changed his diet and lost sixty pounds."

"I'm glad, Becka, but that's not because of me. I was just one person on a team. I think I did CPR for all of sixty seconds before I was relieved. The flight attendants did most of the work."

"As per usual," G.B. said, pretending to cough. Except he was terrible at the fake-cough verbal smackdown and just muttered the words into his fist.

"Quiet, you." To Becka: "Your dad's the one who decided to make the lifestyle changes. That's the hard part, I think."

"I know what I know," Becka said again, pushing her riot of red hair away from her flushed cheeks.

"We might be moving out of hero category and into stalker category," G.B. commented.

"Give her a break, Ghost Baby."

"No. *No.* Don't start that again."

"Then be nice to Becka," Captain Capp ordered.

"Fine. *Shit.* Fine."

"See?" Becka asked, beaming. "Hero."

Epilogue

One month later . . .
Sea-Tac Marriott

Ava couldn't stop staring at the text, though she'd gotten it over an hour ago.

Blake was getting married?

Blake Tarbell was getting married.

Blake? Her Blake? Although that was unfair, and incorrect . . . he was no more her Blake than she was his Ava. But still. The shock of it. As shocked as he'd be if he heard *she* was getting married, which was really funny. *And I have to say, if Tom found me and dropped to one knee tonight (or fell to one knee, which was more likely), I'd have to say no.* Yes, definitely no. Too soon. No rush. Etcetera.

But if he asked six months from now . . . ?

He must have lost a bet. It's literally the only reason I can think of for King Blake of Bachelorandia to get hitched. She felt a little like Sally Albright* when she heard Harry, the most cynical person she knew, was getting married: "Who *is* she?"

"Captain Capp? Don't forget your flowers."

Ava, halfway to the elevator, wrenched her attention from the text, turned around, and shook her head at the bouquet. "Oh, he's *gotta* stop doing that. He can send Hannah to Harvard for a semester with what he's spending on flowers."

"They're lovely," the receptionist said.

Tom had decided to approach courtship by the book. He even had a checklist, to her vast delight. Thus far she'd been serenaded and seduced and was the recipient of letters and love poems. He was taking her out for traditionally romantic dinners and drowning her in flowers. At one point, he'd decided to retroactively protect her reputation by having Abe chaperone.

"If there's nothing else, Captain Capp . . . um . . ."

"Yes?"

"Nothing. You . . . nothing."

"You might as well ask. Did you see my face on the news?"

"It's just I didn't recognize you until I got a really good look and are you the Ava Capp who had to do a belly landing while solving murders?" This all in one breath, like she'd get in trouble if she drew it out.

Ava laughed. "No! Not even close. Maybe a fifth of that is true. Okay, a quarter of it."

"That was . . . wow."

"Yeah."

"I'm glad you're okay."

"Thanks."

---

* *When Harry Met Sally . . .*

"Is there anything else you need?"

"Not from you, m'dear. Now if you'll excuse me, I have to go have Skype sex." She started toward the elevators, then wheeled around and snatched up the bouquet. "Whoops! Can't Skype without a bunch of random flowers strewn everywhere. What? You're looking at me like it's weird. It's not that weird."

"It's a little weird."

"It's how we do things in my family," Ava replied. "That's all."

That's all. And it was enough. In fact, it was everything.

Romance/Horror Trope List

1. Tropes are tools
2. Pilots have a girl/guy in every port (subverted: Ava enjoys a healthy sex life, but her numbers aren't outside the norm)
3. Bitchy gay flight attendant (subverted: while bitchy, G.B. is a raging heterosexual)
4. Sad, dark backstory (literally everyone)
5. Longtime class clown jokes to hide pain of sad, dark backstory (Ava)
6. Bald is evil (subverted)
7. Small-town girl fleeing to big city to leave tragic past behind
8. Stephen King reference (". . . get my mind serene.")
9. Tragic past eventually catches up with small-town girl
10. It's over . . . but it will never be over
11. Breakups are always brutal (subverted with Blake and Ava)
12. Evil is petty (villain)
13. Fatal flaw: pride

14. Eureka moment
15. Red herring
16. Alibi
17. Chronic evidence retention system
18. Clueless mystery—subverted. There *are* clues, but not many; the few there are don't resemble clues; and Ava and Tom don't piece them together until the end
19. The dog was the mastermind
20. They look just like everyone else
21. Mystery magnet
22. Amateur sleuth
23. Improbable coincidences (Ava and Tom are on the same flight)
24. Smart people know Latin
25. This time, it's personal
26. Deadpan snarker (Ava, pretty much constantly)
27. Geeks don't watch much TV
28. Flawed hero
29. Child prodigy
30. Time dissonance
31. Hero is always older (subverted)
32. Heroine is always a virgin (subverted)
33. Badass grandpa
34. Ambiguous disorder
35. Heroine loves children
36. Heroine loves dogs
37. Pretending to be in a fake relationship for a case (Ava, with her "podiatrist")
38. Explain, explain . . . oh, crap!
39. All women are lustful
40. *Good Will Hunting* reference

41. Metareferences (Ava suggests she's living in a romantic comedy)
42. Author pokes fun at her own book ("It's part of why this is such a shitty story")
43. Disability alibi
44. Never the obvious suspect
45. Amateur sleuths are never the suspect (inverted: several people think Ava might be the killer or, at best, had guilty knowledge of the murder)
46. Only bad guys dislike the heroine
47. No more running speech
48. Exposition victim
49. Hurt/comfort (Ava and Tom)
50. Alone with the psycho
51. Bad liar
52. The reveal
53. Heroine comes to an understanding about herself that was obvious to literally everyone else
54. Keep 'em talking
55. Heroes swear a lot (subverted)
56. Good girls don't swear (subverted)
57. Big romantic epiphany
58. Evil gloating
59. Motive rant
60. Happily ever after

About the Author

MaryJanice Davidson is the internationally bestselling author of several books, including the Betsy the Vampire Queen series. Her books have been translated into several languages and are available in fifteen countries. She writes a biweekly column for *USA Today* and frequently speaks to book clubs and writer's groups, teaches writing workshops, and attends conferences all over the world. She has published books, novellas, articles, short stories, recipes, and movie reviews.